THE VAMPIRE'S OPERA

JOY CROZIER
JOSEPH FLOYD

Print ISBN: 979-8-9877915-1-6

eBook ISBN: 979-8-9877915-0-9

DEDICATION

To Ken, my life partner, together we have created a weird, wonderful life, and I treasure every moment with you. Thank you for your endless love and support. To Cara, Ally, Tim, Will, Ari, Caelen and JoJo. Their love for one another, their humor, and insight provide inspiration every day.

To Danny, who believed in me even when I didn't and whose love has sustained me since the day we met. To Joy, who always and only saw possibilities for us despite working with the world's most difficult writing partner. To my sister Joyce, who always knew.

CONTENTS

1

OVERTURE

A sudden roar of cheers thundered inside the vast interior of the Paris Opera House. The theater erupted in applause as the orchestra fell silent and the curtain lowered over the darkened stage. From his vantage, high in the royal box overlooking the orchestra, Maestro Nicolas Portinari was swept up in the wave of appreciation for his latest musical drama. Exhilaration warmed into a deep sense of satisfaction, connecting him to a public from which he most often felt estranged.

In his one thousand years as a vampire, Nicolas had never left the mortal world behind, even as he never truly felt a part of it. Most vampires move through human society as specters, predators driven only by appetites born of the maddening sensations afforded by extraordinary perception. But Nicolas had never lost the desire to live as a human. All his immortal life, he had struggled to hold fast to his lost mortal existence, only to find himself an exile from both human and vampire realms.

It was music that had saved him from the madness that so often comes with the transformation from human to vampire. He was befriended by one of the vampire Elders, Max Scherer, who became

Nicolas's salvation by showing him the power of music in the hands of a preternatural.

"Music does not lie, Nicolas. It will help you understand the counterpoint between reason and desire, between your vampire and human natures. You are both fortunate and cursed. You are one of the few of us who crossed the gulf into immortality with your humanity intact. Thus, what you know will always be at war with what you want."

That advice resonated strongly with Nicolas. He had found solace in music, and it became the subliminal language that allowed him to connect with people and, mysteriously, to himself.

As the premiere of his latest opera, *El Samun*, concluded, and the exultation of that first wave of appreciation faded, his senses were suddenly besieged. The echo of excited voices wafted up from the orchestra below. Mesmerizing light refracted from the mammoth crystal chandelier above. Thousands of thrumming hearts set his vampiric appetite on edge. He focused on his most staunch supporters standing beside him. His anchors: Francois, mortal and steadfastly rational, and Giuliana, his child of darkness, a passionate empath who believed only in what she felt. They were the poles of his existence, balancing him between two worlds.

He pulled Giuliana into his arms to steady himself, and she stood on her toes to kiss him. The applause became even more thunderous when he returned her tender kiss with a more passionate one. She smiled at his reluctance to release her. He closed his eyes and held her tight, the applause drumming in his ears.

She whispered, "Do you feel it? All your dread was for nothing. You've given them a marvelous gift, and they're giving you one in return. No matter what else happens, no matter what the press or the public does with it tomorrow, this evening is yours."

He kissed her again, vowing to own this evening, this moment of pure success, and let her enjoy it, too. Francois offered his hand in congratulations. "You've done it again, Maestro. It was splendid. Opera season doesn't begin until you've debuted."

"Thank you, Francois. I'm glad you're here," Nicolas said as they shook hands. Nicolas faced the audience from the front of the box. Standing against the low balcony wall, he bowed sharply. When he raised his head again, the crowd roared its approval. Tonight, his connection with them burned white-hot. Tonight, by their acknowledgment, he belonged in their world. He closed his eyes, and all that remained was the bond he felt with them at the end of every performance, palpable as electricity. Their affirmation gave him entree into their world, but it also put him at their mercy. This was the price of belonging; their love always translated into ownership.

He bowed deeply once more, then turned away to slip an arm around Giuliana's shoulders. Her pale skin was lustrous and smooth as pearl beneath his hand. A penetrating awareness concentrated in her ice-blue eyes. "I doubt the crowd will clear until you make an appearance," she urged gently.

She was right; they would wait to see him. His reputation with the press was notoriously bad. His reluctance to interact with the public had created a reputation of aloofness and arrogance. He never granted interviews nor gave previews of his work and rarely made public appearances. The press would not leave until they had availed themselves of this rare opportunity for a photograph or an interview.

"Then we must oblige them." He slipped Giuliana's satin stole around her shoulders and took her hand. "After all, what could go wrong tonight?"

Francois pulled aside the red velvet drapery and opened the salon doors. They stepped into the corridor and were instantly swept into the tide of people flowing down the marble hallway toward the grand staircase and the exit. A chorus of shouted congratulations followed them through the crowd.

Giuliana lifted Nicolas's hand to kiss it. He smiled reassuringly at the concern in her eyes. They were linked by blood and five hundred years of life together; she knew his mind and was aware of the tangle of emotions bedeviling him. He had laid the most intimate expression of himself before his public, and now he must face them.

"I'm fine," he murmured softly as he pressed his lips to her gloved palm. She was radiant. The beaded gown she wore sparkled like diamonds. Her satin stole billowed around her in a voluminous, sapphire cloud.

Nicolas disengaged from the hands reaching out to touch him or shake his hand, and from the shouts of congratulations from the people around him. He focused instead on the rhythmic patterns and textures of the ornate decoration of the building. The galleries and salons he passed were a kaleidoscope of colors, sounds, and textures. The marquetry rosette set in the parquet was awash with golden light reflected from the chandeliers. Painted salamanders crawled across the vault of the loggia amid stylized shafts of sunlight. The marble floors were strewn with mosaic roses fashioned out of brightly colored Venetian glass.

He was distracted by this brilliant display when Francois moved ahead to block the path of a young woman in a black velvet gown who was determinedly pushing up the stairs toward them. She was in her mid-thirties, with dark, shoulder-length hair and bright emerald green eyes. Her gaze was fixed intently on Nicolas as she made her way up the stairs through the descending stream of people.

She shouted, "Monsieur Portinari, please, I need to speak to you, privately! You could help so many just by sharing what you know! Please won't you speak to me! Francois stepped deftly in front of her, blocking her path and allowing Nicolas and Giuliana to follow the crowd now streaming down the stairs.

Her frantic words were a familiar refrain from his devotees. Once it had been a fringe element. Now, a growing number insisted that the themes of his music came from some arcane knowledge he alone possessed.

"Madam, this is not the time or the place for this." Francois spoke to the woman calmly, "The Maestro has no time this evening; he's on his way to a reception. Perhaps I can help you?" He gripped her arm to lead her away from Nicolas.

The woman struggled roughly against Francois's hold. "Let me go! He's going to hear what I have to say!"

She shouted furiously above the din. "Monsieur Portinari, you don't understand! I know what you are! The world needs more from you now than your music! You're the only one who can help! Maestro!" Her piercing shout caused Nicolas to falter on the stairs and glance back. The young woman was on her toes, helplessly surveying the distance which had materialized between them. People noticed the disturbance and turned their gaze toward her.

Nicolas's jaw clenched. His gaze locked on Francois, and he motioned his head toward the exit at the bottom of the grand staircase. Francois moved aside, and the woman was instantly pulled into the crowd that flowed down a corridor toward the exit on the side opposite Nicolas. Francois turned and hurried down the stairs to catch up with Nicolas and Giuliana.

A growing ripple of interest slowed the curious onlookers as they craned to catch sight of Portinari moving through the crowd. Giuliana urged him away and, for a moment, they were swept safely down the steps. They paused at the apex of one of the two curving wings of the grand staircase that cascaded from the upper galleries to meet at a wide landing below them. From there, the sinuous curve of onyx stairs flowed out into the main entrance of the building like a stone wave frozen beneath the soaring dome of the opera.

Francois caught up with them, and they hesitated at the top of the landing. An excited murmur swept the room at their appearance, and all eyes turned to face the trio poised at the head of the stairs. They could see and be seen by everyone in the foyer. The crowd applauded and parted as they began their descent.

Nicolas's attention was drawn sharply to a flurry of movement in the mezzanine overhead. It was the young woman again, fighting her way through the crowd to the balustrade. She leaned over it, frantically searching the foyer nearly sixty feet below.

Nicolas watched as her wild eyes searched the crowd and felt a sense of dread as she located him. She fixed her gaze on him. She would not be stopped. *She knows*, he thought. *She knows everything.*

"Nicolas!" Her shriek rose above the din of the crowd. Giuliana gripped his arm, her eyes fastened on the hysterical woman shouting above them. "Nicolas Portinari, you can't hide from the world forever!"

The woman ran along the balustrade, pushing people out of her path until she was directly above Nicolas and Giuliana. The crowd froze, recognizing the start of an ugly scene. Nicolas could not get away now and had no choice but to confront the distraught woman. He peered up at her. Her hands fluttered along the onyx barrier, grasping for purchase.

Her voice was full of aggression and desperation. "We *understand* now! Why do you keep teasing us with these spectacles when what we need is the truth?"

The crowd's attention shifted to Nicolas, forcing him to answer her. "What truth?" he asked softly. His resonant voice calmed the electrified hum around him into an expectant silence.

"Spare us your bewilderment!" she spat, leaning out over the banister. Her eyes had gone completely wild now. Nicolas felt another wave of dread. With a look of determination, she suddenly clamored atop the balustrade. A distressed murmur followed as she swayed high atop the open stairwell. Several in the crowd reached for her, but she screamed, "Don't touch me!" and they drew back, shocked. She laid one hand on a column to steady herself. "You're not going to evade me again. You'll talk to me here. If you leave—or lie—I will jump, and all these people will know you are responsible. Maestro?"

Nicolas registered her every motion; her fingers flicked

nervously against the column; her eyes shifted from him to the crowd. Her other hand twisted the long strand of pearls at her neck. A sense of dread filled him as he caught sight of the falcon tattoo on the back of the woman's hand. She was part of a group he had ignored for too long. Horror buzzed through the crowd. "All right then." Nicolas attempted to appease her in a calm voice that carried through the cavernous rotunda. "Tell me what you want."

"We should leave. She's insane," Francois murmured grimly. Nicolas's eyes fixed on his. "We both know she's not. She thinks I have answers, like all the rest of them. She's scared and confused. I can't abandon her. Besides, we're at her mercy here." He motioned toward the bank of television cameras aimed at them from the foyer below. A cold fear gripped him as he began to realize how this all could end. "Bring her down to me," Nicolas whispered to Francois.

"What are you doing?" The woman scowled as she watched Francois pick his way back up the stairs.

Nicolas stalled. "You're upset. My associate is coming up."

"I am not going to talk to your damned assistant. Tell these people what you are, or I'll expose you, I swear it!" His mind raced through possible outcomes, searching for one that would not lead to more exposure or the woman's death. "Why are you stalling? Are you afraid how your public will react when they discover what you're withholding from them, Maestro?"

She glanced around for support. The crowd looked on with expressions of discomfort and pity. She clung to the column for balance, "You fools! Can't you see it? Do you really believe his work is all just fantasy? Only truth has the power to move you like this. Portinari doesn't just write about immortals! He *is* immortal!" She glared at them.

Those nearest looked away in embarrassment. Bursts of laughter broke out behind her. Nicolas remained motionless, shocked into silence, his face carefully devoid of expression. She searched the crowd for a glimmer of understanding. Nicolas gritted his teeth. He could only count on humiliation to cow her. He watched anxiously as Francois made his way into the gallery on the woman's level.

Nicolas spoke to pull her attention away. "Madame, you are confused. My dramas are meant only to entertain."

The crowd was calmed once more by the hypnotic timbre of his voice, which carried clearly through the space. For a moment, it seemed to work on her, too. Then she shook her head and looked sharply back at Nicolas. "Liar!"

She wrenched her pearls into a fierce knot as the last threads of her sanity and patience snapped. Francois arrived at her side and offered his hand cautiously. "Please, come down with me. I'll take you to Nicolas. He'll speak to you."

"No! Get away from me!"

Francois took a cautious step backward.

"Please, Nicolas! I understand; I swear I do!" Her eyes came sharply to his, and she pointed a finger toward him. "I hear it in your music! We all do!" she cried into the vast, echoing space. "What will it take to make you save us? Do you need me to die first? Is that it?" He gasped as the full force of her torment struck him. "If you think throwing away your life will make you immortal, you understand nothing!" Nicolas shouted, revealing a hint of anger in his voice. He was keenly aware of Giuliana's restraining grip on his wrist.

"Nicky, please," Giuliana cautioned.

"She doesn't want to die, Giuliana," Nicolas said, never taking his eyes from the young woman.

He moved back up a step and shouted to her, "I know what it is to always want more. Like you, I am always in search of meaning. But, trust me, you don't want to die. Dying is the end of meaning. Come down and speak to me."

"I tried to talk to you. You wouldn't hear me!" she cried. Her necklace snapped, and the pearls spilled through her fingers, arcing through the air in a long, silent shower. They exploded in an icy tattoo around Nicolas and Giuliana, then cascaded down the stairs in a clattering hailstorm at the same moment her face went calm and expressionless.

"You believe I'm afraid to die, but you're wrong. I *want* it to be over." Her voice was sad but took on a reflective tone. "I'm not afraid. I trust what I see in you more than I trust your words, Maestro. I see the answer," she said flatly, as if inviting the crowd into her vision. "I see the way now. Watch, and you will all understand."

She is a wraith. She has already relinquished her life.

He shouted to her, hoping to hold her in place. "Only the passion to live can make you immortal!" He stepped forward; in another instant, his physical form would have dissolved into flight, and he would have appeared beside her, but Giuliana's sharp, silent warning stopped him. *Not here, Nicolas! Don't!*

In the next moment, it was too late, for the woman stepped from the balustrade.

For a long moment, she plunged headlong into space. Francois's face registered an instant of complete disbelief. He dove toward the balustrade. His hands clutched the marble. A chorus of screams and shouts of panic rent the air. In the blink of an eye, the woman's body smacked to the floor with a horrifying wet thud only a few feet from Nicolas and Giuliana.

Francois's gaze locked on Nicolas in the crowd below him, and a look of horror passed between them. A riot of shouts and movement broke out as people scattered. Some ran toward the crumpled body sprawled face up across the landing. Some ran away. Her glassy eyes still registered the shock of impact. A stream of blood flowed from her shattered head and trickled down the white onyx stairs in a brilliant crimson stain. Pearls clattered here and there down the steps, to cluster finally against the lifeless body. Giuliana turned away, trapped between horror and disbelief. Nicolas instinctively pulled her back up the stairs and into one of the vacant loges. He slammed the door closed and leaned against it as if to block out the noise outside. In a moment, he began to pace the floor like a trapped animal.

His notoriety had caused the death of the young woman. He was as responsible as the noxious cult behind the falcon tattoo. This news would echo throughout Europe and move him even more firmly into the perilous public spotlight. A tightly wound growl escaped from his throat.

He could hear people shouting questions at Francois as he approached the loge. "Who was she, Monsieur Durand?" cried an agitated voice. "What was her relationship to Portinari?"

Francois's answer was strong and calm. "She had no relationship with Portinari; they never met."

A woman's voice carried clearly from somewhere deeper in the stairwell. "Will the maestro be making a statement? How is he taking it?" This time there was the slightest hint of a warning in Francois's tone as he answered. "I'm sure he's shocked, as we all are. A woman has taken her own life. I have no further comment. Let me through, please."

Chaos flooded into the room when Francois opened the door, and a wave of agitated voices fired off questions in rapid succession. "What's it like working for a vampire? Does the maestro deny the accusations? Was this a publicity stunt?"

Francois closed the door behind him. Clearly shaken, he leaned against it with eyes closed for a moment. When he opened them, he was calm again and his anguish buried. "I'm sorry, Nicolas. I tried to stop her."

Nicolas shook his head. "Don't, Francois, there's nothing you could have done. She had decided to die the moment she shouted to get my attention."

Their eyes met. The fullness of misery in Francois's eyes receded, and he nodded. "I've had the car pulled around to the stage garage. In a while, we can leave from there without going back through the crowd."

2

CON MOTO

A short while later, their limo was whispering through the rain-soaked streets on the way to the Portinari penthouse. Paris glistened in a light veil of rain. Nicolas fell silent. Light from buildings they passed washed over his face as he peered silently out the rain-specked windows at the passing cityscape. Giuliana held his hand in hers. "Nicky?" she asked tentatively.

He did not turn to look at her but brought her palm to his lips. "I'm fine." The image of the woman falling through space, her tortured plea, and the sickening smack of her body falling in a heap onto the stairs repeated in his mind. *Why did I not act sooner?*

Francois poured himself a brandy from the bar. "The foyer was swimming with paparazzi when I went back down to talk to the police." He sipped his drink, the ritual visibly calming him. "Like fucking piranha."

Giuliana stripped off her gloves and tossed them onto the seat beside her crumpled program. "They'll have a field day with this. It's probably being broadcast all over the continent as we speak." Francois glanced nervously at the driver and raised the soundproof partition as his phone chirped, and he answered it curtly. "Yes?"

His voice softened, and he brushed his hand through his hair distractedly. "We'll watch. And cancel the reception. We have nothing to celebrate tonight." He hung up and looked up at Nicolas.

"That was Paul. The reporters have congregated at the reception waiting for you to arrive. And..." Francois met Nicolas's eyes reluctantly, and Nicolas knew the news was not good. "...he said Jules LeCourbe is already on-air, and he's using the suicide as his lead-in for tonight's review."

Nicolas grimaced and touched the control pad on the armrest. A screen in the console flared on. Giuliana cursed under her breath and stared fiercely out the window. Images of the foyer of Palais Garnier appeared. The marble stairs were still stained with the spray of blood. The garish light of cameras washed the color from the faceted glass mosaics and variegated marbles.

Giuliana turned to him. "Nicky, don't do this." A flicker of hurt reflected in her eyes.

"I have to know what they're saying."

A bald, sallow man in his late forties came on the screen. He was painfully thin and wore horn-rimmed glasses, which magnified small, vacant eyes. His expression was scrunched into a permanent smirk. Jules LeCourbe, the arts critic for Television Paris, was the premier arbitrator of culture and the arts in Paris. He had, over the course of the last few years, focused most of his attention on vilifying Nicolas.

"Arrogant worm," Giuliana muttered as LeCourbe's saccharine voice filled the interior of the limousine.

"For nearly a decade now, the reclusive Nicolas Portinari has been embraced by the musical world as a composer of provocative originality." This last word he uttered as if it was something gooey stuck to his tongue. "The Maestro, the arrogant appellation by which he is known to a beguiled public, has composed works from piano concertos to symphonies, all with popular success. It is, however, for his operas that he is most widely known and where his odd, creative virtuosity has found its highest expression. His musical style is hall-marked by an emotional dynamic that battles against a razor-sharp sense of precision and restraint. Some have compared the experi-ence of his music to sitting in a room with a ticking bomb."

"Here it comes." Giuliana looked impatiently at Nicolas and sighed. "Nicky, this is absurd. He has no right,"

"I gave him the right when I let my music be performed in public," Nicolas answered grimly. Giuliana fell silent and listened as the voice droned on from the television.

"His musical style is driven by mysticism. Over the last several years, he has composed and produced a series of operas touted by some as inspired and held by others as impenetrable.

"Though his operas have been credited with spurring a world-wide renaissance in this dying art form, his works are shocking, freakish affairs which flout convention and abuse one's sensibilities. His music possesses an otherworldly tone, designed to disturb his audiences more than entertain them. The lyrically familiar forms of Verdi and Puccini have given way to the garish, atonal rites of Portinari.

"Recently, he has taken his hold on his gullible public one step farther. A worldwide cult has emerged who believe his constant theme of immortality to be true. They worship Portinari as one who can grant eternal life."

"As the tragedy at Palais Garnier tonight so clearly illustrates, there is a price to be paid for allowing such a radical visionary to blur the line between drama and reality. Tonight, one of Portinari's deluded fans accepted his vision and stepped across that boundary with deadly consequences. There are limits to what an audience can and should tolerate. Is Portinari's vision worth the price? For this reviewer, the answer is unequivocally no."

Giuliana reached over and touched the screen. The picture distorted, then went black. Francois poured himself another brandy. Nicolas sat mute, staring at the blank screen, desperately searching for a pattern in the series of events that led to this moment. They rode in silence, the car slicing quietly through the rain-soaked Boulevard Haussmann.

"Where are we going, Francois?" Nicolas asked, tersely.

Francois cleared his throat. and hesitated. "I've asked Cyril to take us to the penthouse. Unless you would prefer to attend the reception?"

"No. I think we've made enough of an impression for one night."

Francois sipped his drink. "I'm afraid the best we can do is try and minimize the impact." Nicolas turned away from the view out the window to watch his mortal companion shift into high gear. Nothing motivated Francois more than a crisis. Nicolas marveled at his competence and willingness to tackle any situation, even this one, which Nicolas suspected had no solution. No matter how seemingly ludicrous the accusations, the suicide would always be a tainted edge to his public life now. It was attention he could ill afford drawing to himself.

"The two of you should probably leave Paris for a while." Francois looked at Nicolas for confirmation.

Nicolas felt suddenly constrained within the confines of the car. The richly woven tapestry of his world was slowly unraveling. What an irony that it all would come apart because of someone he'd never even met; over someone's obsession.

Obsession. He thought of his own and offered a solution to Francois. "Egypt," he voiced. He looked from Francois to Giuliana. "We could go to Egypt for a while; take the Khamsin to Aswan." The Nile steamer seemed like a sanctuary now.

Francois put his glass down. "Yes. That's perfect," he agreed. "Except you have Porrovecchio's ballet tomorrow night in Venice. And the gala..."

Giuli shook her head. "No. We can't go forward with the gala."

"No," Nicolas said. "We can't. But we should go to Venice first. For the ballet and-" He caught Giuliana's eyes.

14

"Electra," she said. "I saw the tattoo, too. "I would not be surprised to find her tangled up in this somehow. I've always suspected she was pulling LeCourbe's strings."

"The Sokaris cult, right? I've heard about them recently, but it's pretty obscure. Do you know more?"

"A bit." Giuliana looked at him. "The falcon is the insignia of one of the vampire houses of Venice."

Nicolas added, "Before that, it represented the cult of an obscure Egyptian demi-god named Sokaris. One of its major tenets was that it offered its followers immortality."

"Good god." Francois shook his head, flabbergasted.

Giuliana looked back to Nicolas. "So, you think she's in Venice?"

He shrugged. "It's possible. But I need to find out. It will only take a couple of nights, Giuli."

"But then Egypt?" she pressed.

"Yes." He smiled at her then looked at Francois.

"It's isolated. You could disappear there for a few weeks until this blows over. If that's acceptable, I'll make the arrangements."

Nicolas nodded. After a few moments, he stopped listening to Francois's words and heard only the soothing, efficient tone of his voice. Its hushed timbre relayed even more than his words. It spoke of tasks to be accomplished, a life to be lived, the future; all things that Nicolas was suddenly aware could be lost to him. The realization was too much to contemplate and made him feel very old. He closed his eyes and thought of Egypt and the desert. How easy it would be to drown himself beneath that burnished ocean of sand, to hide in its depths for years until this incident and all who had witnessed it were dead and gone.

He could do it. He'd done it before. It was a simple matter really, just a breath, and then the gentle sifting downward into darkness. And then nothing. He imagined it. The sibilant hiss of the car as it cut through the gently falling rain became the sound of his body sinking beneath the sweltering sand of that endless dune sea.

3

AN OVERDUE ENCOUNTER

Water sprayed like lace from the bow of the motorboat as it knifed through the oil-smooth waters of the Venetian Lagoon. Nicolas sat in the glass-enclosed cabin, absently composing a melody out of the engine's mournful drone. A theme of lost love and Venice took shape in his mind, a complex blend of mandolins and lutes plucked in time to the strokes of a gondola's winding oar.

Ancient palaces and quays lined either side of the broad channel. St. Mark's Square was obscured by a veil of fog and a light rain. Francois peered through the window, watching the decaying buildings pass outside the tinted glass, lost in his thoughts. It was a short trip from Nicolas's villa on the isle of Giudecca to the busy main island of Venice. Coming back here was as much a journey through time as distance, for the city had barely changed in one thousand years.

The sudden revving of another boat's engine brought the maestro out of his reverie. His eyes flicked open. A small launch sped recklessly out of the fog on their starboard side. Nicolas's driver turned the boat sharply, barely avoiding a collision. The tinny caw of a boat horn echoed suddenly across the lagoon. Francois cursed under his breath at the steep angle of the abrupt maneuver and clutched at the hand loop overhead. The pilot brought the cruiser out of the turn, and the two boats wove slowly through the dense fog at a near idle.

"We understand!" the intruders shouted. Their voices rose in an enthusiastic rendition of the first bars of Nicolas's most famous aria, then fell in a cascade of laughter. The revelers scrambled to keep their balance as wash from the larger boat splashed against theirs. Agitated voices broke through. "Nicolas! Come out to see us! *We understand!"*

Nicolas cringed at the catchphrase. It referenced the title of a duet from his opera, *Immortal Venice*, "Non ci capisco," "I Don't Understand," sung by a human and an immortal as they struggle to comprehend one another. It was the last thing the woman had said before she jumped to her death in Paris: *Watch, and you will all understand.*

Nicolas started as the figure of a young woman suddenly emerged from the stew of fog moving low over the surface of the water between the two craft. She hung frozen in the gloom, gilded in the reflection of the motorboat's running lights. One of her hands pointing upward toward heaven. The other hand held a sword pointed toward the murky depths of the lagoon. A pair of golden wings stretched out behind her. The revelers crossed themselves and huddled closer together, momentarily cowed, as the apparition swiftly overtook them. Nicolas identified the sound of oars beating against oarlocks just as a breeze blew away the curtain of mist to reveal a funeral barge. It was propelled by two oarsmen at each end of the large, veiled catafalque. The carved, golden angel glinted at the vessel's prow.

The young people crossed themselves as the gondola passed within a few meters of their small boat. A sense of relief fell over them to recognize that the craft was not an apparition. The passing from one life to the next had always been romanticized in Venice, which itself seemed to occupy a dream between two worlds. But even Venetians became uneasy when death came so often and so mysteriously.

Almost daily now, bodies were found in churches and parks, crumpled in alleys, and drifting in canals. The cause was a mystery to most of Venice, but recently Nicolas had begun to see that the city was being overrun by rogue vampires. These preternaturals, created by young vampires without the sanction or ancient blood of a coven house, were feeding and killing indiscriminately throughout Venice. It was not the first time Venice had been ravaged by a plague of rogue vampires. It was, however, the first time the ancient vampire Houses had failed to intervene when the delicate balance between the creature underworld and human society was threatened. The barge slipped silently through the rain, and in a few moments, San Michele appeared ghostlike from the darkness. The Island of the Dead had been forced to re-open its gates as a staging point for the steady stream of casualties pouring from Venice. The use of the ancient ornate funeral vessels, discontinued for decades, had been revived in the past few tragic months. Mourning and fear had awakened superstition in all its forms. It reflected in the pale faces of these young people who had turned away from Nicolas to watch the progress of the black-shrouded craft.

As the barge disappeared, an edge of panic sharpened the whispering voices. "Nine of them... There were nine more victims today..."

Nicolas watched, dismayed, as they turned toward his motorboat. Why had they ever come to look to him for answers? "Maestro Portinari! Are you there?" Nicolas rose, gripped by the frightened voices, but Francois laid a hand on his arm. "It's better if you don't, Nicolas."

He stared at Francois for a moment, immobilized, then fell back into the seat and motioned the driver onward. The small boat bobbed in their wake. The sobered youth made no effort to follow.

As they drew closer to the theater, he could see that even in the crowd tonight, there were a disconcerting number of newborn vampires and their revenant makers, lean creatures with wild eyes who normally clung to the shadows. Their presence here in the open and in such numbers was evidence that something was very wrong in Venice. Why had it taken a young woman's death to open his eyes to what was happening around him?

Francois broke Nicolas's concentration. His eyes panned over the crowd. "Are you sure you want to go into Venice tonight? There will be questions about the suicide in Paris."

"I can't ignore Provechio's ballet when he's made such a point of crediting my music for its success."

The craft slowed as it entered a side canal. A brilliant flower of golden light bloomed out of the darkness ahead of them. It marked the location of the Teatro del Amarro where the new ballet was premiering. The boat pulled up to a floating dock, and the engines cut off. At the end of the dock, a long sweep of algae-covered, marble steps emerged out of the black water and rose to the plaza and theater above. The marquee at either side of the entrance bore a poster of dancers superimposed over a gauzy image of Nicolas. His watchful, black eyes staring out at the assembling crowd were the only sharply focused element of the portrait. A cloud of dark hair fell past his shoulders. The rest of his face was almost featureless, a snowy field branded by coal-black eyes.

"Look." Francois nodded toward the crowd milling around in front of the theater. They had recognized him and were making their way toward his boat. Many of them wore Egyptian-style costumes of white linen and gold jewelry. Many in the crowd were vampires.

"Unbelievable," Nicolas breathed. The costumes were reproductions of those from his opera, *Cleopatra*. Fans in front of the theater jostled for a better view. Nicolas sensed a demanding undercurrent flow through the crowd as they leaned over the gate and chanted his name, "Nicolas! Nicolas! Nicolas!"

The sound had once been a sign of his acceptance in the human world. Now, it felt grasping and dangerous. An irrepressible curiosity and the tremble of desperation in their voices drew Nicolas to his feet. Before Francois could stop him, he was through the door of the cabin, onto the dock, and walking toward the crowd.

"It's him! He's here!" someone shouted. The fans whooped and applauded. The revenant vampires vanished into the throng.

Francois cursed and hurried to catch up with him. "Nicolas, this isn't a good idea," he cautioned. Nicolas had just reached the bottom of the stairs when suddenly someone shouted, "Nicolas! *I understand!*"

He raised his head. The mob surged and threatened to engulf him. He took the steps up slowly, then stopped and raised his voice to respond, "What do you understand?"

The cacophony of voices swallowed a confusion of answers. "Nicolas," Francois began uneasily, but Nicolas raised a hand slightly to stop him.

The eyes of a woman in a nondescript gray coat pinned him with their intensity. Holding her gaze, he raised both hands to quiet the noise. When the voices calmed, he said to her, "Tell me."

Her eyes widened. "*Me?!*" She looked around to see all eyes on her and fidgeted nervously until she finally found words. "I believe what I hear in your music; that, if we reach for it, there are mysteries to be revealed. Ways to unlock new potential."

He smiled at her. "We find in music what we're looking for. What you hear in my music is my projection of what I seek in my life. What you interpret from it is yours."

"Yes, of course." She smiled. "But just standing here with you now, I feel it. You aren't like us. You are a man who understands more than most. You aren't afraid, not of the plague, not of criticism, not of anything. You're confident, like you can see the way ahead. I'd like to have that faith in what I believe, too. Your music almost takes me there."

He shook his head. "The power in my music, if there is any, comes only from beauty. Beauty in tone, melody, point, and counter-point. The power is the synergy of instruments and voices coming together. This is an aim I share with all composers, I imagine."

She drew back slightly with a skeptical tilt of her head. "I'm sorry, but I don't believe you, Maestro Portinari. Are you saying that the characters in *el Samun* are not meant to point out the contrast between what we are and what we could be? Floran, a simple mortal human and Helene, immortal, without limits?" The crowd murmured their agreement.

Nicolas was stunned. This is how they interpreted his opera? "Floran and Helene are metaphors about basing one's choices on one's own truth and values. In the end, each draws completion from living with integrity. Like all artists, I try to capture elements of our humanity in my music. But in the end, its primary purpose is enter-tainment." Nicolas looked for a glimmer of understanding among them, but they merely looked at him blankly with a hunger he didn't understand.

His eyes locked on a vampire in the crowd who had been staring at him since he had stepped onto the pier. The creature wore a long, hooded cloak, ridiculously medieval except that he carried it so naturally. No revenant, he could only be a member of one of the old covens. He stood still in the crowd, his posture taut and his eyes alert. He seemed of two minds, caught between confronting Nicolas and fleeing.

The two drifted closer as Nicolas made his way through the crush of people. Nicolas could sometimes sense the thoughts of others, especially vampires of his own blood, humans, and young vampires. From this one, he could only pull a name. Argus. He was old, and his consciousness was clouded, somehow severed from his will. What malignancy was Electra perpetuating now?

Puzzled, Nicolas spoke in a near-whisper that wafted away on the wind for all but the vampire before him. "And you, Argus of Delphi? What is it that you understand? The stench of Electra's conniving is all over you, but you are not one of hers."

"I have a long, complicated history, Maestro," Argus sneered. "Don't mistake me for one of your fans. I know my place in the world. And this—" His hand rose in a gesture that included the theater, the crowd and Nicolas, "—this subterfuge is not where either of us belong. That spectacle in Paris proves it."

"It proved nothing except that Electra has become deranged enough to be dangerous. The woman was one of her acolytes. Do you know where she is? I'd like to let her know how much I appreciate her stunt. But then, you're one of hers. Perhaps I owe you my appreciation, as well?"

Argus stepped a safe distance back. "You owe us more than you think. The sooner you come to that realization, the better for us all. Electra would have you know your time to reclaim Venice is short."

Nicolas scoffed, "This from a woman without the spine to deliver her own messages? You can tell her that my participation in her trickery ended in the ashes of Ca' Portinari a thousand years ago."

"Your hatred for Electra blinds you. You might consider paying heed while there are some of us who still believe you are our kind's best hope," Argus added before the crowd boiled forward. As he was swept away, he shouted to Nicolas, "Don't wait too long, or it will be someone else's order that prevails."

Francois caught up with Nicolas and immediately began clearing a path through the crowd. As they climbed the steps up to the theater, Nicolas caught a final glimpse of the strange vampire as he vanished into the night.

4

CONFRONTING THE TRUTH

After the ballet, a boat picked them up at a side entrance, letting them escape the mob in front of the theater. Nicolas and Francois rode silently for a short while. Nicolas stared out the window. He felt Francois watching him, undoubtedly trying to decipher his strange detachment. In truth, he was struggling to recognize the Venice he had seen tonight. This general sense of fear and unrest was normally not part of the landscape in the town of his birth. They passed by several posters for the ballet with the words," *I understand,*" scrawled across them with red paint. Nicolas exhaled sharply and said aloud, "They understand. What do they mean? I asked, they answered, and I still don't understand. Is it a confirmation or a threat?"

"It may be both." Francois's expression changed. "Or it may be a plea." His hazel eyes seemed unnaturally intense as he spoke. "At a time when all these unexplained deaths have left them hopeless; you've given them immortal characters—heroes of integrity, who seize control over their lives and create something meaningful of their existence. Surely you see how you bring them hope? A sense of freedom? Something to strive for?"

Nicolas smiled. "That's high praise coming from you. I don't think I've ever heard you venture an opinion on my work before."

"I'm not really qualified to have one." He looked down thoughtfully, then added, "But I don't know, somehow this season feels different, everyone seems so polarized. It's as if they're no longer talking about art but about something else."

"They are, and that's probably my fault. I've been a little too direct and carelessly pointed in my productions lately." He crossed his arms over his chest and exhaled heavily.

"Nicolas, no one else has ever done productions like this before. No one has integrated multimedia, video, and music the way you have. I think these works have become so realistic, so immersive lately, that audiences don't realize they are watching something fictional. Your productions literally break down the 4th wall between observer and participant. The experience is powerful, and it feels real. You're not to be faulted for that. It's what gives your work its power."

"Yes. It's also what makes people see more than is there."

"Some of them may see the real substance behind the spectacle."

"The woman in Paris thought she did, too, and look how that ended. These people want more of me than my music. They look so hungry for something. An answer, maybe?"

"They want you." Francois voiced the impossible demand as if it should be a comfort. "To have a connection to the man who inspires them. Even if that connection is just a moment when you acknowledge that you are connected to them through your music. Fantasy meets reality." François lit a cigarette. "It's a strange time. They're terrified. You bring them comfort."

"Comfort?" Nicolas chuckled. "Do you see the irony in that, Francois?"

"I do. But I can also see their point."

Nicolas looked at him sharply. "Can you? Because seeking comfort from a vampire means death for a human. It's that simple."

Francois blushed and withdrew back into his seat. Nicolas knew that in Francois's mind the crowds, the notoriety, were just problems to solve. For Nicolas, the prying public, the relentless press, and the unexplained deaths were all evidence that his carefully constructed life was threatening to come undone. Nicolas listened for escape. He tried to find the music once more in the sound of the water lapping against the bank. Francois stubbed his cigarette out. He never seemed to finish them. "Reviews, aside from a few from LeCourbe's camp, are all glowing." Francois hesitated. "El Samun may be your most popular opera, yet."

"Yes, and now it's tarnished irreparably." Nicolas sighed, thinking of the efforts of so many that had gone into the production. Preparations for opening night had consumed his attention for weeks. Normally, an opening left him elated but ready to be home, which was why he and Giuliana always returned to Venice after his premieres. The city seemed to forgive her native son for opening his works in Paris, so long as Giuliana held her famous galas celebrating those openings in Venice. The post-production respites were usually joyful and relaxing. Not so this year.

Francois continued to recite the necessary details of the past week's business. Nicolas gazed at the lights along the shoreline and struggled with an inescapable truth. The greater his popularity grew, the more the public sensed his strangeness. The more they praised his work, the plainer it became that the source of their love for his art was his otherness. Every attempt at self-expression invited public exposure of his true nature.

Francois's voice stopped, waiting for a reply. Nicolas stared at him blankly. An amused smile played over Francois's lips. He leaned forward to speak to the pilot, waving them to shore a bit short of their destination. Nicolas and Francois stepped onto the rocking wooden wharf. A row of small shops, mostly darkened for the evening, lined the cobbled walk, but a soft glow still illuminated the small jewelry store that was their destination.

Gustavo created the famous jewelry that was a tradition between Nicolas and Giuliana to celebrate the creation of every new opera. With each new work, Giuliana gifted Nicolas with a spectacular opening night gala, and Nicolas gifted Giuliana with an equally spectacular creation by Gustavo to wear that evening. Nicolas was especially pleased with his idea for this year's gift.

Passersby, even when they did not recognize Nicolas, turned curiously as they passed to take in the unlikely pair. By all appearances, both were nearly the same age. Both were tall and lean with angular features. Nicolas invariably wore tailored, Italian-made suits in dark colors which followed the natural silhouette of his body, and gave him a sleek, cat-like grace. Francois's suit reflected the exquisite cut and understated detailing of a high-end Parisian couturier, and his gait was sure and purposeful. Nicolas's hematite eyes and mane of ebony hair were a counterpoint to Francois's bright hazel eyes, neat chestnut hair, and close-cropped beard. Nicolas had a romantic aura about him; Francois was the consummate French financier, crisp, self-assured, and focused. Nicolas was always slightly distracted, especially in Venice, where he tended to hold his surroundings in a deep sort of reverence.

Francois brought them to a sudden stop to look more closely at the display in the tiny window of a bookshop next door to Gustavo's. A pyramid of Nicolas's compact discs and vinyl albums was surrounded by a scattering of paperbacks bent on deciphering the supernatural and philosophical themes in his musical dramas.

"I've never seen anything like it. You're everywhere I look." Francois looked up at Nicolas and smiled, then hesitated. "You don't seem pleased."

"They display this trivia alongside my music, as if it's all the same thing." Nicolas slipped away into his thoughts for a moment. He pondered the idea that his music could, in the end, have no more worth than the sensationalism.

A book on display caught his eye. On the cover was a photo of

Nicolas conducting an orchestra. He was on his toes, shoulders lifted, arms raised. His hands floated like talons at the end of arms bent forward like the wings of a bird about to take flight. The title cut across the black and white photograph in bold red ink: *Some Understand, an Unauthorized Biography of Nicolas Portinari by Jules LeCourbe.*

Nicolas glanced at Francois, who seemed braced for Nicolas's reaction. "Paul read the advance copy. I didn't realize it had been released," he said quietly.

"And what does LeCourbe have to say?" Nicolas asked wearily.

"At his least offensive light, he says you're power hungry, a fanatic who seeks nothing but to be idolized, like all leaders of cults," Francois answered frankly. The quiet timbre of his voice concealed any hint of emotion. "In his darker moments, he accuses you of capitalizing on this tragedy in Venice. He alludes to the popular rumor that you may be gathering a following for some more perverse purpose." Nicolas was forced to remember the treacherous balance his mortal friend was forced to maintain between his own humanity and exposure to a darker reality others could scarcely fantasize. When he looked up at the reflection in the glass, Francois was watching him with a disturbing intensity. An emotion Nicolas refused to name steeped in the sudden depth of Francois's eyes before his expression dissolved back into its normal detached professionalism.

Nicolas quickly took the opportunity to withdraw. "Gustavo will be waiting," he said crisply.

At the small jewelry shop, Gustavo let them in, then locked the doors. The reflective surfaces produced a riot of light in the narrow space, stunning Nicolas's senses. The clutter of glass and wood cases seemed smaller each time he visited. Photographs of celebrities wearing Gustavo's renowned designs lined the red-flocked walls.

"It's good to see you again, Nicolas." The old jeweler pulled his glasses perilously close to the end of his stubby nose and peered over them at his customer.

"Thank you, Gustavo. Were you able to work with the stones?" Nicolas asked.

Gustavo smiled broadly. He took a fringed scarf of black velvet from his arm and draped it over the counter, setting the case at its center. "You gave me quite a challenge, but I think you will be pleased."

Nicolas flexed his long fingers, opened the box, and lifted out a necklace. The glitter of gems in his hands was mesmerizing. It had taken Nicolas more than a year to procure the rubies. The gems had once been sewn to the bodice of a gown worn by Isabella I of Castile, the queen of Spain during a time when Giuliana's family were first among Castilian nobility. The long-anticipated necklace spread over his fingers in a spray set in an impossibly fine gold web. He imagined the concoction of chain and stone as it would tumble over Giuliana's pale neck and scatter blood red across her breast. It was an abstraction perfectly realized, a gift to represent Giuliana's heritage, their long life together, and their love.

"It's exquisite," Francois said. Nicolas held the necklace up so that the light caught in the scattered jewels. "You never disappoint me, Gustavo. It is exactly how I imagined it. Giuliana will be enchanted."

A satisfied smile lit Gustavo's face. He glanced at Giuliana's photo, displayed in a gold frame inside the glass case. She wore the twined snakes of red gold he had created as a tiara and necklace for the *Cleopatra* gala last year. The snakes' sapphire eyes glittered in the photo, their intensity a pale echo of Giuliana's cool, kohl-lined stare. "It's always a pleasure to design a piece for Giuliana. I was sorry to hear the gala had been cancelled."

Gustavo lifted the necklace from Nicolas's hands, rearranged it in its velvet case, and handed it to him. Nicolas slipped it into his coat pocket as Gustavo reached beneath the counter for a decanter of brandy which was the ritual ending for each transaction between them. He sighed dramatically, "You should have been allowed your celebration, Maestro, not vexed by the superstition of fools. All this talk of the occult is an embarrassment—they've all gone insane. One minute you're a devil, the next a savior. Bah!" he spat in disgust. "Your wonderful operas should be enough for them. Still, they want to pick the skin from your bones."

Nicolas watched the old man pour, then downed the amber liquid gratefully. The shop's warm light and Gustavo's friendship were harbors in the frigid darkness that had engulfed the city. The liquid warmed him. He was grateful for this moment, in the company of this man, who felt nothing for him but goodwill, even though he had known Nicolas for what he was for decades. These small points of grace that allowed him meaningful intersection with normal human life were a lifeblood to Nicolas. "It's nothing, Gustavo. The price one pays for being in the public eye."

"No one deserves to pay such a price, let alone you, Maestro. That poor woman was deranged." Suddenly, there was a shouted chorus outside of, "I understand," followed by the sound of running feet.

Nicolas smiled at Gustavo, "Thank you for this, my friend. Giuliana will be pleased."

Once outside, Nicolas watched Francois walk slowly through the murky light along the wharf toward the awaiting boat. Nicolas watched him until he boarded, and the boat pulled away toward the rim of sparkling lights on the horizon that was Villa Giuliana.

When Nicolas turned back, he was frozen by a sudden, putrid scent and footsteps in the alley beside the jewelry store. He touched the box in his coat pocket and willed himself to remain still as an apparition emerged from the dark shadows. It was a vampire, one of the young ones, watching the window where Gustavo could be seen closing the shop inside. Judging from the way the revenant peered furtively into the window, he had a purpose and knew he had no right to be there. Nicolas watched him fall back into the shadows, settling in to wait.

Before the intruder could draw a breath, Nicolas was behind him, his hand clutching the vampire's throat. He forced the struggling creature back against the wall. "You are violating a very ancient covenant by being here. This place is under my protection." Nicolas snarled; all trace of the elegant maestro was gone as the ancient vampire emerged. His fangs extended; his eyes blazed in a mask of rage and perpetual hunger. "The penalty for breaking my aegis is not pleasant."

The young vampire cowered, but still hissed, "That protocol is as dead as the Coven that decreed it." His bleary eyes bulged. "Who are you to interfere in Venice? You've abandoned your kind here!" it gasped, grappling with Nicolas's hand at his throat. Nicolas hissed close to his ear. "I am Nicolas Portinari, and all preternaturals know that the mortals I consort with are under my protection. Why are you here?

Nicolas's gaze fell to the gleaming falcon pendant dangling from the vampire's neck. Electra. His anger grew. "Speak before I tear the answer from you."

The creature lost all hint of bravado, trapped by Nicolas's horrifying expression. "Have mercy, father. It would be death for me to tell you. My queen..."

Nicolas choked him until he gagged. "It will most certainly mean your death if you don't answer me." He reached out and let the creature feel the cold force of his will. The connection to the creature's mind was sudden and painful to the revenant. "Or shall I squeeze the answer from your blood-sodden brain?"

Images from the creature's mind flowed into Nicolas's consciousness; he had left a bloody trail tonight, starting in a place dear to Nicolas. The vampire clutched his head in his hands and gasped with the pain of Nicolas's enraged invasion, barely able to speak.

"To observe!" The words bubbled from his mouth trailing a dribble of crimson. "That's all to observe. To discover which of your acolytes you are likely to turn."

Nicolas's hand loosened on the revenant's throat as he broke their connection. "What makes you believe I'm likely to turn any of them?" he asked, thoroughly bewildered.

The creature stuttered, "They say... they say... you must. The revenants, father, can't you see? They are overrunning us! The ancients are gathering their loyal ones around them. Anyone bound by blood to your House of Rialto is a sworn enemy to all other Houses and a danger to us if you will not join us."

"My house is dead," Nicolas snarled.

"But *you* are not! *You* are House Rialto!"

The words struck Nicolas like a physical blow. "Please, father! We have the right to protect ourselves if you won't!" the vampire cried.

"I have sworn never to bring another soul into darkness," Nicolas growled. "But coven or no, I guarantee that the penalty for interfering with any human under my protection will be death." He shoved the revenant away from him and through the gate. "Tell your grasping queen that I am not quite dead yet," he spat.

The vampire walked backward down the street, his bravado returning the more distance he put between them. "Your rule is ending! A new, powerful house has risen in Venice. Electra will prevail."

Then his courage deserted him completely, and he sprinted down a side alley.

Nicolas cursed and took a few steps after the wretch. He hesitated, then drew a deep breath. It was better not to confront Electra or her brood when he was angry. He would find another way to remind her of her place.

5

ANDANTE

As the vampire's footsteps echoed down the alley, Nicolas felt suddenly cold and discouraged. He cast a thought toward the villa where Giuliana was still shutting down preparations for the gala. He reached out through their blood link and gently brushed her mind. *"Venice is waiting, Mio Cuore."*

He felt her smile and maintained their connection as she gave final instructions to the staff then hurriedly left the house. She moved down the pier toward the boathouse, and he quickened his pace, glad that she would be joining him soon.

He moved through the markets, passing merchants covering bins of walnuts and chestnuts for the night. Luminous persimmons were piled alongside bushels of new pears. The sweet smell wafted on the bitter wind and reminded Nicolas of eras past. He continued walking, avoiding all eye contact, moving through the streets with the air of a man who knew the city intimately. He trusted no one; not the public who would cling to him, the press who hounded him, nor the pale vampires he passed occasionally in the crowd. He trusted only Giuliana, Francois, and this decrepit old city whose ancient heart harbored as many secrets as his own.

Nicolas was born in the year 1008, when Venice ruled over the Adriatic and balanced power between the Holy Roman and Byzantine Empires. He was the eldest son of Dominic Portinari, a politically astute magistrate and wealthy shipping magnate. Dominic and his five sons were all pioneers in the burgeoning trade with Egypt and India. Like his father before him, Nicolas was fascinated by the sea and ships, and even more so by their exotic destinations. His life had been one of privilege and reckless adventure at a time when the boundaries of the world were still unknown.

In 1047 he had been dragged unwillingly into immortality by Khaldun, his chief business rival and the elder of the House of Rialto. It was a cruel end to a life filled with possibility. Miserable over the metamorphosis, Nicolas vowed never to create another vampire. It was a promise which sentenced him to centuries of loneliness and led him to the bitter discovery that the drive to create more of his own kind was as strong as the need for blood.

In the nearly thousand years since he had broken his vow only once by turning Giuliana de Cordova at the end of the 15th century. He had been completely captivated by her, and she had come to him willingly, with such openness and honesty that he had surrendered completely to their need for one another. She had been his only companion ever since. They passed their centuries together as soulmates and lovers, bound to one another in a way that surpassed mortal understanding. He interfered with other vampires only when they threatened his life with Giuliana. Because of his vow, Nicolas and Giuliana were the last survivors in Venice of the once mighty House of Rialto.

He came to a halt in a pool of darkness. He had arrived at his destination; the old deserted Arsenale. The vast network was full of wavering shadows and light. The old complex had been closed for decades. Its bones glistened in the moonlight, damp and water stained, a half-buried skeleton.

A sound like a flock of birds taking flight rose from within the crumbling complex. Nicolas peered into the darkness until he found the source; heavy plastic sheets fluttering over a long row of sculpture stored here for a restoration that had never come. The statue's quivering winding sheets animated their wraithlike forms. Beneath the shrouds, the ghostly figures stood frozen eerily in place under the shelter of a collapsing roof; prisoners struggling to be. Nicolas edged closer, drawn to their veiled secrets.

A gondola glided out of the darkness to dock at the battered stazio, just a few dozen feet away. Nicolas recognized his own gondolier at the same moment Giuliana emerged from the cabin to step up onto the quay. Pulling her cape around her, she strode from the streetlight into the pitch black of the deserted loggia. His keen eyes saw everything in the scant light, her shoes and dress glistening, the puddles on the wet pavement shattering like mirrors where she stepped. Even in the darkness, he could see her eyes were a storm of shifting blue and gray. Crossing diagonally across the pitted cobblestones, she headed directly toward him, moving with perfect intention, a woman who never took an indirect route anywhere. Her hair had slipped free of her hood and whipped around her face in flashes of gold, her eyes darted over the Arsenale's decaying facade, missing nothing. Nicolas knew that she, too, was distracted by the sensual symphony around her, though it manifested for her as a visual and tactile feast. Now and then, she paused to touch the bricks with her fingertips.

He reached for her softly, silently, with the psychic connection born of their shared blood *"Giuliana. Beloved."*

The marble figures appeared to move on their pedestals, a deceptive trick of the light and wind. He watched them, transfixed, lost suddenly in the strains of a melody born in their motion. He reached out and touched a pale statue of Apollo, absorbing its music through his fingertips. Another alabaster figure floated through the shadows toward him, her unearthly eyes filled with compassion. He reached for her, and his heart stopped beating as she spoke his name.

"Nicolas? What's wrong?"

His confusion evaporated at the sound of Giuliana's voice. He folded her in his arms so suddenly that she gasped. He inhaled her scent and found a moment of peace. "Nothing now, beloved."

"I've been thinking of you all evening," she breathed against his neck.

"I wondered why I couldn't concentrate on the ballet tonight." He smiled and kissed her, then pulled away, knowing her kiss was only the sweet frontier of his longing. He released her to pull the jeweler's box from his pocket and place it in her hands. "I've brought you something. It was for the gala, but..." He shrugged his shoulders and fell silent.

She took it from him, opened it, and exhaled sharply. The rubies floated before her face in a galaxy of fiery points as she lifted the chain up to the light. "Nicolas!" she gasped, as pleased as he had hoped. "It's exquisite!"

Taking the necklace from her hands, he stepped behind her to fasten the web around her neck. "Wear them for me," he whispered against her hair. "I want to think of you and know you are wearing them."

He turned her and adjusted the golden strands over her throat. The effect was stunning. Her alabaster skin and intense eyes reflected the cold, radiant beauty of the stones. "From one Spanish queen to another," he murmured as he adjusted her cape around her shoulders and kissed her forehead. She looked at him quizzically, and he chuckled. "I will explain another night." He took both her hands in his. "Giuli, did you know about LeCourbe's book?"

"Yes," she sighed. "I knew."

He smiled sadly and shook his head. "Why didn't you tell me?"

"I saw no reason. You've been so concerned about the press lately; I didn't want his vindictive little missive to interfere with the opening. He's a gnat, Nicolas. Not worth an ounce of your attention."

"I hope you're right." He considered for a moment. "Giuliana, one of Electra's brood, followed me tonight. I caught him outside Gustavo's."

She drew back, surprised. "At Gustavo's? Have they lost their minds?"

"I don't know. She may be having us followed to guide her to potential acolytes. More likely, she's worried that I have designs on her power in Venice. She's not above using our friends to threaten me."

"Then she's gone insane. Aren't a thousand years of experience enough for her to know that you won't be threatened?"

"If I know Electra, she intends to take advantage of this moment. The city is paralyzed by fear, and I appear to be trapped into submission by my own public. I can't move anymore without making the news."

"What will you do?" she asked.

"The revenant had been to the Arsenale. I need to go there. But I don't want you mixed up in this. I should go alone."

"I'm not afraid of Electra—or her issue, Nicolas." It was true; she was not afraid. It was reflected in her intrepid manner and the confidence with which she moved through the world. She still carried herself like the Spanish nobility she had once been.

Nicolas spread his hand over her cheek and looked into her eyes. "I'm thinking of the night we met. Do you remember?" Giuliana brushed his lips with her fingertips, then reached behind his head and unfastened his hair from its tie so that it fell loose around his shoulders. She smiled at the effect and caressed the raven strands around his face. "You wore it down then." She sighed, remembering their first passionate nights in Egypt. "Come hunt with me."

"I have no heart for it. Electra and her spawn own Venice now. At least for the moment."

"Then let's see for ourselves what haunts the Arsenale. It's a good night to hunt revenants." She cocked one eyebrow, immediately game.

Nicolas nodded. "Yes, perhaps it's time we made an appearance." It riled his temper to think of Electra's spawn roaming the Arsenale.

They entered the old structure. Nicolas heard the faint sound of footsteps falling behind them and voices echoing from far away. The lagoon lapped against the quays. Wind creaked through deserted buildings. Entry these days was forbidden to the public, but there was nothing Nicolas didn't know about these yards, including paths of entry that had not been discovered in modern times.

A breath of stagnant air rose from the lagoon. Inside the Arsenale was another quieter, darker world. Nicolas and Giuliana turned down an alley which was sheltered between towering shells of buildings that created impossible shadows. It would have given the bravest man pause. There were humans about, their hearts pounding at a lethal pace as they intuited danger. Other, more dangerous creatures also scuttled through the complex's depths. Above the staccato of their own footsteps, they heard lighter, more hesitant ones following.

He slipped his arm around Giuliana's waist and guided her through the entrance to one of the oldest buildings sitting on the lagoon, one constructed centuries ago to manufacture ropes. Inside they followed a long ramp which led to the upper stories where rigging had once been loaded onto the passing ships. Its floor was pocked with holes, but Nicolas kept to the stronger side supports and climbed up to a loft. Giuliana picked her way deftly behind him. Large parts of the wall facing the water were gone. Orange city light misted through the gaps, illuminating the vast, murky interior. To Nicolas, it still smelled of rope and canvas. They paused, and Giuliana leaned against him, her head on his shoulder. "What are you thinking?"

"I'm just dreading the night it will no longer be here." Across the canal, the cemetery island of San Michel floated on the dark water, silent and white as a skull. Beyond it, the lights of Murano dusted the horizon. Nicolas surveyed the view, standing in a gash of light that spilled in through the ruined walls. He turned as the steps behind them came closer. A woman in her twenties emerged from the gloom. Ringlets of red hair fell around her face in a damp cloud. Nicolas could read her thoughts easily. She was confused, drawn to this place by some force she couldn't explain.

The woman's breath was short and labored. Nicolas stood perfectly still, willing her to pass. It was her last chance to save herself. He smelled death here tonight.

But she stopped, then stepped inside the shattered building, drawn inexorably up the ramp. She moved through the shafts of light that poured here and there through places where the roof was missing. From somewhere in the darkness beyond, Nicolas heard others moving; nothing more than a whisper of fabric as if the building had sighed. The woman stopped a few feet away, and Nicolas and Giuliana stepped out of the shadows before her.

Nicolas spoke, his voice barely revealing the urgency he felt, "Signorina, you are unwise to walk these ruins alone at night. Do you know how much danger you are in?"

The girl gasped. "Senore Portinari!"

Nicolas stopped short, and Giuliana inhaled sharply as both caught the sudden crisp, metallic scent of blood in the air. "You need to go."

He was beside the woman in an instant. He grasped her arm and forced her down the ramp and toward the entrance just as two revenants dropped out of the dark levels above. A half-dozen more appeared suddenly, crowded along the rails. They hovered at the edge of the darkness, hypnotized by the girl's pounding heart.

Nicolas's attention was pulled away from her momentarily. The two young ones before him were agitated, captured in the spell of the blood fever. They stood their ground, unmoving. He growled and lunged toward them. Just as he had the first in his grasp, the girl screamed behind him. He whirled around to find her in the grip of a third fledgling, blood already seeping from a fresh, deep wound across her breast and collarbone.

The fledgling could not have been more than a day or two old, judging by his agitation and the fire of irrepressible lust in his eyes. He lifted the girl off the ground, bringing the scarlet cut to his mouth. Her back arched violently, and her scream cut through the night. The newborn tore his own wrist. In a moment, he would give the blood back to her, and the girl would be damned for eternity.

With a swift motion, Nicolas ripped the head from the vampire he held, dropping him dead to the floor. But before he could reach the woman, Giuliana was there. She wrenched the fledgling's head off. His decapitated body stood for a moment, then fell to the floor. Giuliana sank to her knees, cradling the ravaged girl in her lap. Nicolas growled and looked around warily. A pack of revenants was a threat, even to vampires as old as he and Giuliana. But they had realized who they had provoked and decided the lone girl wasn't worth the fight. They vanished into the night with a chorus of shrieks.

Nicolas looked at Giuliana, and she met his gaze steadily, shaking her head. They couldn't save the young woman without turning her. She stood as Nicolas lifted the woman in his arms. Far away, the flutter of plastic shrouds covering stone statues thundered in a cold burst of wind, threatening to release what they held bound.

The woman's white hand floated up into the air. It trembled, disoriented, then found his face. He was totally defeated as her fingers ran along his cheek. Her hand closed in his hair. He leaned into her neck and took a long draught of her blood, sending comfort through the blood link.

Death tainted the elixir quickly. He released her vein but could not force himself to let her go. Giuliana followed him as he stepped down the slick bank and crouched to let the slight body slip into the dark canal. She stood beside him as he dipped his hands into the cool water and washed the blood away. He could not find motivation to stand and leave.

Giuliana inhaled sharply, and he was suddenly aware of a presence above him. A voice pierced the darkness from the loft where he had just been.

"How sweet, Maestro. I must say, it's gratifying to be reminded that you're still one of us. But don't you have a public waiting to adore you somewhere?"

Giuliana rested her hand on Nicolas's shoulder, standing protectively close. Nicolas stood and forced himself to focus on the figure above them in the loft. Her long, white dress with its billowing train, recalled the costumes worn by the *Cleopatra* fanatics, but she bore herself more like a queen than a disciple. The wind caught the layers of her clothes and moved them around her in a blur. She was slight, her expression brittle and defiant. A sleek helmet of raven-blue hair fell to her thin shoulders.

Electra faced him as he approached up the ramp with Giuliana, reminding him of the plastic-shrouded statues, broken, with only the appearance of life. He loathed her. He stopped before her, closing his eyes to fight the rage her voice loosed in him. When he finally allowed himself to speak, only the disgust he felt in himself remained to curdle his response.

"What's lured you out of your grave, Electra?"

"Why, I've come to see you, Nicolas." Her body was a study in angles and planes. She was too lean and too pale for the thin, white silk she wore, a dazzling corpse. "I've heard that you've been asking for me."

"So, your minion conveyed my message."

She chuckled, and her expression softened. "Nicolas, don't be naïve; when you spill blood, every vampire in Venice knows it."

He stared up at her. "Electra, I'll be brief. Get your House in order, or I will."

Her face froze back into insolence. "That's all? Good. Then you can listen to me."

Giuliana snarled. Nicolas laid a calming hand on her waist and pulled her close. "I suppose we're due. How long has it been?"

"Only years this time. Not like the decades when you were hiding in Paris," she said, sauntering slowly down the stairs. "Or the century when you were hiding in Egypt."

He cut her off. "I thought you had left the city. You have been quiet these past years."

"Maybe because this time you've taken a different tack and forced all the rest of us into hiding instead."

"Not far enough. Your spawn is thick in Venice. Everywhere I look, they're lurking. How could you have brought so many into this life with no care for the consequences? You used to have a conscience, Electra."

There was a flash of something human in her eyes. It may have resembled regret. "A conscience is a luxury some of us can't afford. We're not human anymore, Nicolas. You are not one of them."

Nicolas turned back toward the canal and its soothing view. "Get to your point.

She walked in a slow semi-circle scrutinizing him. "Why all the remorse? It's the girl's death you're agonizing over, isn't it?"

"You are boring me, Electra."

"See if this interests you then. The spawn you see throughout Venice are not all mine." He raised one eyebrow and waited. She let a cool second or two pass before continuing. "They are revenants bred from revenants from tainted vampire lines outside Europe—most of them are dozens of generations removed from any ancient's blood. They have no community and no one to lead them."

"I am not interested in the power politics of Venice's undead."

"But you do care to remain living amongst them, don't you?" He turned away from her while she continued. "Nicolas," she said more gently. "I know what your life among them means to you."

He forced himself to meet her eyes. "What do you want?"

"Without you, there's only me in Venice, and I can't control them without spawning an army."

"Electra, I am not responsible for every vampire in Europe."

"Then I have to be!" she hissed. "These revenants will soon make the lives you and I have built in the world impossible. The mortals are becoming superstitious again. How long do you think it will be before they get past the gossip about cults and plagues and make the obvious connection between you and the mysteries around you? How many lies have you been forced to tell just tonight to maintain your great farce?"

Gustavo's face appeared to Nicolas unbidden. Even Francois if sins of omission counted. He sighed, "What would you have me do?"

She tossed her head angrily. "You know what you must do. Take back the power you abdicated."

Nicolas allowed himself a tired, amused smile. He hadn't expected this. "Surely you do not mean to say you would trust me any more than the revenants, Electra?"

"This time, I have no choice. You two are the last of the Rialtos, since you chose to destroy the rest. Doesn't that make you responsible? Shouldn't you at least try to save the world for the sake of those mortals you are so fond of?"

"It is hubris to think we deserve to have influence on humanity, Electra. Lest you have forgotten, we are the evil in the world."

"Hubris is *human* pride, Nicolas. Our supremacy is not hubris; it is fact. It's only your monumental ego which makes you believe you are evil."

"Then why interfere? Why not let the revenants overrun the mortal world if we are not evil?"

Electra moved upward toward the peak of the ramp, where the sight of Venice was most breathtaking. She fed on the sight of the city, just as he did. Her expression was almost tender as she said, thoughtfully. "You know why, Nicolas. We need humankind. They sustain us, not only with their blood but by linking us to the culture and the world we crave. If not for them, we would become feral, hopelessly out of touch with the times, and trapped in the past. We have no ability to focus on the mundane. Can you imagine any one of us operating a power plant or collecting refuse?"

"So, we are parasites then?"

Electra spread her hands before her. "And you feed more lustfully than any of us. I've been to the opera, Nicolas. I've followed the progress of the artists Giuliana nurtures so lovingly."

"What is your point?" Giuliana growled, revealing a flash of hatred that hinted at the ugly history between them. Electra ignored her and said to Nicolas, "You need the undead in Venice to respect you. If you don't step forward, they will learn to despise you."

"The other Houses will have to control their own misbegotten broods. My House is long dead."

"The other houses can't. The bloodlines are too polluted—the fools feed from one another, diluting their strength—and there is too much in-fighting between them. Increasingly, half-bloods like me, born from vampires carrying more than one bloodline, are building their own covens. These weaker broods are rising everywhere. You're the only one to whom the remaining ancients will pledge allegiance. This new breed of vampire has no restraint. Their excesses will expose us. We will be forced out of the cities like we were in the dark ages. Do you remember what it was like for us when the world believed in vampires, Nicolas?"

He leaned his head back against the wall and sighed. "Electra, what you want is impossible. There is no room for compromise between us. The Elders are fractured."

"As long as you and I live, it's not impossible," she growled. "Rebuild your House. Re-establish order. They all fear you because of what you did to House Rialto. But, right now, they also believe you could resurrect Rialto and bring order back to our world. If you don't act soon, they will abandon all thought of you and look to someone else."

She took a few eager steps toward him. "There were once conventions for making vampires, Nicolas. You could force them to stop this mindless replication. Just gather enough of your own brood around you to protect your way of life."

"I do not want a coven, Electra. I am not a leader. I never was."

She turned to look at him. "What of your hordes of fans who swear publicly they would do anything for you? What of the prodigies Giuliana coddles and supports?"

"It is not the same."

"It's exactly the same. You're only following your nature, Nicolas. We will always gather a clan. The only difference is that you stupidly refuse to pass on the strength of your blood and re-establish Rialto as the first house. Have you forgotten that your line once ruled the preternatural world from this city? From this very complex? They would follow you! Give them your ancient blood. What a mighty house it would be!"

"That legacy died with my maker, Electra. The undead cannot be lead. Giuliana and I have built a life together. That is all we need." Giuliana stepped closer to him, her body taut and primed for a fight.

"I shouldn't need to remind you that you weren't suited for the role of faithful husband, even as a human," she threw back hatefully. "Haven't five hundred years of that particular masquerade been enough? You are a vampire—you don't need a mate; you need a coven. So does she. There are those around you who could be turned, those who could make a difference. For all the guilt you are carrying around, you could have saved that woman tonight- and the one in Paris. I would have. You could have; instead, you *chose* death for her."

"What you would have chosen for them is not salvation, Electra."

"It's *our* salvation. Without the strength of the old ones, the whole race of us will be driven wild. Think what that will mean for humanity, Nicolas." She hesitated for the first time. "I hear rumors and whisperings. Sokaris is struggling to rise again. He'll call followers to him soon. He could well be behind all of this. I have witnessed, myself, his ability to control others."

Nicolas turned on her coldly. "Sokaris again? After the woman with your mark on her arm took her own life at a public event? After all these centuries, I would have thought you could come up with something more believable than a mythical deity. My patience with you is wearing thin."

"Your patience, where Sokaris is concerned, has always been too thin—thin enough, at least, to keep you from seeing the truth."

"Then let your invention come and make things right for you," Nicolas said dryly. "If he is real, as you have always said, he is truly the most ancient amongst us. Let him come sort out your mess." He glared at her, his anger threatening to erupt. "He's been a convenient excuse for your evil before. I will not do it."

Anger flashed in her dark eyes, eyes remarkably like Nicolas's. "I'm warning you, Nicolas, because, for some reason, I'm still fond of you. But know that I hold you responsible, and I am not the only one. If reclaiming Venice means allying myself with Sokaris, I will."

"Then do it, Electra. And leave me out of it. And if another of your brood intrudes again on my domain, or stalks a mortal who is under my protection, or uses my name for your insane end, there will be hell to pay for all the House of Delphi. This conversation should hold us for another century. We are done Electra."

With an effort of will, he forced himself to vanish, pulling Giuliana with him, back to home, back to safety, back to the villa. The last sound he heard before he dissolved into the fog rising above the lagoon, was her angry scream whipping into a tempest.

6

ENTR'ACTE

Six Months Ago

E lectra woke from her sleep at sunset in a hotel in Qena. She hated Egypt's unrelenting dust and sand. She especially hated the sameness of the landscape, rolling away from horizon to horizon in unending waves of gray dunes. She imagined it might have been beautiful under a blazing sun but viewed through the filter of night, which drained it of all color, it made her long for the liquid, light-filled canals of Venice.

All that kept her going was the possibility that somewhere in the sea of sand was an ally who could help her gain control over Sokaris. Sokarian writings held that an ancient vampire named Khaldun had once commanded the spirit. Legend said that he had sought sanctuary and oblivion in the desert of Egypt at the end of the last great vampire war, a millennium ago after Nicolas had destroyed his coven. A passage in the chronicles of the cult had given her a clue to where she might find him.

She rose and made her way to the lobby, where she found Argus waiting for her. He led her to their car and slid behind the wheel. They didn't speak until they reached their destination, Luxor.

Their car pulled into a guard station, where an officer tapped on Electra's window and motioned for her to roll it down. She spoke to him fluently in Arabic and, after a brief negotiation, handed him a thick roll of money, and he passed them through the checkpoint.

The tourist parking lot that led to Karnak was deserted as Argus parked the car. "We'll have to walk from here."

She opened the door and stepped out into the cool night air. Their destination, the temple at Karnak, was an oasis of light in the near distance. An avenue of sphinxes lined the sandy trail they followed. The route ended at a soaring sandstone pylon at the entrance to the complex. The bribe had worked. The entrance was unattended. What few guards there were had withdrawn a distance away and stood clustered around a glowing fire smoking cigarettes.

They crossed through the portal and instantly plunged into a dark colonnade with columns so tall that, even with their vampiric vision, they could not see the top of them. They made their way through a maze of open courtyards, followed by claustrophobic passages which branched open suddenly into vast pillared rooms peopled with broken statues. They traveled silently through the stone labyrinth. Electra stopped several times before walls covered in hieroglyphs only to turn away after a few moments and continue their trek through the darkness.

Finally, Argus said, "Perhaps if you share what you're looking for, I can help?"

She huffed. "I doubt it." Arrogance tinged her voice as she paused in front of a wall covered in deeply carved ankhs. "And what I'm searching for is this."

Her pale hands fluttered over the wall like birds as she pressed a combination of the carved ankhs. In the next moment, a thunderous rumble filled the air, and the wall began to slide, revealing an opening. She pushed him through the entrance ahead of her and then followed quickly just as the wall began to slide shut again.

The darkness was absolute, the sudden silence deafening. Electra focused, then reached into her pocket, removed a small flashlight, and flicked it on. The light spilled liquid into the room and over Argus, who was crouched in the sand where he had stumbled. She played the light around to reveal a large rough-hewn chamber hollowed out of the stone.

As her eyes adjusted to the light, more details appeared. What appeared to be a large stone altar sat in the center of the room. On top of it rested an immense alabaster bowl. She shined the light onto the other side of the room and nearly dropped it when it revealed a group of faces staring at her. Startled, it took a moment for her to recognize the faces as a line of mummy cases which stood upright around the perimeter of the altar.

She was startled again when there was a sudden flare of light behind her. She turned to find Argus exploring the chamber with another brilliant flashlight.

"Don't touch anything," she hissed and took a few steps further into the room.

She motioned him to stay next to the altar, which she began to examine with the light. The stone itself was covered in hieroglyphs. There was an array of silver vessels, small figurines and a gold dagger laid out around the central bowl. It seemed to be set for a ceremony. She wiped sand away from the altar stone with her hand and a look of wild excitement sparkled in her eyes. "This is it!" She gasped breathlessly.

Argus looked at her with questioning eyes. "This is the Shrine of the Ancients! We stand before the altar of Khaldun, the oldest of our kind."

She ignored Argus and walked around the altar, her fingers smoothing frantically over the carved hieroglyphs as she read them aloud in a guttural voice. The spell echoed through the chamber. She moved down one side, then another, her voice growing louder. When she reached the final side, where Argus stood, she emitted a sound like a wail. In the flicker of an eye, she simultaneously pulled him over the bowl, grabbed the dagger, and slashed his throat.

He gasped as the blood gurgled from his wound into the bowl. A look of terror, then confusion, played across his face as she held him in place. He struggled at first but weakened quickly as his life poured out into the bowl. Just as it seemed all his blood would be taken, the wound began to heal itself. Another moment and the hemorrhage stopped. She pushed him aside onto the ground, and he crawled weakly away into the corner.

A burst of blue light flowered in the bowl, and wind moaned around the chamber. The lid of the largest sarcophagus crashed open with an awful din and a swarm of sand. Argus moaned and shrank back.

"Khaldun?" Electra said breathlessly.

The ancient vampire moved so lightly toward them that he seemed to float from the shadows. The stained and torn linen robes he wore could have been centuries old. The withered paleness of his face was not the translucence of an ancient; it was the fossilized remnant of something truly dead. Pallid, uninterested eyes were framed by dusty braids which had once kept his hair neatly in place but now were woolly and unkempt. He worked his hands at his sides as if his fingers were stiff. His nails were curled under and unnaturally long. Electra and Argus peered into the darkness to see other, similarly clad vampires emerging from other coffins, and clustering in the shadows to hide from the scant light.

Electra went to one knee, trembling. Argus prostrated himself behind her, fear radiating from his every pore. Keeping her head bowed, she lifted her eyes to Khaldun. "Father, I have searched for you for many years. My servant and I have disturbed your rest only out of desperation. I fear we are being led to the edge of extinction. We need your wisdom. Your help to reclaim what we once were."

"Help?" His voice was raspy and uncertain, as if he hadn't spoken for a long time, and carried the feeling of another age. "Our kind stripped me of power, decimated my bloodline, and forced me into the wilderness. What we once were has been extinct for a very long time."

"You would find the world, and our place in it, much changed since that time. I assure you; it is worth saving."

"You assure me?" Khaldun hissed, violently. "Who are you, to intrude on my refuge and ask favors of me? What do I care about the vampire world?"

Electra cringed. "I am Electra, keeper of the secrets of Sokaris, and queen of the resurrected house of Delphi." Despite her bowed head, her voice was prideful, and she raised her eyes to meet his.

The old vampire drew back. His face twitched. Finally, he scoffed incredulously. "Sokaris. I haven't heard of that one in an age." For the first time, he looked at Electra with mild interest. "What do you mean, 'resurrected house of Delphi'?"

"I intend to take back the power of the original House of Delphi. There are others, Elders, who would join me."

"Would they?" A thin chuckle escaped him. "Have I been buried here long enough for the world to have changed so much as to see the Elders agree on anything? As I recall, there was one of unexpected power who tore everything asunder. What of him?"

"Nicolas Portinari lives, but he does not rule. He has broken the power of the Elders and they are scattered to the four corners of the earth." From her knees, Electra recounted the highlights of Nicolas's story since Khaldun had left the world, his increasing wealth, his fame in Venice and Paris, his reckless interactions with the human world through business and particularly through his music. Khaldun stood still as a mountain before them. But he listened through the long story.

She finished. "But for all that, he is nothing but a joke now, a puppet, for the entertainment of humans. His very existence is a threat to all vampires. Nicolas has abandoned his nature and thrown away his power. With the right allies at my side, I can eliminate him."

"Yes," Khaldun mused, "his name was Nicolas, wasn't it?" A light flickered to life in his dead eyes. He studied her face. "Tell me how you would destroy this Nicolas. He had strength unimagined in a vampire."

"It is a power he has never used again; it lives only in legends." She lifted her head to meet his gaze. "He lives his life on a stage. He denies his vampire nature and lives on the fringes of humanity. He is neither one nor the other now by his own design. It is a weakness I intend to exploit to turn both vampires and humans against him."

His interest intensified a bit. "But he is powerful and dangerous. Perhaps more so, should he be exposed."

"That's why I need Sokaris. I once possessed an ancient gold ring engraved with roses that bound Sokaris to my will. I used him to bring Nicolas to his knees. I could do it again."

Khaldun laughed outright. It was a dry, cruel sound. "You would subjugate your own god?"

Electra dared to smile conspiratorially. "I don't believe in gods. Only in the means to my end. But the ring is lost, and Sokaris has disappeared."

"I see. And your lore tells you that I may be connected enough to Sokaris to know where he might be and how to control him?"

"Yes."

"And so then, am I also to be a means to your end?"

A look of caution played across her face. "Of course not. How could I ever command one such as you? I am your servant and only call on your mercy and knowledge to help us all."

Khaldun considered—the machinations of his mind playing out on his face, which had subtly softened. Finally, he said, "Get up, child. It is your good fortune that you have piqued my curiosity." Electra stood, her face luminous. Argus rose behind her but kept a safe distance. "I may be able to help you. I do know something of

Sokaris and how to bind him. Perhaps we can form an alliance of sorts if you are willing to follow my guidance."

"Of course! Please accept my humble gratitude." Electra's bowed head concealed her self-satisfied smile. "What would you have me do? Command anything within my power, and it will be done."

"You are already on the right path. You must wreak havoc with Nicolas's public life and make him suffer the consequences of his folly. His knife-edged walk between worlds must be made to cut him deeply. We must take away all that he loves and needs and leave him desperate and alone. He will be vulnerable then. That's when we'll strike."

His features settled into a smile full of malice. "And you must, as you say, find Sokaris. You are clever to have identified him as the tool you must wield. If contact has been severed with his acolytes, he must have been bound. As strong as he is, he is still susceptible to simple sympathetic magic. Return to the old knowledge to find him. The earliest spells are the best. Find a way to release him and I will know it. Then my family and I will come to your aid. Only then will I share with you what I know of controlling him."

"I will do as you say, Father. I have schemes and traps already laid. Pieces already in place."

Electra and Argus bowed once more and departed. Khaldun watched them leave, then mused, "Nicolas, Giuliana, and Sokaris. What can it mean that the triad have all returned to my orbit in one fell stroke?"

He turned to the ragged group of followers behind him. His bearing had straightened, and his eyes were alight. A frightening smile stretched across his face until it seemed as if his hoary skin would crack. "It seems where I thought I had two enemies; I may only have one. One Nicolas to bring to hand, and he has been served up to us on a delightful silver platter by that simple, waspish queen, along with a weapon that could finally bring him down."

His smile faded. "That servant, Argus, is not as devoted to her as he seems. I can use him." He beckoned to the vampires, and three women stepped forward. "Bring him back to me, alone, in a few days. Then prepare yourselves, children. We have a mission ahead of us that I think you will enjoy. It is long since we have roamed the earth. Do any of you remember the glorious city of Venice?"

7

PROTEGES

Giuliana came downstairs at dusk the next evening_and encountered the comforting sight of Francois and Nicolas together in the Villa's cavernous kitchen. Francois was cooking; Nicolas sat at the thick, deeply marred baker's table marking up musical scores. They were in the middle of a lively debate over the rights to *Cleopatra*.

Nicolas was dressed simply, in black slacks and a sweater, more relaxed than he had been since they'd arrived in Venice. His expression was vibrant as he laughed at the notion of sharing the rights to his music. The rich sound echoed from the vaulted ceiling and gave life to the space.

Francois was good for Nicolas. He was the latest in the lengthy line of Durands, who had been caretakers of Nicolas's fortune for many hundreds of years. His acceptance of the nature of vampires allowed him to challenge the formidable Maestro as few dared. Giuliana wondered if he knew how much Nicolas trusted him and if he understood what a rare and costly gift it was.

She smiled at Francois, grateful that he had distracted Nicolas for this moment. "Are you going into the city tonight?" Francois asked cheerfully.

"It is my last chance to visit with the Puentes before Egypt." She laid her cheek against Nicky's. "You could come with me."

Nicky folded his hands over hers at his chest. "We would only attract attention together. I may join you in a while." His thought barely brushed against her consciousness. *Drink deeply, Corazon.*

She left through the old garden, the scent of cypress and roses hanging heavily in the dusky air. At the end of the pier, her form quivered and vanished as she took flight. A net of stars and the humid night quickly embraced her. Moments later, she shimmered and reappeared as she touched the ground again in the heart of Venice.

The urge to hunt was suddenly powerful. Humans moved past, hearts pounding, setting off a primordial urge to turn and follow. There were only two reasons for a vampire to associate with humans: companionship and blood. Aside from his interactions with Francois, and a few associations in the music world, Nicolas avoided close human entanglements. Due to his advanced age, he seldom felt a craving he could not quell. When he did give into the urge to feed, he drank only from strangers. They were left alive and with no memory of their encounter with him.

Unlike Nicolas, Giuliana's relative youth meant she still felt her hunger profoundly and still required deep draughts of human blood for sustenance. Nicolas understood her need, but he rarely shared it. Thus, Giuliana often fed alone. Through many years of hunger, Giuliana had come upon a way to give something back to those whose blood she craved. She was an accomplished artist and art conservator. That passion naturally drew her to gifted human artists, whose blood carried a creative spark she found heady and satisfying. Over time, she translated her need to feed into a network of mutual support. She had become a mentor, a muse, and a patron.

With few exceptions, the artists did not consciously remember the moments she fed, but the act left them with a gift. In exchange for their rich blood, she left them infused with passion, a sense of possibility and a breath of creative energy. Her attachments to these artists had become a rich and fulfilling component of her life.

Over time there had appeared a few of such talent, with whom she bonded so completely she allowed them to see and remember her true nature. Carlo and Bianca Puentes, whom she visited tonight, were one such couple. If discovered, this offense would further vilify Nicolas and Giuliana among powerful vampires.

Electra had spoken the truth at the Arsenale. History proved that human awareness of immortals ultimately led to suffering and slaughter. Secrecy and discretion were the paramount rules of vampires. It was the most sacred covenant between immortals. Breaking it was considered an unforgivable transgression.

Giuliana had little regard for convention and had never known a world where the Elders wielded power. It was not intentional and had happened gradually, but there was no doubt that she had breached the rule of secrecy. Now Electra and the Elders would see that they paid the price. Giuliana feared the inevitable showdown. She had never seen Nicolas's strength tested by a greater force, but she worried that he might not be able to protect them against a coalition of Elders.

Though Nicolas did not sanction Giuliana's friendships with humans, he was keenly aware of all her proteges. She knew that he often came to watch them work in the pre-dawn hours. He saw their exhibits, knew their character and associations, and catalogued their habits. His purpose was twofold. The ancient law of Aegis gave shelter to humans whom a vampire had chosen to protect. Nicolas's shadowy presence around these humans prevented their falling victim to any other of Venice's undead.

More importantly, he came to witness the powerful effect she had on the humans who gave her the gift of their blood. It kept alive his belief that vampires could have a positive impact on the human world. It was a belief he had almost abandoned. Giuliana left the mortals she touched cocooned in her effect. It left them victims to their senses and in a state of heightened perception. The most promising among them took this gift and translated it into stunning works of self-expression. It not only enhanced their art, but also the way they approached their lives.

These vicarious relationships had become a window through which Nicolas experienced connection with the human world. He was always aware of the destructive potential that lurked in every encounter between vampire and human. His brutal history colored his interaction with the mortal world. He knew what it meant to be made a prisoner of death and darkness.

And now there was another threat. Giuliana's gift sent these mortals into the world burning like flames. It was the spark that ignited their talent and made their lives shine. It was this fire that had brought them the attention of the world and made them stars. It had also drawn the attention of critics like Jules LeCourbe. Though her proteges were devoted to Giuliana, Nicolas counted them a danger to her as well.

The back door to the Puentes's apartment was hidden beneath the first landing of the exterior staircase and propped slightly open. She closed the door silently behind her and lingered a moment, adjusting to their nearness, breathing in their scent, managing her hunger. These visits always began this way, on the cusp of desire.

The Puentes's studio was a single room stretching from the front windows all the way to the rear of the building and its courtyard. It had once been a ballroom and was still equipped with an elaborate chandelier of Austrian crystal and two fireplaces with mantels carved with richly detailed lions. The fireplaces were empty, and the chandelier was dark, but there was still an intense vitality in the room.

Carlo stood on a platform painting an oversized canvas tacked to the wall. A bed had been pushed to the center of the floor alongside an antique wooden table inlaid with a brilliant pattern of blue tiles, worth a fortune had it not been covered with drips of paint and faded from turpentine. Bianca lay sprawled on the bed, tangled in the sheets, working at her lover's portrait on a sketchpad while he painted hers. She wore one of Carlo's shirts which swallowed her. Her hair was black as coal and cropped close in a ragged pixie cut. Her eyes were large, dark, and liquid. She was intent on her sketch.

Carlo's head turned. He tried to hide his surprise as Giuliana moved into the room. Without speaking, he turned coldly away and stretched across the ladder to correct a patch of flesh. All the color in the painting was pooled in its shadows, blue in the hollows of the girl's eyes and cheeks, red in the fabric, a deep purple beneath her thin, dusky face. He was angry again. Giuliana noted the signs picked out in color.

"Giuliana!" Bianca said, delighted, bouncing up to a sitting position. The girl was slight and spirited. Willing to go to any lengths to fulfill a whim, she burned with a passion for experience. She quickly dropped her sketchpad and leaped from the bed. Giuliana hugged Bianca happily and looked up at Carlo. "This one is nearly finished, no?"

Carlo shrugged. His ebony hair fell in a tangle of curls to his shoulders. Giuliana's eyes traveled slowly over his bare chest, torn jeans, and paint-splattered boots. Her gaze came back to his eyes to find them filled with hostility. He challenged, "What difference does it make? It will never see the light of day."

Giuliana was exhausted by the old argument and said wearily, "Carlo, an exhibition is a distraction you don't need right now. Show your work too soon, and you'll waste your best opportunity to make an impression." She did not add the rest of her thought- *you must learn to harness your emotion so that it becomes integral to the work and not a distraction.*

Having heard this argument too often, Bianca ignored them, retrieved her sketch, and sat down on the edge of the bed, frowning. "This one is a challenge. There's something missing… in his expression. I can't pin it down. It's like…"

"Bitterness," Giuliana finished softly, turning from Carlo's scowl to sit by Bianca on the bed. Carlo turned back to his work.

Bianca sighed thoughtfully, looking back at her work, and began to draw. Slowly, what had been a simple charcoal sketch became a wonder of light and shadow, more animated, a more exact rendering of expression than a photograph. Giuliana was fascinated with the way a few simple lines and shadows had somehow captured Carlo's frustration, his loneliness. Bianca saw the world with the eyes of a vampire and had faithfully translated that vision into a breathtaking drawing. Few vampires could do the same; this kind of result required human alchemy.

After a long while of drawing, with Giuliana sitting quietly by her side, Bianca looked up and said suddenly, "You make me so much more." Her voice was full and husky with the same emotion threatening to overflow in her eyes.

"I only make you *want* more," Giuliana sighed. She let her lips meet Bianca's upturned mouth. Bianca pressed herself into Giuliana's kiss, breathless, poised in expectation. There was a sharp glint of pearly fang, then a long kiss, sweet and tender as a lover's, beneath Bianca's narrow jaw. The blood ran salty and pure over Giuliana's lips, exploding with life. She drew more deeply as Bianca swooned, electric against her skin.

Carlo had come down the ladder, unnoticed. He reached to grasp Bianca's arm and jerk her out of Giuliana's embrace, sending her sprawling across the bed. "That's a dangerous game you two play. How long before she forgets herself and kills one of us, Bianca?" Bianca stared at Carlo, bewildered. He glared at Giuliana. "Or is killing us the ultimate plan?"

Bianca rose from the bed. "You are an idiot, Carlo. It's only a little blood."

"A little blood? You do realize they are predators?"

"We're all predators," she snapped, annoyed, then stared dangerously far into Giuliana's eyes. "Giuliana, less than us. She takes what she needs and leaves life in her wake."

"Life!" Carlo snarled. "Tell that to the dead!" His eyes met Giuliana's. "How long do you think you can keep it up before someone figures out that the only plague in Venice is vampires?"

Giuliana sighed, but she was grateful his vitriol had finally risen to the surface. "Carlo, what's happened? Why are you so angry?"

"Don't you know, with all your keen insight?" He jerked an oily rag from the back of a chair and wiped his hands, then hurled it aside. "Other vampires have begun to haunt us, Giuliana. They've singled us out." He met her eyes. "They follow us like they're hunting us, because of our relationship with you and Portinari, I assume." His eyes grew narrower in his stony expression. "Why did he bring them here? Why does he want us all dead?"

Giuliana shook her head. "You are mistaken. Nicolas has nothing to do with the vampires who have invaded this city. Neither do I. We thrive on connection, not death. You are safe with me, as you've always been." She reached for him, but he shook her off.

"Can you swear that to me, Giuliana? Your first interest is our art? Even above our blood? Weren't those dead also once connected to vampires, just like we are connected to you? Can you swear that you will never take our lives?"

Giuliana cringed. "Do I need to swear it?"

Carlo stepped back from her sudden intensity. His mouth clamped shut on words he was obviously desperate to speak. "Don't play with me, Carlo. Say what you have to say."

He tilted his head to the side, and his eyes flickered a bitter dare. "Why don't you stop pretending I have any power here and just take it?"

It was the wrong night to test her. His pulse pounded in her mind as she watched the artery contract rhythmically just below his supple skin. Faster than his eyes could follow, she slid her arms around him, laid her head on his shoulder and sank her emerging fangs deep into his throat. He made a feeble attempt to push her away, but he was hers now, lost in the power of her hunger and his need for connection with her. She growled and drank him in. It had been him that she needed, the depth that she could not find in Bianca, the anger and frustration that echoed hers tonight. Where Bianca's blood was full of light and promise, Carlo's was full of longing, regret. And guilt. She pulled away and stared at him a moment as she processed what had passed to her through his blood, what he had wanted her to know but could not say. "Carlo, what have you done?"

He sank down to sit on the bed, his anger swallowed by fear. "Can you fix it?"

"At least have the courage to say it out loud, Carlo," she said miserably, knowing she would not be able to protect him now.

"I made an agreement with Jules LeCourbe," he choked out. "He promised me full press for an exhibition in Paris in return for an interview about you and what you are. And photographs from our evenings here in the studio."

Her anger rose swiftly. "You fool! I warned you about betraying us!" She hovered over him, her body taut and poised for attack.

"But he seemed to already know everything!" he shouted as if the words could ward off an impending blow. "And I haven't done it, yet!"

She froze, suddenly aware of another presence just outside the window.

Carlo looked up dazed, his fingers wiping blood from his throat, his eyes a question. Bianca blinked her eyes slowly, as if remembering to breathe. She rose from the bed and said desperately, "He's not going to talk to them, Giuliana, no matter what he said."

Giuliana held Carlo's miserable stare. "I know he won't," she said sadly, turning away. She sighed and shook her hair from her face, and looked through the window into the inky shadows beyond. A familiar presence brushed her awareness. Nicolas had come, after all.

Grief and despair overtook her. She had to be away. She left quickly, without another word. Refusing to acknowledge their stricken expressions, she barreled through the door, only to encounter Nicolas standing motionless against the garden wall, as hopelessly trapped as she was. She stopped short, facing him, tears beginning to fall. Nicolas grasped her by her arms, bringing her back, and said gently, "Giuliana, you know what has to be done."

"Do it then. I cannot." She spun out of his grasp but turned to face him, crimson streaks running down her cheeks. "Electra did this."

"You don't know that." He was cautious, knowing she was navigating a thin edge.

"Don't deceive yourself, Nicky. You know she controls LeCourbe. He doesn't have the brains or the courage to act alone." She turned and moved blindly away from him toward the sidewalk.

"Giuliana, Corazon, where are you going?" The distress in his voice wrapped around her, asking her to stay.

She didn't answer; she took flight instead. He could have followed her in an instant, but she knew he wouldn't. He knew her well enough to know what she needed and that she would have it at any cost.

She took form on the land side of the moldering palace that served as the residence of Electra's coven, as well as the headquarters of the Sokaris cult in Venice. A black steel falcon in a circle of gold was set into the iron bars of the courtyard gate. She entered the derelict garden. The courtyard was large for Venice. At one end was a fire pit and benches in a tidy square surrounded by low hedges. On the other was what remained of the original gardens, black with rot.

Several vampires and humans were congregated there, looking toward her. She hissed a warning. They moved away.

Electra remained where she was, sitting on a swing hung beneath a trellis, which itself was obscured by an overgrown vine. She had one leg tucked beneath her and pushed herself back and forth lightly with the other foot. A languid smile spread across her face. "Are you sure you want to be here, out of Nicolas's shadow?"

Giuliana bared her fangs and snarled. "Don't offer me sarcasm. It sickens me. You've caused the deaths of ones I care about tonight, Electra. Did you set LeCourbe on the Puentes?"

Electra relaxed into her seat. "I'm sure I have no idea what you mean." She continued to swing.

"Be careful Electra, Nicolas may not have me on the leash you think he does. I'm a different woman than I was the last time you stepped between me and someone I loved."

Electra put a finger to her temple, as if struggling to remember. "Let's see. You must be referring to that impressionable boy, Ramon. He was your son, wasn't he? A very entertaining young man."

Electra met her gaze, a challenge flashing in her eyes. Giuliana's fingertips burned as she resisted taking the bait. They had never tested one another. Nicolas had always stood between them, preventing them from coming to blows. Would Electra's greater age prevail in all-out war? Or would Giuliana's gift of fire prove stronger? Giuliana stood firm, full of rage. Electra tensed. The swing stopped.

There were certainly enough years of bitterness between them to fuel a war. They had first met when Nicolas brought the mortal Giuliana and her son, Ramon, home to Venice from Egypt in 1495, after a great fire and the tragic death of Ramon's younger brother. Nicolas had simply wanted to take Giuliana away from that sorrow in Egypt. But when Electra heard that Nicolas's home in Egypt had burned and that he had left on a ship bound for Venice, she wrongly assumed he was coming back to Venice after so many years to rebuild the House of Rialto and reestablish the coven hierarchy he had destroyed.

So, when other vampires fled the city upon hearing of his return, Electra had stayed. She alone had come to Nicolas at the old house of Rialto where he and Giuliana had taken shelter while Villa Giuliana was built. When she had seen Giuliana, still mortal, moving ghostlike through the world and wearing tragedy like a cloak, Electra had laughed, mockingly. "Really, Nicolas?"

It was a hateful, brutal sound. Giuliana had been terrified of her. Electra and Nicolas had argued bitterly about events deep in their pasts. Giuliana could not help but see how like Nicolas Electra was; dark, slender, and pale. They were also alike as vampires, both lethal, preternatural, and full of venom. Giuliana felt unmoored in this new world.

But then, Nicolas had brought Giuliana into the dark. Electra was shocked, and this time she was not amused. She found every opportunity to remind Giuliana that though she had once been a strongminded, privileged noblewoman, in the vampire world she was weak and vulnerable. Electra played on Giuliana's self-doubt and declared that Nicolas would not stay long, that a fledgling like Giuliana, even in all her feral beauty, could not possibly hold the interest of an ancient like Nicolas. Giuliana was wild still, a slave to what she felt, and Electra made her feel dread and helplessness. Electra found many ways to taunt her, and the most terrifying was to threaten Ramon.

Giuliana had been wed to Nicolas's mortal steward, and her son was of the line that would eventually produce Francois. Ramon despised Giuliana, first for the events in Egypt and then for choosing to become a vampire. Nicolas had been the one to win him over. They had much in common; a love of the sea and adventure, and exotic, faraway lands. Nicolas was generous with Ramon. He became Nicolas's steward and ran his business affairs in the sixteenth century as his direct descendant, Francois, did today. Electra's threats against Ramon went just far enough to frighten Giuliana without activating Nicolas. Electra blamed Giuliana for keeping Nicolas from rebuilding his coven and accused them of pretending they were human. But, in time, Electra returned to the Delphi house in Greece, and for centuries was not a presence in Giuliana's life.

Until now. Giuliana considered the woman before her. Why now? Why had she become interested in Nicolas and Venice again now? Reason overcame her rage. There was something more important to be dealt with here than Giuliana's personal revenge.

The space grew noisier. Giuliana looked around. There were humans in finely tailored robes of white wool with silver trim coming from inside the palace and taking seats on benches on the far side of the gardens, which were arranged in a square around the fire pit. Two of the acolytes opened the gate and invited others in from outside.

"Just say what you need to say, Giuliana. As you can see, I have other commitments." Giuliana realized that the gown Electra wore was like the others but woven in a translucent gossamer. She wore a large golden falcon pendant, inlaid with lapis lazuli.

The clock struck midnight. Something clicked. "Who are the Sokarians, Electra?"

Electra looked about the courtyard at the new arrivals, some of whom were beginning to take notice of their standoff. She said calmly, "The acolytes of Sokaris are mystics who keep alive the truths of ancient beliefs. We believe that there are great gifts to be discovered in abandoned lore, including the potential for immortality."

Giuliana's eyes narrowed. "That's the propaganda. What's in it for you?"

"Why, nothing. What else could there be?" Electra said primly for the benefit of the onlookers, who noticed her watching them and moved away to join those gathering around the fire. "You heard Nicolas. He is not concerned about our little group."

"Nicolas believes you are deranged and that Sokaris never existed. You've hidden safely in his certainty about that for quite some time. But me, I'm not so sure. Playing with powers beyond your ken seems exactly like something a power-hungry egomaniac would do."

Electra's eyes flashed and something seemed to be unleashed within her. "Your arrogance is unbecoming, Princess. You're so self-satisfied with your neat little existence that you believe Nicolas has shared all he is and all he has done with you. Maybe it's time I share some history with you." Electra grasped Giuliana's upper arm and steered her to the gate, away from curious ears. "As usual, you have things backward," she hissed into Giuliana's face and jabbed a pointing finger toward her own chest. "I had the power. I commanded Sokaris."

Repugnant as it was, it felt like the truth. Giuliana threw off Electra's grip. "To what end?"

"Revenge. My sister needed to suffer. I used Sokaris to take hold of Nicolas's mind and heart. I led him away from Portia and into my bed. His life was ruined on my whim. And I was a mere mortal then. Imagine what I could do today if Sokaris was unbound. Or rather, imagine what I could make Nicolas do, should Sokaris rise again." Giuliana's shock drew a self-satisfied smile across Electra's thin lips.

"You truly are malignant." The blood ran cold in Giuliana's veins. "Here's a warning. You may be a blind spot for Nicolas, but I see you clearly. I believe you are behind all of it; the suicide, Jules LeCourbe, the Puentes, the carnage in the city. And it won't be long before I am able to prove it. I don't know what vile scheme you are perpetrating, but you will suffer for your crimes."

"Do your worst, Giuliana. I welcome the challenge."

Giuliana turned toward the gate. Before exiting, she flung her palms backward, releasing two imperceptibly small balls of fire from her fingertips. They swirled through bare branches leaving a tiny sparkling trail. With a final loop, they descended to burn through the throat of one acolyte, then another. Clutching at the gaping, seared holes in their necks, the two fell. With cries of horror and confusion, the others ran to gather around them.

Giuliana continued through the gate, her face twitching with anger, hoping for Electra to follow. But the only sounds were the clang of the gate as it closed and the eerie lament of the supplicants' rising chant.

8

REPERCUSSIONS

They flew from Venice before dawn and spent the day at a hotel in Cairo. Just after dusk, a car delivered Nicolas and Giuliana to the private dock near Saqqara where the steamboat, Khamsin, awaited their boarding. While Nicolas went directly to the pilot house to speak to the captain, Giuliana paced the width of the stern beneath a trellis of miniature white lights strung between the decks. Her eyes passed hungrily over the familiar vista, the ink-dark stream of the Nile, the brief, rebellious eruption of lush greenery cradled by the protective desolation on either shore. She wandered restlessly along the deck, reliving the dread she had felt since she had looked up at the Palais Garnier to find the doomed woman's mad gaze fixed on Nicolas. One lone member of the pack circling Nicolas's blaze of popularity had become crazed enough to cross into the light, and now others would surely follow.

Her conversation with Electra still haunted her, but she had not found a way to broach it with Nicolas. Logic told her that the story about Sokaris had to be a lie; no one could have manipulated the man she knew in such a way. But a ghost of dread hovered. It had the ring of truth. He hadn't asked her where she had gone when she had closed herself off and fled the Puentes, and she hadn't asked what had happened after she had left. They had closed a door on that night with an unspoken agreement that it was too fresh and painful to face.

She glanced up anxiously to find Nicolas leaning with one shoulder against the glass door, gazing back down at her. She warmed and found her smile reflected in the subtle softening of his expression. He was as impatient as she to begin this journey. The two-week voyage from Saqqara to Abu Simbel was a ritual of renewal for them, and for more than one hundred years, the Khamsin had been their sanctuary. Now the steamer's huge paddle was motionless. There was no sound but the river's patient purling against the hull of the ship and her dock; no light beyond the ship except the strange, orange glow of Zoser's pyramid in the distance and the starlight bathing Nicolas's deserted estate, El Samun, on the cliff above them.

Giuliana reached for the rail and breathed a soft sigh of relief as the ship's engines shuddered and roared awake. A flock of egrets, flushed from a grove of date palms fringing the water's edge, took to the air and wheeled suddenly southward as a single body. Her heart caught and lifted with them as they found their own rhythm and scattered, a handful of velvet shadows, their silver wings vanishing, one by one, into the web of crystalline stars. The ship began to move and pushed slowly after them.

Giuliana had first seen el Samun through mortal eyes more than five hundred years ago. She had arrived at the garden palace with her family in the shimmering midday heat as a guest of the enigmatic Nicolas Portinari. By the time she learned what he was, it no longer mattered; they were irrevocably in love. The tragedy that had unfolded there had left her unable to return to the palace and gardens she had loved so well in the five hundred years since. At the beginning of every voyage, the abandoned complex stood as a reminder of the price to be paid for crossing between two worlds.

Giuliana was wholly absorbed in the throb of the engines awakening and the ship moving forward as Nicolas's arms slipped around her waist. "I love watching you watch the desert."

She leaned into him, relieved to hear the passionate nuance the desert had restored in his voice. "Let's stay here, Giuli," he whispered against her neck. "We can lose ourselves like one of the relics buried here in the sand."

"Egypt is our respite. But the vitality of the cities fuels our lives. We need the world."

He let her go and leaned forward on the rail with his forearms. "Maybe there is no place for us in the world. We take so much, and what do we give back?"

"We give them insight and vision with every drop of blood we take," she rejoined, stung by his unhappiness. "And, in this case, you gave them music, the like of which had never been heard. When there is no place in the world for that, it won't be fit to inhabit."

"And if my music comes at too high a price?"

"It's not your fault that one crazy woman's response to brilliance is self-immolation."' she tossed back, unreasonably nettled.

"That woman wasn't responding to brilliance or to my music. She was responding to what I am. What I *am*, surely you see that? Our very presence among them is destructive."

"So, what is our alternative? Should we give up our lives because they lose their will to live when confronted with the truth? There is no 'vampire' world separate from the 'human' world. There is one world, and we are a part of it."

He inhaled deeply and shook his head. "Giuli, we have the power to take more than we deserve. It is up to us to make sure we don't, not just for their sake, but for our own."

"And who gets to decide what we deserve? Them? Why shouldn't we, like every other creature on earth, let our need determine what we have the right to take? What choice do we have? We are not gods, Nicolas. We're not responsible for the order of things."

He reached and smoothed his palm over her flushed cheek. "No, Giuli, we're only responsible for the integrity of our own lives."

She stared at him, defiantly. "If integrity is to be the standard, I would gladly measure your life against anyone's. We will always be alien to them, no matter how much we give or how little we take. That doesn't make us unnatural."

"Tell that to the family of that woman who jumped. Tell it to the Puentes. Tell it to your sculptor tonight."

"Khali doesn't think me unnatural." She searched Nicolas's grim face. "Nicky, I don't have to go. He's insulated from Venice and the greater world."

He closed his eyes and shook his head. "You should go check on him."

"Come to the desert with me, and I'll make you forget every miserable, petty irritation of the human world, I swear it." Her voice trailed off into a low, sultry murmur. She bit at his throat and pressed her fangs against his flesh so his slightest motion of resistance would result in complete penetration. A challenging growl resonated softly, deep in her throat.

He foiled her threat; he tilted his head and melted submissively against her with a graceful motion so sensual and bewitching she could not doubt which of them had surrendered. His pulse beckoned, responded instantly to her every subtle move, trembling velvet soft at her kiss.

She sighed. "Let's drink our fill of Egypt. If there must be two worlds, then just tonight, let the mortals have theirs while you and I claim ours."

Hunger flared distantly in his eyes as he peered into hers, but he shook his head. Her heart fell at his words, so gentle and final. "You go, Giuli. I need to phone Francois and find out how much damage has been done." He leaned in and brushed her lips with a kiss, then turned and walked away. She watched him go, feeling the distance his great age placed between them at such moments.

Closing her eyes, Giuliana focused her power inward, until she felt the very substance of her body dissolving into the damp wind. With a thought, she vanished and willed herself southward along the river's course toward the desert and a need of her own.

She materialized on a familiar rock path, lustrous with starlight and dusted with sand. The hematite river returned the moon's illumination. Behind her lay the halogen streetlights and pink granite curbs of modern Aswan.

She followed the road until it ended in a final spasm of scattered stones which had once formed the wall enclosing the ancient village below her. Giuliana picked a path to a segment of the wall still standing along the escarpment. She leapt up warily to crouch upon the wall, her fingers splayed wide against the stone, her hair shimmering in a liquid curtain around her.

She inhaled the scent of the village, leapt from the wall, and became a silver specter crossing a moonlit field of rubble. She vanished like a shadow into the inky depths of the ancient town.

Her mind cast outward toward the Khamsin and brushed softly against Nicolas's. Their psychic connection, amplified by centuries of shared blood, linked his perception to hers in a state of mutual awareness. She perceived for a moment through his senses, and he through hers.

The pages of an unfinished score were scattered beneath his idle hands. She listened for the fragments of chords and rambling musical phrases that would dominate his thoughts while he composed. There was only silence. She hesitated, disoriented. No music. She was within a heartbeat of turning back when a familiar sight drew her up sharply, and the connection with Nicolas dissolved. She had nearly passed her destination.

Golden light poured through the open window of the mud-brick structure. The house embraced a small courtyard on three sides. The yard was paved with cracked limestone and covered with sand. A few wayward sprigs of oleander wafted over the wall from the garden next door.

Giuliana closed her eyes, frozen in place, trapped by the sight of an intense, dark-skinned man moving into view through the illuminated window. He came from another room deeper in the house, sipping from a cup held in both hands. His dark, honey skin was smeared with the same fine, ashy powder that coated the floor, the crumbling window frame, and every other surface in sight. He sat on the deteriorating windowsill between an overflowing ashtray and a regiment of deserted cups and half-empty bottles of golden beer. He set the cup beside him and bent forward to light a cigarette in cupped hands, engrossed in thought. He shook the match dead while smoke wafted around his head, then out the window and into the night where Giuliana closed her eyes and inhaled it like incense.

While he smoked in slow, unconscious gestures, his attention was focused on a large, shapeless block of red granite on a pedestal dominating the center of the room. It was surrounded by tables and shelves supporting other masses of stone and sculpture, some that could be complete, some only scored with a few sketchy gouges. Each piece of his work was intimately familiar to Giuliana, even the discarded fragments of unfinished pieces shattered in nights of angry frustration, now being ground to dust on the studio floor.

Giuliana passed through the open gate into the intimate space of the courtyard, concealing herself in the shadows. His scent filled her senses; she could not prevent the craving that sighed through her as she instinctually cataloged its inviting elements, sweat, granite dust, the peculiar masculine musk. And blood. Above all, blood.

His pulse pounded in her head, and she felt his frustration with the stone. Like every object of his passion, its hold on him enraged him. Peering toward the star-pricked northern sky, she cast her thoughts again toward Nicolas. He had abandoned the dark study and moved to the gaslit promenade outside their sitting room. What she saw through her own eyes vanished, and she saw only through his. Giuliana felt the exhilarating power of the old ship pushing forward beneath him and the kiss of the damp breeze on his face. She heard the wind as he did, fluttering against the scalloped edge of the canopy overhead.

Nicolas was remembering, sifting restlessly through the years. Memory after memory misted over his sight as he recalled centuries long past, centuries before Giuliana's birth, other catastrophes, other deaths, other reasons to start over. He saw the many lives he had crafted over decades, only to see them destroyed over and again by the necessity of adapting his existence to a world fashioned by beings perpetually engaged in a struggle with mortality. It was the price of living in a mortal world, to be haunted by endings. He felt as brittle and ancient as his surroundings. The temptation to bury himself in the warm, desert sands enticed him irresistibly, but even on the verge of succumbing, his relentless instinct for survival rebelled sharply. Hunger closed in on him.

Giuliana startled as the image of the desert in his mind was replaced suddenly with an image of her as she had stood on the deck an hour ago in his arms. Caught in his memory, her hands caressed him again. The folds of diaphanous gauze barely concealed the glow of her body beneath it; the recollection coaxed his appetite forward. He was torn between her invitation to hunt and his new aversion toward humanity, which transformed his hunger into a distasteful affliction.

Her image wavered before him; his thirst surged forward. Her image sharpened, the balance shifted; Nicolas surrendered abruptly to his hunger and reached out to locate Giuliana. As his consciousness touched hers, he was ensnared by the tempting tableau before Giuliana's eyes, the provocative vision of the tawny sculptor, and the alluring rhythm of his heartbeat. Nicky's head lifted sharply. Their connection vanished.

Giuliana's vision wavered, and the sculptor turned his head suddenly toward her. His dark brow arched in an almost imperceptible frown, as if he had sensed something disquieting. It was the unmistakable prescience of the hunted, the instant before panic explodes into the chase. Giuliana shook off the last shreds of her connection with Nicolas.

The artist crossed the room to circle round the block of unfinished stone. He scooped a rolled sketch and a noisy handful of chisel points and gouges from a sideboard and, defying the silence, dropped them to clatter onto the pedestal beside the granite. Turning to the stone, he lifted a dusty hand to test its surface with his thumb and forefinger.

His savage excitement the moment he began the execution of a new sculpture was intoxicating. She had rarely witnessed such an effortless translation of vision into reality in centuries of patronage. She waited expectantly, anticipating the next moment when his vision would express itself in the ringing bite of steel into stone.

He took a few hesitant steps and smoothed his hands cautiously over the unshaped mass. He searched its surface hungrily with his palm until his caress turned into a demand, and then a fist pounding the marble. He picked up a drill, but his focus evaporated. He was unable to work.

Disgusted, he flung the drill onto the workbench and stepped back, defeated. He turned suddenly and peered toward the window with a strange look of awareness, then padded to the door and threw it open.

He was barefoot, wearing nothing but a colorless pair of sweatpants rolled low on his dark, slender hips. He leaned one shoulder against the doorway to fix his smoky eyes on her without the slightest evidence of surprise. The barest shadow of a mustache and beard enhanced his expressive mouth. His dark hair was pulled away from his face in a short ponytail. His own features could have been sculpted in stone for their regal symmetry and remote demeanor. He was too serious, too intent, and too obsessed; exactly the profile that most often drew Giuliana to the artists she chose to champion.

"Hello, Anna."

"Your Paris show was remarkable," she said.

"So, you did see it." He regarded her solemnly behind a thick fringe of sable lashes. His gaze passed boldly down the front of her dress, the challenge as palpable as a touch.

"Of course."

"I guessed you lived in Paris. I thought I might see you at the exhibition."

"I won't come to you in public."

"Oh, yes. Your great need for secrecy."

She moved closer and brushed her fingers along the familiar, beguiling curve from his neck to his shoulder. His jaw tensed at her touch.

"You're angry. Why?"

"You stay away too long." He looped his arm around her waist and crushed her against the door. "Your eyes are hungry," he said soberly, exploring their depths possessively. "You need me, too." His arms folded around her more gently, and she was too bewildered to resist. He whispered, "I look for you everywhere. When you leave, all I can think is that you're gone."

"When I'm gone, you have your work..."

"When you're gone, the work is not satisfying. You come, and I am inspired for a while until your effect fades; then, I can only think about the next time you'll come or obsess about where you are."

His eyes clutched at hers, and she felt a note of dread. "Tell me the truth. Who are you with when you aren't with me? Where do you go when you leave? Do you ever even think of me?"

She drew away, putting a safe distance between them. "Khali, what's wrong? Why this sudden interest in my life? Our arrangement never troubled you before."

"No, it never has, but I thought..." His voice stopped as if the words had caught in his throat.

"What?" She was exasperated. "What did you think?"

"...that you were mine," he admitted. "I imagined that the life you left to come to me was unfulfilling, that I was your inspiration, as you were mine, that together we are something more than either of us alone. I never dreamt that when you left me, you went to a lover who makes me seem like a provincial fool."

"Lover?" Her voice trailed off. Nicolas. He knew about Nicolas. Starlight rushed eerily through dust swirling over the decaying walls as she absorbed the jolt and connections fell into place. "You've seen photographs from the suicide at opening night in Paris."

"Yes, Giuliana. Giuliana de Cordova." He tested the name she had never shared with him, and then gestured his arm toward her in a sudden sarcastic flourish. Hurt in his eyes battled with his rising anger.

"Imagine. Giuliana de Cordova. Mistress to Nicolas Portinari, champion to scores of floundering artists. Tell me, does he allow you to feed in all their beds? Or is an unsophisticated Egyptian artist just not enough of a threat to attract the Maestro's attention?"

"Stop it, Khali," she warned.

"You lied to me, *Anna*," he said hurtfully, emphasizing the name she had used with him. "Did you think I'd never find out? Even Aswan has wi-fi. Do you know how it felt finding out who you were that way? Do you know what it did to me to see you clinging to that arrogant bastard, knowing that you spend the rest of your life with someone who can be with you in a way I can never be? They talk about you as if he owns you!"

Disgusted, he turned away and stood at the iron gate with arms crossed over his waist, peering toward the river. "Khali," He stiffened, then relented to her fingers traveling gently down his sides. "Please don't do this."

"Why me, Anna? Why did you come here? Weren't there enough fools in Paris to feed you?"

She pulled away and fixed him with a level stare. "I revealed myself to you because of your strength and your damnable pride.

Because you were arrogant and self-contained and because you trusted only your own vision. I chose you because I thought you could take what I had to offer and not lose yourself in it! Was I wrong?"

His eyes came back to hers. Their disorienting depths caused her a moment of unsteadiness. They were very much like Nicky's might once have been. She was seized with a sudden impression of the musician's penetrating gaze. The connection flared and bridged the distance between the claustrophobic studio and the prow of the Khamsin where Nicolas was poised uneasily, finally aware of his own hunger.

The image of the sculptor was brushed away from Giuliana's awareness like gossamer in the gush of wind tearing at Nicolas's clothes. The Khamsin surged against the satin smooth current. Nicolas examined his hunger with detached ambivalence, mildly taunted by the image of the sculptor he had plucked from her mind. Her disappointment and distress, mixed with a distant echo of pure human jealousy, washed over him, and his indecision vanished. His sudden hunger sent him beyond her reach with a thought that took him away toward the desert. He was gone, and there was only blankness, while Giuliana wondered despairingly if he had gone to hunt or to bury himself in the sand.

She roused, lost again in the simple, vital eyes of the young man in front of her, waiting, inches away.

He extended his hand to her. "Come to bed. Take what you came for."

She shook her head. "It's not what I came for. Not tonight."

"Anna," he sighed. "I don't understand. Why did you come tonight, if not to feed?"

Giuliana suddenly felt old suddenly. "Ironically, I needed to remind myself that my presence in the world doesn't always end in suffering."

"Well then, consider this. After I saw those photographs today, I tried to remember what it was like to sculpt without you. I can't remember what inspired me then. You've taught me to see, not with my eyes but with something finer." His eyes were flat. "I sculpted before you came, Anna, but it was not the same. I was groping in the dark. Does that help you understand your impact?"

"That's not true, Khali. It was your talent that drew me to you in the beginning..."

"Come with me." He grabbed her wrist and pulled her inside. She stumbled after him to the center of the large, dusty room and a hulking mass draped in moth-colored canvas. He released her and jerked the cover away from an enormous, alabaster sculpture beneath it. He gave her a moment to feel the effect, then he turned his head toward her triumphantly. "Had I done anything like this before you came?"

Giuliana stood in stunned silence and stared up into her own features frozen in stone. The life-size female figure stood in the cutaway prow of a sailboat, her slender, perfectly formed hands grasping each side. Her flowing chiton was carved in elaborate detail. Her body beneath it was captured with a startling, modern realism, and a lover's accuracy. The dress and her hair blended and billowed behind her until they became the shape of the wind. Head tilted back, eyes on the stars, her expression was the perfect representation of Giuliana's intense, inquisitive nature. Her bare feet were anchored far apart as if it was her intention alone that both powered the boat and kept it from taking flight. It embodied the essence of feminine power, fragility of form combined with a fierce indomitableness of spirit.

"When did you do this?" she whispered when she could breathe again.

"After your last visit."

Giuliana stared at him, astonished, then turned again to the statue, circling round it. The stone was gouged away in an angry rhythm of tiny, deep whorls arranged in precise and complex patterns. The channels and ridges created a violent interplay of light and shadow, which eddied around the serene figure in a disturbing tempest. Giuliana's influence had expanded the artist's vision in a way his intellect couldn't comprehend. The heightened perception he experienced when she fed from him had allowed him to capture his impression of her perfectly.

There was a moment when neither of them could find words. She forced herself to move. "Khali, it's magnificent. But it's finished." She scooped his sketch from the floor and offered it to him. "It's time to start something new."

She reached out for Nicolas and found him walking listlessly through silver dunes. Hunger stirred as insistent and unheeded against his consciousness as the wind against his skin. He scanned the horizon ceaselessly, as if searching for something lost. By design or instinct, he was following the same course she had taken earlier this evening.

"Beloved," she murmured, hopelessly. Far away, she felt him lift his head and listen to the wind. There was a surge of bitterness, and then the scene disappeared as he vanished in flight. The room was suddenly suffocating. "I have to go," she murmured.

She was jarred aware by Khali's voice. "You can't leave me, Anna." The humiliation in his voice, his eyes, was agonizing.

She turned to stare out the window. "It's time, Khali. You must go the rest of the way yourself. You will sculpt. You can't help but sculpt; it's in your blood."

There was a bitter bark of laughter. "Sculpt, you say, as if it's a simple thing! The work I will do will mean nothing in the shadow of this!" He waved his arm angrily at Giuliana's alabaster image.

"But this one is yours, Khali. Look at it! Who else could have made it? No one!"

"But it's not mine! It is unfathomable. I can't even wrap my mind around what it means, let alone claim it! It makes me loathe every piece I've done before."

"It's phenomenal."

"It makes everything ordinary unbearable! Can't you see the utter cruelty in exposing the mediocrity of a man's work, of his life and then leaving him with it? Damn it, Anna!" His anger flared.

The connection blossomed again, and she was suddenly aware of Nicolas close by. Her connection with him lasted only a moment before it was severed abruptly by the dark veil of flight. He was not far away, on the shore of the Nile. Khali's angry voice echoed from her mind to his, bleeding into the shouts of the crazed woman before she jumped. She grasped dizzily at their tenuous connection, disoriented by Nicolas's rage rising in response to Khali's. He moved along a familiar rock path at the river's edge, along a stone wall, through the arched gate into Khali's tiny courtyard. She glanced anxiously toward the open doorway.

Khali looked involuntarily to the statue. When his gaze came back to her it was full of venom. He jerked her around with one hand and seized a mallet off the table with the other. For a moment she thought he would attempt to strike her, but he just dragged her to the feet of the sculpture and thrust her aside. "If you are going to leave, take it all!"

He raised his arm over his head and brought the mallet crashing down onto the prow of the carved boat. An explosion of alabaster chips shattered across the tile floor. Giuliana cringed to see the hatred in his eyes as he bludgeoned the delicately carved bow again. She could not move herself to keep him from destroying what he had every right to hate. The truth of her whole short interlude with him crashed in on her with sudden clarity. The vision she had inspired hadn't enhanced his, it had overwhelmed it. In wanting to give him something, she had robbed him of everything.

The reality of her leaving possessed him. His voice was only barely human as he unleashed a stream of epithets which struck her with the same shattering force as his mallet against the marble. "You —heartless—parasite! You can't leave me here to live with this!"

84

Her eyes were fixed to the mallet as he raised it again, this time taking aim at the statue's exultant face. Giuliana followed the sweeping arc of his arm as he swung with brutal force. He grunted in surprise as the momentum of the blow stopped abruptly in mid-swing. He twisted beneath his pinioned arm to find himself staring up into the enraged visage of Nicolas Portinari.

Khali's expression contorted in horror, but he was saved from the full force of the vampire's anger. In the split second it had taken the mortal to turn his head, Nicolas's attention shifted from his violent rage to the statue. Nicolas hesitated, poised between anger and awe. He hissed a warning in the man's ear, "All that stands between you and death is her inexplicable affection for you." He wrenched the mallet from Khali's hand and sent it skittering across the tile floor away from them, then thrust the man away from the statue.

Khali stumbled into the wall and slid down to the floor, his fearful eyes fastened to Nicolas who glanced at Giuliana, cataloguing her position and measuring her condition. He stepped toward the statue as if simultaneously attracted and repelled by it. He moved closer still, through the harsh light of the studio, then turned to look at Giuliana, his eyes bruised, before he reached for the light switch, and darkness fell into the room. Giuliana's mind linked with his as the lustrous quality of the stone emerged more distinctly in the vampire's sight; Giuliana, rendered in marble in radiant, intimate detail, stirred to life beneath a curtain of starlight. Here was the essence of his lover which he, himself, had often set to music, captured in stone by a mortal.

His steely voice knifed through the dark into the heart of the night blind man. "You could destroy such a thing after having the vision to create it?" Before Khali could find his voice to reply, Nicolas shoved a row of half-finished sculptures crashing to the floor. "Destroy it all, then. It's only a *human's* vision, after all."

Giuliana cringed as he swept another shelf of pieces to the floor.

"What does stone mean once you've renounced the humanity that shaped it?" He whirled suddenly and pulled Khali back to his feet, spreading his hand over the terrified sculptor's throat. Giuliana gasped. Khali pressed himself against the wall as if he would escape through it. Nicolas growled into his face, pinned Khali's head fast against the stone and demanded, "Do you know what I would give for the life you dismiss?"

Nicolas shoved Khali away and rose to circle the statue, giving it wide berth, as if he found it disturbing. He raised his fingers to brush the statue's alabaster features, and Giuliana had the heady sensation of his hand against her skin. He searched the stone face then looked into her living eyes.

"Do you see what happens when we try to connect with them, Giuliana? This *negation*." A cold strand of despair twisted into the complex pattern of his voice. He swept the heap of discarded points and gouges off the pedestal. They clattered to the tile floor in a cascade of ringing steel.

Guilt possessed Giuliana. She had lured him here for this. She moved quickly to his side and wrapped her arms around him. A jealous anger racked Khali's expression and fueled his dormant aggression. He was swallowed in a blind rage as their shadows merged into one.

"I warn you, Anna, I won't let you leave me. I would rather see us both destroyed!" Giuliana blinked curiously, as if he had spoken in an unknown language. A feral growl escaped Nicolas. His shadow uncoiled from Giuliana's, quavered, and edged toward the man with a single threatening step.

Khali lashed out, "Leave me here, and that spectacle in Paris will seem like a whisper next to the furor I will cause! Everyone will know you for the monsters you are, if I must spend my life to prove it!" The echo of Khali's threat reverberated in the still room. A horrible moment of silence followed. Nicolas took another wavering step toward the artist whose cockiness melted into fear at the feral expression on the vampire's face as he moved into the moonlight. He stumbled back a few steps, his eyes darting between Nicolas and Giuliana.

Nicolas snarled. He snapped the man's head back by the jaw and sank his fangs savagely into his throat. Khali's back arched unnaturally; his arms spasmed. Giuliana reached automatically to grasp Nicky's arm, but it was too late. Blood gurgled from the dying man's mouth, stifling his scream, and splattering a strand of dark pearls across her dress. Nicolas growled and drained Khali's blood with a terrifying, ravenous sorrow. Giuliana vanished from the labyrinthine courtyards before the sculptor's body fell to the ground. She escaped across the river in a desperate whirl of energy.

She materialized amid a sandstorm at the foot of the escarpment where she had first seen Khali's house. The wind blustered, and the sand seethed around her. The veil of sand drew closed over the obsidian dome of sky, consuming the field of platinum stars and silvery light. She trudged aimlessly to the top of a dune and stopped. There was nowhere else to run. The storm approached her; the wind circled around her with an electric hum.

The sand became a wave on the horizon, engulfing the sea of dunes as it flowed toward her. She crouched and plundered handfuls, then let it flow from her hands in a glittering double spiral as she turned. Longing willed her downward into the glistening desert with a promise of sleep and sanctuary. In a few moments, she would fall into the deathly sleep where no living thing could wake her.

Beyond the curtain of the rising sandstorm, a luminescent figure walked toward her across the crest of a distant dune. Nicolas materialized through the vortex of sand, approaching slowly, his black hair whipped about his face in a tangle. He reached down and pulled her from the dune, gathering her resistant body to his, speaking a litany of sorrow into her ear in a voice of velvet and gravel. His tears boiled against her shoulder. His body shuddered in her arms.

"Nicolas. Beloved." She hadn't known until she spoke that she was weeping. Sand sifted from her fists as she opened them to drag her hands over his chest. "Let the desert swallow us. The world will never know or care."

He shrugged off his shirt and draped it around her. She brushed her hand through his hair and along the arc of his cheek. His skin was luminous as porcelain. Only the essence remained of the refined Maestro who had seduced all of Paris. His eyes burned with an intensity that would have frightened his devotees. There was no trace of lethargy or despair in his eyes, only a gleam of anger and a chasm of need.

The double-edged hunger roused before the stone figure in the artist's studio was still only half satisfied. He offered no apology or rebuke; if he had, she would have resisted. Instead, his hands slipped possessively beneath the shirt to clutch her waist and bring her close again, as if she was the only thing of value left in the world.

His mouth scourged a trail from her lips to her jaw to her neck while his fingers swept aside the shirt at her breast. Her hands closed on his burning shoulders in a spasm of intense pleasure, then opened and slid down his chest, absorbing the delicious, humanlike heat that had once been Khali's passion.

His fangs pierced the flesh above her breast suddenly with savage force. Her consciousness twined with his and then was absorbed into his overwhelming need. An eternity of moments later, his hold on her relaxed, and he laid her down gently against the dune.

Poised above her, he brought his lips to hers, and briefly, the connection was gone. She moved with a feral instinct to reclaim it. She rose and plunged her fangs into his throat as he threw his head back to offer the sculptor's blood freely now that it was indistinguishable from his own. He groaned in a sharp meeting of pleasure and pain. She tasted Khali with a spasm of grief and drew his life back from Nicolas ravenously. Blood sparkled over her lips and tongue, rich and full as scarlet silk, embroidered with the vital, golden strands of memory and music. Khali's thread was inter-twined there, distinct and now inseparable from her own.

The blood heat pulsed through her immortal body, giving her, for these precious moments, the pleasure of her lost humanity again. The instinctive drive for human connection aroused, and she pulled Nicolas down, his own body charged and craving her. She pushed away his clothes and wrapped herself around him, pulling him toward her until she was one with his body, his taste, his scent. Their mouths came together again, still hot from the feed, drawing the bottomless need from one another with human impatience.

Desire swept through them, burning with blood and screaming with the howl of the sandstorm. The connection burned white hot as a wave of pleasure broke over them like the buffeting wind. The storm wailed past them to vanish into the horizon.

Finally sated, she opened her eyes and felt the tingling on her skin as the wound healed. The sky swung back into place above her. She was cradled in a nest of sand, still warm from the heat of the day. Nicky leaned on one elbow beside her, smiling sadly. "You considered bringing him among us."

She dropped her head back against the dune and sighed in remorse. "I only considered it for an instant. I don't think I will again."

"You will." He smiled sadly. "It's our curse."

"Do you? Consider it?"

"Not in five hundred years." He smiled at her. "And even then, even with you, the decision almost broke me."

"Did you regret it?"

"Not for a moment, but we were fortunate. Your humanity and your sanity survived the transition. That is rare. Even so, those first years were agonizing. Watching your pain as you transformed, your overwhelming hunger that could not be sated, connections with your human life slowly ebbing away. Not knowing whether you would survive as one of us. Knowing I was responsible. It was not a simple thing, Giuliana."

She turned toward him. "Nicolas?"

He lifted his eyes to hers. She kissed him and then settled against his shoulder. "I'm sorry if I caused you..." His eyes were deep, and the pain still raw. "Tonight and all those years in the beginning," She couldn't finish; she couldn't bear thinking of the pain he'd been through if what Electra had said was true.

"Having you by my side these centuries has been worth any amount of pain." He lifted her fingers to his mouth and then pressed her palm flat against his heart. "And I couldn't blame him for his obsession with you, Giuli. I share it."

"You've only one obsession, Maestro Portinari, and it is most assuredly not me."

"You take too much pleasure in underestimating my obsession with you, Giuliana." He stood and pulled her up with him. "Does it frighten you so much to be loved?"

She tilted her head and met his eyes squarely. "It frightens me to claim too closely something it would kill me to lose."

He bowed his head in a rare moment of acceptance. The power between them flared. The wind brushed by them and whispered on over the vast desolation toward the horizon. She realized, with a pang of regret, that they had already been to Aswan.

"I hope I didn't lead us to the end of our voyage too soon." He walked a few steps away to the top of the dune, watching the receding sandstorm in the distance. He looked over his shoulder to see her.

"This voyage has no end for us, Giuliana. We are destined to repeat it, over and again."

She shuddered. "I hope I never repeat tonight's journey."

"But we will if we remain among them. Even the best of them, the strongest, the visionaries, like Khali, will break under the weight of what we are." He sighed and looked away.

Something connected in her mind, and she finally voiced the question that she had been waiting to ask since they had first broached the subject of leaving Paris. "Nicolas, what of Francois?"

He closed his eyes for a moment. "Francois is part of the world we must leave behind. Portinari Enterprises will cease to exist."

Giuliana smiled sadly. "There is more to your connection with Francois than Portinari Enterprises, Nicolas. He won't be left behind easily. He's devoted to you."

He ignored the possibility, his most effective tactic of evasion. He extended his hand to her, and his eyes met hers squarely. "Come, Giuli. We have a journey to begin."

9

MEMENTO MORI

Their journey brought to a premature end, they turned the Khamsin around and traveled back towards Cairo and home for two days. The memory of what happened in Aswan haunted them both. Nicolas never left his stateroom. Giuliana came out only late at night to pace the deck and watch the dark landscape slip by.

On the third night, he emerged to find her on deck with the boat anchored off Luxor. She leaned against the railing, eyes closed, gusts of wind pulling her gossamer-thin kimono and robe into a fluttering cloud around her.

He wrapped his arms around her waist. Instinctively, she leaned back against him. For over an hour, they stood silently, neither speaking. The lights of Luxor glittered on the distant eastern bank while darkness cloaked the west. The Nile was a rippling artery of quicksilver reflecting the stars. The desert moaned dolorously with the sound of the wind.

She turned in his arms to look into his face. "Where are you, Nicky?" Her hand brushed his face. "What are you thinking?"

He took her hand in his and kissed the palm. "I remember the first time we made this voyage and am wondering if this is meant to be the last."

"The last?" She looked at him through questioning eyes. "Why would it be the last?"

He released her and grasped the steel railing, lost in memory. "You were human then and had lost everything. I have never known such sadness. I wasn't sure you would survive that trip, and all I could think was, how would I survive if you did not?"

She moved to the railing beside him. "There is so much about that trip I don't remember. It was like moving through a dream. I remember a night here, in Luxor. The wind was the same, the stars were the same, even you were the same."

He stared at the reflections of light rippling against the boat and the memory flared open like a curtain pulled apart in a darkened room. The second sight dilated as he cast the vision to her.

Five hundred years ago, they left el-Samun the same night it burned, its ruins still smoldering on the plateau above the Nile. The galley that was to take them to Venice was not due for weeks and his only thought had been to get her away. They descended the esplanade leading from the house down to the river quickly, in silence, like survivors fleeing a disaster. The quivering glow of the fire blazed against the night sky, illuminating their way. Crackling flames punctuated the darkness along with the crash of falling timbers and collapsing walls. At the dock, they boarded the big dahabiya kept there for river excursions, Nicolas, Giuliana, and her surviving son.

"To Luxor," Nicolas uttered to the captain, who greeted his employer with great deference and immediately began calling out orders to his men in Arabic. Nicolas led a dazed Giuliana and her sleeping son to the suite located below deck at the stern. The crew, terrified by the inferno at the house and by this hasty departure, wasted no time casting off. The great lateen sails, one on the stern, one on the bow, unfurled with a crackling like the wings of a bird.

The wind filled them and tugged the boat slowly upriver against the current.

For four nights the ship sailed south, lost in the relentless desert which ended at the ribbon of dark water that was the Nile. Nicolas rose at first darkness to check on Giuliana and her son, and to see that food was brought to them. She hardly acknowledged his presence when he came to her, answering flatly that she needed nothing. The rest of the night he paced the deck, watching the dusky landscape slip by. On the fifth night, they reached their destination.

Luxor was a dusty, forgotten village built amidst the ruins of a sprawling, ancient temple complex. Massive walls, gigantic columns, and soaring obelisks, half-submerged beneath the sea of sand, littered the desert for as far as the eye could see. Above this broken landscape floated a great orange moon, drowning everything in its luminescent glow.

On this night, she finally emerged and found him on deck, staring out at the ruins and flickering torch lights and fires of the village. She wrapped her arms around him. He leaned back against her. They stood for a long while without speaking, the passage of time marked by the slowly rising moon. Finally, he turned in her arms and looked into her eyes. "Where are you, Giuliana?" His hand brushed the hair from her face. "What are you thinking?"

She took his hand in hers and kissed the palm. "My life feels as if it is over. I have no home, no family, no husband. I don't belong anywhere, not anymore."

He kissed her tenderly and wrapped his arms around her. She pulled away and moved to the railing, gazing out over the landscape as if seeing the ruins for the first time. The shadows of broken columns and shattered temples shimmered beneath the moonlight. Fires speckled the landscape, marking where people populated the desolation. "It feels as if time has run out for me, Nicolas." She choked back tears.

He moved to the railing beside her. "Look around you, Giuli. You are in a place where time has no meaning. The natives here say time begins and ends in this river. They believe the world was created out of the waters of the Nile and that eternity flows in them." He reached out to grasp her by her shoulders. "Giuliana, your life is far from over. In some way, it is as if it were just beginning. You have a chance now to be reborn, to shape your life as you would have it, without anyone ever telling you what form it must take or what you must do again."

Tears began to well up in her eyes and flow down her face. "Nicky," she moaned softly. "I'm afraid. I'm afraid of the gift you offer, afraid that I may not be up to that journey, afraid that I don't know what I want my life to be."

He wrapped her in his arms. "Do not be afraid. You have me and I will be with you, always. I cannot imagine my life without you. Whatever you choose will be right. Whatever new life you make will be perfect. That is how you move through the world." She melted against him, relaxing in his arms.

He kissed her and continued. "People have come to this place for thousands of years to celebrate the rebirth of life. So can you, beloved. So can we. This can be our new beginning, our new life. Together we will shape them into dreams beyond those of anyone who has ever wished for new life here."

The sound of the river purling against the boat brought him back to the present and the memory dissolved between them. For a moment, Nicolas was unsure where he was in time. "Once more, beloved, we have come to Luxor and are facing yet another rebirth. This time, it comes at great cost. It is not one we can celebrate." His voice trembled, low and detached.

Only then, when she lifted her gaze to his, did Giuliana see the blood streaking down his face. "Nicky, what do you mean? What's wrong?" She reached up and wiped his tears away with her fingertips.

"Everything beloved," he exhaled heavily. He grasped her hand

and kissed her palm. "We cannot continue to live in the world as we have."

"Nicky, there must be a way..." Her voice faltered as he continued.

"For three nights now, I have struggled to find a way out of this disaster, only to arrive at the same answer."

"And what is the answer?" she whispered.

He hesitated before replying. "There is only one obvious thing to do. You must see that too, Carino." He lifted her chin, her glittering eyes fixed on his "We must give it up. We must give everything up."

"Nicky, we've done this before and not so long ago. We can again." She embraced him, her hands sliding around his back.

"I'm afraid, Giuliana. I'm afraid I may not be able to face the journey ahead, afraid my life will become meaningless. I'm afraid my only refuge lies beneath the sands."

She kissed him again. "We've faced that before, my love, here at this very place. You helped me to see that even immortals can be reborn again." She lay her face against his chest, holding him tighter.

"Nicky, don't be afraid. You don't have to worry about your life having no meaning. Don't you see, that's how you move through the world, shaping meaning where there is none? You're incapable of anything less. Whatever you decide, I am with you. Whatever life you choose, I will be a part of it. I will be with you, always."

He pulled her tight against him and leaned his face down to hers and whispered. "Do you suppose there is still time?"

She smiled at him. "Someone very wise once told me that time begins and ends on this river, that eternity flows in it. We have eternity, my love."

10

A NEW DESIGN

The evening after returning from Egypt Nicolas came downstairs to find Francois standing in front of a roaring fire in the fireplace of the library. The flickering light was the room's only illumination. The myriad of Carnevale masks decorating the walls seemed alive with it. Their bejeweled and decorated faces were overpowered by the dark, blank eyes that stared from them out over the room.

"Good evening, Francois." Nicolas leaned against the doorway with one shoulder, his arms crossed over his chest. The vampire's glittering onyx eyes seemed to absorb all the light in the room. They focused on Francois.

Startled, Francois turned toward his voice. "Welcome home Nicolas. How was Egypt?"

Nicolas straightened and walked into the room. "It was a relief. A visit to the desert always seems to put things back into perspective. It's impossible to take your own problems very seriously when you're standing before monuments which have endured so many centuries."

Francois reached to turn on the lights, but Nicolas stopped him with a shake of his head.

"Giuliana is well?"

Nicolas chuckled softly, with the affection that was always apparent when he spoke of her. "She is indomitable. They say time fears the pyramids, but my friend, I believe the pyramids fear Giuliana."

The two men gravitated to the huge window that looked out over the Grand Canal. "She is well and glad to be back. It's nearly time for Carnevale and you know how she loves that. He answered gently, the connection between them tangible, even in her absence. "She will be down momentarily."

"To tell you the truth, I've been glad both of you have been away."

"The press is speculating of course?" Nicolas guessed sadly.

"I'm afraid so. The papers have been full of bizarre headlines, lurid photos, and wild theories."

"I'm glad we were away then." It was drizzling rain outside. The crackle of the fire and the water hitting the windows were the only sounds. Nicolas stared out at the dark waters of the canal which were spangled with the lights of passing boats. He mused for a moment, distracted by the view, lost in the grip of a sorrow that registered precisely in his expression. He glanced at Francois. "And you? How are you Francois, besides the obvious fact that you're working too much?"

"Not too much really." Francois stood next to him at the window, taking in the view. St. Mark's Square burned with light beyond the wide swath of dark canal. His shoulder brushed against the vampire's. Their proximity was evidence of their unguarded state. Francois glanced at Nicolas. A peculiar magnetism held the men together for one uncomfortable moment while Nicolas resisted making the connections his preternatural senses begged to make.

Giuliana entered the room and Francois walked over to greet her with a hug, then escaped to the bar. She went to stand by Nicolas at the window, where he pressed the palm of one hand against the pane of glass, blocking out one part of the city, then another. He imagined the way it had evolved down through the centuries. The falling raindrops traced a silver path of tears across the reflection of his ivory features.

He looked up to find himself the focus of Giuliana's uncanny perception. "LeCourbe was right. That woman's death is my fault."

"LeCourbe is a viper, Nicky. And that woman was insane."

"Was she insane? She died to achieve the aberration I have come to represent. They sense the gifts of immortality, but not the price we've paid for it. My notoriety has given Electra and that damned cult influence she doesn't deserve."

He drew her into his arms. Her body tensed in resistance. He clung more tightly to her and spoke intently into her ear. "It's time to tell Francois. Are you ready?"

Her body gradually relaxed against his as she surrendered to the inevitable. "Nicky." She slipped her arms around him and pulled him close, her own fear drowned in her concern for him. "You and I could be trapped in hell's heart and still shape a life to dazzle the heavens." She leaned forward and kissed his lips, gently. "As long as we are together."

He smiled at her dauntless confidence. "Well then, maybe our course is already charted and all that remains is to begin the journey."

He slipped from her embrace, his attention captured by the display cases built into the far wall, and the sudden play of light glinting over Lalique glass. Slowly a design formed, out of lines and light and hard, cold glass; a plan for their survival began to take shape.

Francois returned with their drinks, and they sat in a grouping of lacquered wood and leather chairs. "Francois," Nicolas stopped short as something on the low table in front of them caught his eye. He plucked a gold Faberge picture frame from the tabletop and fell silent while he stared at the picture it held.

Francois sought to fill the sudden, awkward silence. "Nicolas, one deranged girl taking her life will only provide tabloid fodder for a few weeks."

"If this had just been another spark of unsubstantiated rumor nursed by the press, that may have been true. But that woman was willing to kill herself to make her point. He continued speaking without once looking away from the picture in his hand. "This is too close to the truth. It's already turned into a wildfire and nothing we do now can stop it."

He handed the frame to Giuliana and watched her expression change. It was a hand-colored photograph of them taken near the turn of the century. Both wore evening clothes: he, a frock coat and cape, she in an empire-style ball gown. It had been taken on the landing of the grand staircase at Palais Garnier.

"It's not just about us anymore, Francois," Nicolas continued. "Something has incited other vampires to attack Venice. Francois closed his eyes as if accepting an unpleasant truth. "Yes. The deaths in Venice are the work of renegade vampires. Surely, you've suspected?" Francois nodded. "Circumstances don't allow us to live in the public eye. The world is close to discovering the truth, and after that, there will be no place safe for us." He looked again into the man's eyes. "But I need your help to prevent that from happening."

Francois removed his cigarette case, a gift from Nicolas years ago, and clenched it tightly in his hand. He smoothed his thumb across its gleaming gold surface, feeling the letters engraved in its lid. It was a peculiar nervous habit: a means of knowing when Francois was unsure. The action gave him a few moments grace in which to collect his thoughts. He lit the cigarette, inhaled deeply, and exhaled a jet of blue smoke. "What sort of help?"

"Francois, what would happen to Portinari Enterprises if

Giuliana and I were to die suddenly?" Nicolas asked very matter-of-factly, his gaze never leaving the other man's eyes.

Francois laughed out loud. "Excuse me, Nicolas. Did I miss something? Are you serious?" He took another drag from his cigarette.

"I'm serious, Francois. You must understand how important it is that the truth of our nature does not come to light. Imagine the panic such a revelation would cause in the world at large."

"Yes. Yes, I can imagine, Nicolas."

"Think of what such a disclosure would mean for Giuli and me. Other vampires will not look kindly on us drawing all this attention to ourselves. We will become hunted and despised among our own kind, and in the human world; creatures to be destroyed or, worse." Nicolas watched as Francois digested the latter comment. "I can assure you, I have no desire to spend eternity as a laboratory specimen."

"You must have dealt with this situation before. How do others of your kind deal with this?"

"We assume new identities. We last had to do so during the revolution here in France. At that time, it was a simple thing to arrange. After we went underground, we went back to Venice. Times being what they were, it was easy to see to our financial affairs and establish new identities there. We were already wealthy then, but not well known."

He paused to give Francois a moment to absorb this information, then continued. "The world now is a much smaller place. Given our present circumstances, my fame, our affluence, the resources available to those who might pry, I imagine that would be a more tricky thing to arrange today."

"You're serious, aren't you?" Francois reached over and stubbed his cigarette out. "You and Giuliana will assume new identities?"

"More than that," Nicolas said. "Nicolas and Giuliana must appear to die; unmistakably, undeniably, so no question remains in anyone's mind."

"Accidents happen, Nicolas. Your resources open certain avenues which might assist in establishing new identities for the two of you." He took a drink of the amber liquid. "The transfer of your assets is another story, altogether. I'm not sure it's possible to do that invisibly. Every financial transaction leaves a trail, a trail that anyone persistent enough could follow. I need some time to consider some options."

"I would prefer to maintain control over Portinari Enterprises. It's my last real connection to my human life."

Francois looked puzzled. "That's an odd way of putting it, Nicolas."

"You don't understand, Francois, it's not about the money. Immortality provides abundant opportunities to make many fortunes. Portinari Enterprises began as a small trade consortium formed by my father in the year 1001. It is my inheritance from him. It would be a terrible blow to see that legacy dissolved. It means something to me."

Francois stared at him; a look of surprise played across his face. "Then we'll just have to make sure whatever we come up with doesn't allow that to happen."

Nicolas smiled and watched as Francois rose to the task he had been given. Here was a man who could chart the course of the future. He watched the man shift into action, could almost see him begin to play out scenarios in his head. Nicolas sometimes envied the mortal their limited conception of time; the lack of perspective to know that everything in their life was interwoven and connected. The flow of warp and weft begins before their brief existence and goes on unendingly afterward. Life's tapestry was complex and pulling a thread *here* eventually unwound the design *there*.

But he was loathe to disillusion the man. Let Francois do what he could, ignorant of the forces already set in motion against them.

11

INTERMEZZO

Venice floated in the wine dark lagoon like an exotic flower. Scintillating halos of golden light shot through the midnight sky and bloomed in the clouds over the city. Its gilded reflection shimmered across the water to reach Nicolas who stood poised at the great window of his office at the Villa Giuliana. The city beckoned, but he resisted her pull, just as he had resisted most everything in the nights since their return from Egypt.

Giuliana had gone into the city hours ago. She had done her best to temper his mood but even she had finally given up and left him to work his way through it. He turned and walked back to the documents littering his desk. There were notes from Francois about arcane business details Nicolas no longer cared about, contracts that needed signing, the first pages of a musical score that now would probably never see completion, and a letter from his old friend Max Scherer. This he picked up and read again.

Nicolas, my dear friend,

I've heard what happened in Paris and have a distraction to offer you. Remember the concerto I've been working on? Well, it's finished. It would be wonderful if you joined me some evening for a run-through. I've recently acquired a new piano that will meet with your approval. It's been too long since we've had time together so, surprise me and come to Salzburg. I remain yours in the blood,

Max

Nicolas smiled. Leave it to Max to find a way to engage him when everything else seemed a distraction and pointless. His old friend had been turned almost five hundred years before Nicolas was even born. Somehow, in all that time, he had managed not to get involved with the infighting that broke out amongst the vampire clans with irritating regularity. His calm, dispassionate manner gave him a certain cachet of objectivity and the vampire houses had come to defer to him as a kind of de facto magistrate. Bringing opposing sides together had always been his gift and he had resolved many potentially bloody conflicts.

Nicolas dropped the letter and, before it had time to hit the desk, his body shuddered and morphed into a whisper of wind as he wrapped himself in flight. In a blink of light, he vanished and was racing towards Salzburg. His awareness focused sharply, and intention pulled him inexorably towards the place where he might find answers and music again.

The uncertainty of the last few days wheeled away in a penumbra of shadow that twisted around and drove him forward. He exhaled as the Venetian lagoon vanished behind him in a rim of golden light. *What a fool I've been to think we could live amongst people with no consequences.* The grim reality of the suicide had clearly revealed he could no longer ignore the chaos engulfing the vampire world.

In the next moment, his shape quivered into form on the terrace of Max's villa. The sound of a piano drifted through the closed French doors off the terrace. Nicolas stood motionless as his senses refocused and he peered inside. A fire scintillated in a wall-sized stone fireplace. The room was part library, part music room; floor-to-ceiling bookcases lined its walls and various musical instruments were scattered about it.

In its center sat a man playing a grand piano, unlike any piano Nicolas had ever seen. Rather than wood, a sinuous, gold metallic exoskeleton formed the body of the instrument. The casing flowed vine-like over the piano in a series of interlocking curves and sweeping lines which intertwined and snaked down to form legs, then overlapped one another to surround the piano's core. Its lid and sides were inset with clear Lucite panels so that the inner frame, strings, hammers, and soundboard were completely visible. The effect was sculptural and organic, an insect's carapace and a piece of futuristic machinery.

He opened the door and was immediately immersed in a deep current of music which washed over him, liquid and dark, and pulled him further into the room. Max sat at the piano, his fingers ran over the keys and the notes flowed from the instrument smoothly in a clear, fluid cadence.

Nicolas moved to stand silently by Max's side. He listened for a long while, mesmerized, as the melody split into two themes that attacked and fought one another as they built in intensity. Allegro ma non tanto, fast but not too fast, the variations began to wind round one another, one succumbing to the other until finally, they blended seamlessly back into one.

Max's hands were a blur of motion when finally, the piece reached a crescendo in a cascade of trembling notes. The final measure still hung in the air when Nicolas finally spoke.

"You don't need an accompanist, Max, you need an orchestra. That was magnificent." He smiled as Max turned to him.

The vampire's appearance belied his great age. He looked to be in his early fifties. His golden-brown hair hung to his shoulders and framed a pair of lustrous hazel eyes that glinted in small flashes of light as they darted over Nicolas.

"I think it's you who's in need of supporting players, Nicky." He smiled and slid over on the piano bench to give Nicolas room to sit.

"Do I, now?" Nicolas wrinkled his brow and sat down, smoothing his hand over the undulating frame of the piano as he cataloged its every texture and curve.

"I think you might, my boy." Concern sounded quietly in his voice as he wrapped his arm around the younger vampire's shoulders. "What happened in Paris has put us all in peril, but none more so than you."

Nicolas moved his hands over the keyboard as if absorbing the notes from the keys themselves. "What happened in Paris came from hundreds of years of my denying the reality of my situation." Effortlessly, he began to replay the concerto from the point where he had first heard it outside on the terrace.

"I was a fool to think we could live amongst them," he stated emotionlessly, relishing the feel of the keys beneath his fingers. "Our presence in the mortal world is devastating for them and ultimately damning for us." Once more the twin themes filled the room, circling warily around one another in opposition. "That woman's death only made it clear how wrong I've been."

Max slid from the bench and stood for a long while beside the piano, listening as Nicolas played the piece. After a while, he spoke again. "That woman's death was a tragedy, Nicolas, but it wasn't your fault, and it didn't happen because you made a life among them."

The maestro's gaze fixed on Max, who hesitated a moment before continuing. "It was a sign of what happens when no one takes responsibility for maintaining order among vampires. Calamitous events, things that you can no longer ignore, are overwhelming our world because you toppled that order, and no one had the courage to take your place. Now it is up to you to do something about it."

The themes wavered, echoing one another as they began to build in intensity. "Not you too, Max." Nicolas scowled. "Have you been consorting with Electra?"

His fingers darted quickly across the keys in a glissando. His hands were a blur as they stabbed out the melody which had reconnected into something more powerful and complete now. He closed his eyes, lost in the music as he began the coda. He replayed the piece exactly as he had heard it. The concerto built to its climax as the theme soared. A cascade of notes flooded from the piano, surging into the room in a torrent that ended in a shimmering quiver of notes.

Only the sound of Nicolas's breathing broke the silence that filled the room. Max waited as he came back from wherever the music had transported him. When his eyes reopened, Max spoke to him. " and self-serving but, I've heard her argument, and, in this instance, she may be right."

Anger flared for a moment in Nicolas's eyes. "Even if she is right, what can I do? I have no coven. I lead no one. I have no power. Are you forgetting what happened to House Rialto?" He slammed shut the fallboard of the piano, stood suddenly, and walked quickly to the French doors to peer outside. Max joined him and they stared at the dark river beyond the terrace.

When Max spoke again, his voice was calm but firm. "I remember what happened. I remember telling you at the time that it was a tragedy. I still think it was. The thing is, there are those who might be able to help you restore order now."

Nicolas sighed heavily and leaned his forehead against the glass door. "The Elders?" He turned and looked into Max's eyes, skeptically. "I destroyed the hold of the Elders over the vampire houses the night I massacred House Rialto. What makes you think they would help me?"

"I think they may have no choice, Nicolas. Things have gotten bad all over. Revenants are overrunning cities all over the world now. Something is happening and we, you, need to at least find out what's going on." Max said emphatically, uttering the choice Nicolas did not want to face.

"Even if I wanted to Max, and I don't, I wouldn't know where to begin, how to contact them. There hasn't been a convocation of the Elders since," he stopped talking, his voice suddenly weary as the memory overtook him.

"Not since House Rialto." Max completed his thought. "I know, Nicolas. But some of them still exist who may have interest in helping you." His hands reached out and grasped Nicolas's shoulders, holding him to the spot. "The survivors scattered to the four corners of the world. The old order was dead. It was a time of chaos and fear for all vampires. They waited for you to track them down and destroy them, too, and when you didn't, they rebuilt their lives. The Elders still exist. They are concerned by this outbreak of chaos. I believe they are ready for someone to lead them again. It's time you faced them."

12

DISSONANTE

Giuliana saw new resolve in Nicolas after his visit with Max, though she was surprised to find that his thoughts had turned to the Elders. It had been centuries since they had come together, but Max had convinced him that there were still some who might help. She supported the decision to call them to convene to discuss the sudden onslaught of revenant vampires. Still, it left her anxious for Nicolas.

Nicolas had immediately sent invitations to the houses that might be open to an alliance. She suspected he acted so quickly to make it impossible to back out. But, when the appointed night arrived, he and Giuliana traveled down the Rio d'San Angelo to the Rialto coven house via boat.

When first built, the Rialto coven house would have towered over the oldest part of San Polo. Now it seemed small next to the grand sixteenth-century palaces on either side. Its rows of closely spaced pillars and ornate stone tracery appeared to float above the canal, giving the structure a sense of weightless grace.

The water gateway, where arriving passengers once disembarked at the palazzo from their gondolas, was padlocked now. Murky light smeared along the polished wood of the motorboat as Nicolas guided it deftly to dock at the entrance of the old building. Even after Nicolas cut the engine, inky water still pushed against the hull in insistent wavelets, urging them forward.

Nicolas stood and unlocked the gate while Giuliana gazed up at the façade. The three-story structure was punctuated by narrow arched windows and studded with marble medallions and stone panels. Moonlight ricocheted in pinpricks from surfaces once gilt. Giuliana picked out the writhing figures of mythical creatures looking down on them. These grimy guardians had held their silent vigil over the house through centuries of neglect.

They slipped through the dark water portal just before midnight. Nicolas frowned. "I hope we don't come to regret this," he murmured as he helped her onto the dock.

Giuliana felt his resistance battling his resolve. "We may. But we had to try. If our life is to fall away beneath us, we need to understand why."

It had been decades since they visited the palazzo. Once it housed the powerful Rialto coven. During the time the Council of Elders wielded power, it had also served as their meeting place, as Rialto was first among covens. Vampire covens had strong roots in Venice, dating all the way back to the original twelve founding families of the city. Nicolas rarely visited the building anymore except when the occasional need arose to interact with other vampires.

Nicolas held the door open for her and they entered the portego, the traditional entrance hall which ran the length of the house, from the water entrance on the canal to the garden entrance on the land side. She had forgotten how stately it was. The floor of the hall was a mosaic of flowers and twisting garlands in rich browns, reds, and white. White marble fireplaces, fraught with carved figures framed either side of the entry hall. A fresco depicting the lion of Venice, battling fantastic beasts, topped each mantel. Giuliana wondered at the wealth and craftsmanship that came together to create this place. She grieved over its neglect.

The building was musty and nearly empty. Gone were the long velvet benches and mahogany tables that once made this a warm and inviting place. Now the few furnishings were broken and dusty, and perfectly reflected the current state of relations between Nicolas and most of his kind.

At the next door, Nicolas hesitated. He leaned down and kissed Giuliana. "Ready?" he asked. She smiled and nodded. He grasped the door handle and whispered, "Into the lions' den."

The door opened to reveal a magnificently appointed hallway. Its cobalt blue floor was a star-field, spangled with gold comets and inlaid mosaic stars of Murano glass and colored marble. An enormous, gas-fueled, crystal chandelier bathed the room in golden, flickering light. Immediately to their right, Max stood in front of an immense, red porphyry fireplace. This one set with a roaring fire. Beyond it, was a round mahogany table which was varnished to a brilliant shine.

Giuliana watched apprehensively. Neither Nicolas nor the visitors seemed sure they wanted to be here. All of them were wary and seemed reluctant to engage. The others were unknown to her, and the shadowy group in the scant light radiated mystery. Her keen curiosity about the Elders chafed against her loyalty to Nicolas and his decision to separate himself from them. She hoped they knew more of Nicolas than his current public image and his violent destruction of his coven a thousand years ago.

Max smiled at their appearance and came over. He greeted Nicolas and took Giuliana's hand in his to kiss it. He had a human-like animation and warmth. Giuliana knew him well and was as fond of him as Nicolas was. Max motioned with his head towards the others seated at the table. "Only half of those invited are here. It's disappointing, but not a great surprise. The others are hostile or afraid that this was some sort of trap." He motioned towards the table. "We should get started. Our guests are already restless."

The others watched warily as Nicolas and Giuliana took their seats, then glared at one another as if poised for a fight. For a moment, the only sound was the crackling of the fire.

Giuliana surveyed the room, pointedly ignoring Electra, who sat several seats away from her. She glanced up at a fresco depicting a similar meeting that decorated the dome above them. Images of both Max and Nicolas stared back at her, and, other than the clothes they wore, they looked exactly as they did tonight.

Giuliana turned her attention to the vampires around the table. The Elders' expressions provided no clue as to how they felt about Nicolas's past and the act that had shattered their authority. Their lack of eye contact and reluctance to talk among themselves suggested they had as little affection for one another as they seemingly did for Nicolas.

Nicolas watched them, too. He had never shared what had happened to the Rialto coven with her, but she was certain that he felt no regret for it. He was slow to anger and never acted without assessing the possible consequences. Of one thing she was certain: if they were expecting an apology tonight, they would be disappointed.

Nicolas was about to speak when a woman with a startling mane of auburn hair entered the room. She walked by them to take a seat and cast him a wary, distrustful look.

"Persephone," Nicolas said carefully. "Thank you for coming."

"Just show me it was not a mistake." Her expression turned into a snarl as she slid her chair under the table.

"Yes, I'm hoping for the same thing, myself," he said with a sardonic smile, then began by thanking the rest for coming. He described the situation with the rogue vampires in Venice, how their numbers had surged wildly in the last few weeks as they created scores of savage revenants.

He was interrupted by a tall vampire sprawled across the chair directly across from him who threw off the dark hood of his cloak to reveal a headful of unruly orange-red curls. "Enough. We all know there's been an explosion of vampires in Venice. But why should any of us care? You shattered the Council's power centuries ago and abandoned us to a war of your making. Now, you've let your life get out of control, and suddenly you need us?" The vampire's mane of unruly orange hair and shaggy beard accentuated his fierce expression.

Nicolas did not take the bait. "My life isn't out of control, Eoghan. That incident in Paris was unforeseeable, and I wasn't responsible for it." He leaned back, his thumb tapping against the table, waiting.

Eoghan leaned forward; his exceptionally green eyes narrowed, and his voice went lower. "You're lying to yourself. Any fool could have predicted it." He fell back into his seat. "Those cursed musicals beg the public to speculate about you."

Nicolas countered, "Men have written about fantastical creatures since they invented writing."

"Yes, *men* have written about them, not one of our own kind." Eoghan scoffed. He shook his finger at Nicolas, "You've put us all in danger."

Giuliana glanced at Nicolas as he drew back, stung. He had expected Eoghan to be an ally. His voice was controlled when he continued. "I've broken no covenant. This wasn't something I planned. I'm not to blame for every insane thing that happens around me."

"Gods' blood man!" Eoghan bellowed, slamming his huge hands on the top of the table, and stood. "Who do you think is to blame, if not you? You've acted recklessly since the night you destroyed the power of this Council! Was that someone else's fault, too?"

A current of apprehension spread rapidly through the room, and the meeting teetered on the edge of ending before it had ever begun.

Max stood up, laying his hand on Nicolas's arm, "Please Eoghan, sit down. We can all agree that there were tragic mistakes made in the past, but we are not going to solve that tonight. Tonight, we all face a common threat, and fighting among ourselves only puts us in further danger. Surely none of us want that?" His eyes rested boldly on each of them in turn. Eoghan glared fiercely at Nicolas for several moments, but then he resumed his seat. Nicolas's jaw was tight, his face stony. Anger and something else flared in his eyes. Giuliana recognized his struggle for control.

An intense look passed between Nicolas and Giuliana. Eoghan didn't miss it. He studied them shrewdly, then said pointedly. "So, this is the consort, Giuliana." He addressed her in his native Gaelic, "Cead mile failte, a thousand welcomes, Lady. You are developing a reputation of your own. I've heard of your fierceness in keeping Electra's kin sorted. A bold move. You should keep in mind that she is vain but not weak."

Electra snorted. Giuliana nodded curtly. "Repayment for a violation of the law of Aegis. We may not live as a coven, but we do protect our own." She looked directly at Eoghan and added, "Vanity is its own weakness."

Eoghan looked startled for a moment, then roared with laughter. He leaned back in his seat and plopped his booted feet onto the table, ignoring the looks directed his way. Electra glared at them both.

Eoghan spoke again. "Alright. So, we're facing a plague of revenants. This isn't our first experience with a rogue insurgency." His gaze fixed on Nicolas, "Though it is the first time we've had one without a Council to rein it in. We know how to deal with rogues; we just beat them into submission. As I see it, this is the least of our problems. The bigger problem is that rumors and the press threaten to expose our existence. What are we going to do about that?"

Nicolas replied. "In a few days or weeks, the world will have forgotten that crazed woman, but we will still be facing this plague, and we won't know any more about what's behind it unless we work together to find out." He glanced around the room. "Did any of you know it was spreading outside your own domains?"

There was a reluctant head shaking around the room. "Do any of you have any idea who's responsible for it?" Again, there was a murmur of voices responding in the negative. "I know there's no trust among us. No one dares act for fear of inciting the others. We've not moved in concert for a very long time. We've been fortunate to have enjoyed a relative peace for nearly a thousand years, but I think that peace is over."

Eoghan laughed out loud. "Fortunate? We've all been fucking terrified of you and your infamous temper."

"You know, Eoghan's right. Nothing like this has happened in centuries." Persephone looked pensive. "So why now, then?" she challenged. "Why Venice? Is it a coincidence that it's arising from the seat of the Council's former power?"

Max answered thoughtfully, "Yes, it did clearly start in Venice; that's unlikely to be a coincidence. The events here and in Paris indicate a calculated effort to reveal our existence to humans. You live on the edge of discovery, Nicolas, and these events are bent on making that sort of life impossible. What if they aren't attacking Venice?" He paused and looked around the room, then concluded. "What if they are attacking you?"

Nicolas looked up. "Me? No one has attacked me in a thousand years. Don't be ridiculous." His gaze raked around the room; his jaw set resolutely.

Giuliana recognized the coming storm and knew she must choose her words carefully. She was beginning to see a new possibility spread before her, an invisible hand behind it all. Incite humans by hinting at the immortality withheld from them. Expose Nicolas, the beloved son of Venice and Paris, as one holding the secret. Demonize his popular music. Release a horde of the worst kind of vampires into the city to turn minds against them. Suppose someone *was* targeting them?

"Max may be right. What if someone has set them loose intentionally?" she asked. "Someone whose goal is to destroy you and the life that you've built?"

"Giuliana, what would that accomplish for anyone?" he asked dismissively. "I don't have a coven. I have no power over any house, not even my own." He took a calming breath. "Who would do this? Who could? And, more importantly, why? What would it accomplish?"

Max tapped his fingers on the tabletop and mused. "All our kind know that you've lived among mortals unapologetically for centuries. There are many of us who resent vampires who do that. Some feel that it's dangerous and puts us all at risk of exposure. Others just think it is wrong."

He looked at Nicolas. "To drag your life into the spotlight, then strike at you, could be a statement- a public condemnation of your lifestyle. And that force of feral newborns wreaking havoc makes it a doubly effective statement, powerful enough to be noticed—to terrorize both human and vampire. That could be why." Max's brows knit together in concentration, and he bit his lip thoughtfully. "But who? Now that's a puzzle."

"Perhaps someone who wants to see vampires cling to the old ways?" A woman spoke. Her skin was the color of café au lait, and her hair was a mighty aura of blackish-red curls falling loosely to her shoulders. She was easily the youngest vampire present, yet she exuded an uncompromising confidence.

Delphine, from New Orleans, Nicolas sent to Giuliana. *One of the most respected among us.*

"There are some vampires of every age who simply prefer anarchy," Delphine offered in a soft patois that had been nearly polished away by time. Glints of ethereal bronze light from the chandelier caught on her curls. There was a velvety sureness in her voice that commanded the group's attention. Her delicate features, patient expression, and halo of hair gave her a saintly appearance.

Argus, who sat beside Electra, nodded enthusiastically. "Many vampires thrive on chaos. There are more than a few who believe that the complete subjugation of humankind is unavoidable," he said. Giuliana watched him curiously. She sensed that he was working out a mental puzzle even as he spoke. His struggle to solve it ended with a flare of his eyes that indicated a startling epiphany, but it was quickly snuffed out as Nicolas's gaze fixed on him.

Argus sensed Nicolas's anger settling on him and rushed to explain. "No! I don't mean me! I don't believe it! But some do. You all know it." He fell into a distressed silence. For a moment, Giuliana saw something more complex in him, a muddiness in his intention. Nicolas snarled and looked away. Argus perplexed him, too.

Eoghan's eyes flashed hatred, and he pointed at Electra. "Why aren't we asking her? I've heard she's been busily expanding her house the last year. Shouldn't we start with the answer that's staring us in the face?" His tone declared that he had no use for Electra. Perhaps because they were very much alike; bold, clever, and headstrong.

An ancient with matted dreadlocks nodded his agreement. "I, too, suspect that Electra's hunger for power in Venice is the source of this plague."

"That's a lie!" Electra struck the table with her open palm. "This did not start with me! The House of Delphi has been overrun at every turn!" She glared at Nicolas. "What else was I supposed to do but increase my numbers?"

Her face flushed nearly the color of her scarlet dress as she stared Eoghan down. "Delphi is only one House, and I am only a half-blood. Yes! I'm doing everything I can to battle this, to save my house. But I'm not creating rogues! To save Venice, the old Houses must be reborn from pure blood, and if Nicolas will not do it, then one of you must intervene."

She met the eyes of one vampire, then another, until it was clear no one would volunteer to support her. No one would challenge

Nicolas's right to rule Venice. Giuliana thought, with some satisfaction, that the lack of support must be eating Electra alive. She wondered if Electra was adept and patient enough for such a long game. Electra did look agitated. Her eyes darted nervously from one vampire to another. Though she was the obvious choice, it didn't seem likely to Giuliana.

"I swear to you that this is not me. Nicolas, you know that I've done nothing but beg you to find a solution to the revenants. Why would I do that if I had set them loose?" Electra pled.

Nicolas hesitated, then said reluctantly to the others, "In this, I believe her. She fears for Venice, as I do." Electra gave him a grateful look.

There was silence for a moment as the group considered. Then, Delphine's dulcet voice emerged once again. "Has anyone considered the possibility that one of the very ancient vampires may have resurfaced?"

A confused silence. Giuliana guessed that the proud Elders in the room thought of themselves as pre-eminent and seldom considered those who had come before them. Nicolas had been silent on the subject, and she assumed the primogenitors had long degenerated into madness or buried themselves in the earth, or both, and taken the truth of their beginnings with them.

Delphine continued cautiously. "I spent my first centuries as a vampire in Egypt, fixated on understanding what we are. Our history is palpable there; like many, I believe it is where we began. Last month, I visited a shrine in Thebes, and there was evidence of recent blood sacrifice in the sanctuary of the Numina." Astonishment rippled through the gathering. "Could it have been Khaldun?" She looked first toward Argus, then toward Nicolas. "It was he who first subscribed to the idea of human decline, and he is known to have generated a great deal of chaos."

Giuliana felt a throb of distress from Nicolas. "Who is Khaldun?" she asked.

A current of dismay spread through the room, and all eyes fell on Nicolas.

Eoghan cried out, "Cor! You mean you've never told her the tale?" He caught himself and went quiet.

"Who is he?" Giuliana asked Nicolas.

Nicolas sighed. Max laid a sympathetic hand on his shoulder and said, "Khaldun is one of the eldest amongst us. He's older than anyone can remember. The vampires of his era believed that to thrive, life must be in balance in all its aspects. They held that there were those who were even older still, known as the Numina that safeguarded that balance. Chances are that those legends partly inspired the pantheon of Egyptian deities."

"Yes," Electra interjected. "It is also said that the Elders of that time once worshipped one of these beings, called Sokaris." Argus made a sound as if to speak, but she flashed a cold stare at him. He fell silent.

"The Numina and Sokaris are fantasy," Nicolas asserted. "But Khaldun is real. He was real." He looked at Giuliana. "Khaldun was the head of the Rialto coven, and he fled Venice after I destroyed most of the coven a thousand years ago."

Giuliana flinched as a missing piece of Nicolas's history translated into a dagger of pain. She looked at him and saw her pain reflected in his dark eyes.

"We know that he disappeared, but do we know that he is dead?" Max asked.

Nicolas drummed the table. "Even if Khaldun was alive, why would he emerge now?"

"Sokaris is rising. If Sokaris, why not Khaldun?" Electra said petulantly. Giuliana sensed deception, as she did every time Electra mentioned Sokaris. As Nicolas opened his mouth to speak, Electra held up her hands to stop him. "No, don't even say it. I am sick to death of your disdain. Just wait. Do not act, and Sokaris will take you unaware. This swarm of revenants will sweep you from your damnable high road. You will end up having to transform every human connection you've cultivated just to survive, just as I have."

"They are not mine to transform," Nicolas said.

"Then the hordes will overrun you. Who else will stop them? This sorry lot?" Electra gestured around her scornfully.

"Beware your contempt, Electra," Max warned her.

"You deserve contempt!" she snapped. "You're too cowardly to act. You're all just irrelevant relics! You had the power to rule, and you let one man throw it all away."

"Did we?" Max questioned, anger coloring his voice. "Even though the Council suffered violence and upheaval, our conventions endured. Because of that, our kind has survived, despite our tendency toward self-destruction. Be grateful. The only reason you have a coven in Venice is because the Council wasn't around to put a stop to it." Rage filled her eyes, but Electra remained quiet as he continued. "We may need a new way of governing now, but we will come together, or else we will all perish."

Max looked away from her back to Nicolas. His voice softened. "But I'm afraid she is right about one thing, our need to act, and soon." Max sighed. "If something isn't done, we will soon have a world where humans live in terror and vampires devolve into feral packs. Who benefits from that?"

"Are you suggesting that we start a war, Max? Because that's what it's likely to become," Eoghan said. "The moment any of us acts against the rogues, the power behind this atrocity will show them- selves. Are you ready for that?"

"No!" Persephone interjected. "I have no stake in this and no reason to make enemies just so you can continue to pretend you are human." She rose. Her eyes shifted around the room nervously. "My house will not see the benefit of risking our peace to interfere in events that don't affect us. It was a mistake to come here. Even the fact of our meeting could provoke them." Giuliana watched as the vampire left with a feral growl, and the fragile peace in the room began to disintegrate. Whatever had motivated them to come tonight, they were certainly not prepared for the potential of a modern-day preternatural war. She wondered if this group had ever agreed on anything.

"She's right. Coming together could be seen as a threat." Eoghan slapped his hands on his knees and stood. "I would join an alliance of Houses, but we don't even know who we're fighting against." He stood and began walking toward the exit. "Nicolas, give me someone real to fight, and the House of Sandel will join you." With that, he turned and walked out into the night.

The others mumbled their reluctant agreement, and then there was quiet for a moment as everyone absorbed what they had heard. Eventually, it became clear that the meeting was over, they all stood, and the group began to say their goodbyes and exit one by one.

Delphine stopped beside Nicolas. Her tawny skin glowed as she turned her empathetic eyes on him and grasped his shoulder. "Though I sympathize with you, I must agree with Eoghan. Until we know who or what we're fighting, there's little to be done. I fear the one you will fight is stronger than all of us. My coven is young and cannot take on such a force." She smiled at him, "I know you have history with Electra, but she is not completely wrong or totally insane. Something is happening. Look to Egypt, Nicolas." With that, she followed the others through the door.

Only Nicolas, Giuliana, Max, Electra, and Argus remained. They were silent for a moment as disappointment took them. "Well," Max sighed heavily. "At least we know where they stand."

Argus looked as if he was about to speak. Nicolas's eyes narrowed, and he said, "At the theater, you said that someone else's order might prevail. Whose order?"

A fog of confusion clouded Argus's expression as he held Nicolas's eyes for a beat or two. When he spoke, it sounded as if he was reaching deep into his memory. "Someone less thoughtful. Someone who does not understand the balance of things." Giuliana was sure that something just beyond Argus's grasp was struggling to be said. Then he finished flatly. "You should take the reins while you can. Enough of the covens would support you if you would lead. No matter what they say, hope brought them here tonight."

Nicolas paused, looking as if he had once again seen something strange in Argus. Giuliana heard it in his haunted voice, a perception that went deeper than his actions suggested.

Giuliana said to Argus, "You can't force Nicolas into power he doesn't want. He has no responsibility for this."

"No?" Electra sighed impatiently. "Think how it was when you arrived in Venice, Giuliana. Do you remember vampires here in the sixteenth century? No, you don't. That's because when Nicolas returned with you from Egypt, vampires *fled* this city. He had decimated his own coven before he left, and we all feared what might happen to us. So, you see, he shaped the city more than you know. Without legitimate houses, what is there to stop the revenants?"

Argus said, "Don't you see that you were the only one who ever cared a whit for humanity? If you want to protect mortals, tell the Elders how your plan will benefit them. Otherwise, the only question will be which of the rest of the sorriest lot will rise to the top of the heap." Electra glared at him, and he fell silent.

Nicolas covered his face with his hands for a moment. When he looked at them again, his eyes seemed infinitely old. "I don't even know how to begin."

Max said, "Nicolas, there is already a war against you on two fronts perpetrated by both human and vampire adversaries. On one side are the rogue vampire hordes, maybe even someone powerful controlling them. On the other are the humans who half worship you, half distrust you. LeCourbe clings to you like a tick. Remember your history, Nicolas. His ilk is the next round of scum we will be up against. Begin there."

"Max, I can't. I admit that I am responsible for my human following. That, at least, is clear to me now. But if the vampire unrest is also my doing, I don't need to have more of a presence; I need to have less."

Max embraced him. "Don't be so sure of that. After being here tonight with all of them," he nodded his head towards the table, "I'm not." He kissed Giuliana, then smiled at Nicolas. "Whatever you decide, know that you have my support and that of House Salzburg."

Electra made an impatient sound and headed towards the door. But before she exited the salon, she turned to say, "Run away from this if you will, Nicolas, but know this. I will do what I need to do to survive, and I won't let you stand in my way. And don't be surprised when things start hitting you a little closer to home."

Argus shot a pained look at Nicolas, as if he wanted to say something, perhaps a warning, but then he turned and followed Electra out.

Nicolas walked to the fireplace as Max left and closed the door behind him. Giuliana joined him. The flames flickered in his dark eyes as if a fire burned within him. "Nicky, why have you never told me about Khaldun?" She reached out and turned his face to hers.

"It's not my proudest moment, Giuli." He grasped her hand in his and brought it to his lips in a kiss.

"Will you tell me what happened?" She sat on the hearth.

He sat down and leaned against her. For a long time, he didn't speak; then, a long sigh escaped him. "After the death of Portia, I felt as if I had betrayed everything and everyone. I wanted my life to be over. But I had children to consider. So, I lost myself in keeping my father's business alive. I turned all the guilt, anger, and loneliness I felt into something to drive me. I lived and breathed every waking moment, expanding and keeping my father's shipping trade alive.

"Khaldun lived in Venice then and ran a rival trade consortium. I didn't know he was a vampire, didn't know such things existed. He was a business rival, and every major trade agreement out of Venice became a contest between us. Of course, I challenged his encroachment into my father's territory. He undermined me at every turn; he

125

had my business partners killed, and he upset deals I'd made. I couldn't escape him or his influence. Finally, he demanded that I work for him. I fought it until he threatened my children."

He looked into her eyes. "I'd lost so much already. I couldn't risk that. So, I surrendered to him. I worked for him for years, all the while plotting my revenge, waiting for the moment when I could strike back." He looked away. "All the while, not knowing what he was."

He sighed deeply. "I had a plan. It took years for me to put pieces in place that would break his hold on me and allow me to take everything back." He looked into her eyes. "And on the eve of springing my trap, he discovered my plan. That was the night I learned he was a vampire. He took me prisoner and fed from me for weeks. Always leaving me more dead than alive, but not releasing me. He showed me the savagery of preternatural vengeance. I longed for death, and when I thought I could stand nothing else, he made me watch while he took the life of one of my own brothers." His voice trembled, and Giuliana wrapped her arms around him, holding him close. "I watched him die, heard him crying out for me to help him. But there was nothing I could do." He pulled away and looked at her. "I begged him to stop, to let him go. I told him I would do anything he wanted. But he killed him anyway."

He stood and turned to face the fire. The flames turned his face into a mask of despair. "It was so long ago, but every time I close my eyes, I can still see it. Still hear Pedro's screams, still hear Khaldun's raspy voice asking me, 'Anything? We shall see.'"

"And then he turned me." His voice went flat, and she could barely hear him over the fire. "Though I wanted to die, he wouldn't let me. You know what it's like as your life seeps out of you, you crave it. You see, hear, feel, think nothing except that your life is ending. So, I drank and my hatred of him wound its way through my veins in his blood until I couldn't tell if it were him or me, I hated more. My misery was complete. Or so I thought."

126

He stepped away from the fire, his back toward her, his shoulders slumped. "He left me alone that night, and the hunger for blood raged through me like a fever. I remember I howled for it until the sunrise left me in a stupor. The next night it began again. Khaldun returned with his coven. He said I must feed, and that he had brought me someone." His voice cracked. "Then he brought in a child."

Giuliana gasped, "Nicky please, no more." She went to his side and held him tight in her arms.

"I remember the child crying out in fear. I remember Khaldun whispering to me, 'Drink. You must drink,' urging me on with his coven echoing him. I wept. I screamed no. I cursed him. But in the end, the hunger built until it overwhelmed me. I took him, took his sweet life. Khaldun laughed. The whole coven roared with laughter. I felt something build inside me, some ugly awareness, part hatred, part self-loathing. Something happened, and I still to this day don't know what it was—a connection with some mysterious energy, a frisson of some unknown power surged through me into the room. As I looked at them, their laughter turned to shrieks, and then they turned to ash before my eyes." He fell silent.

"And what of Khaldun?" she asked. "Did he die that night, too?"

"I thought he had. I hoped he had. But I didn't see him. In the panic and terror, I didn't see him."

"Do you think Delphine is right then? That he survived and has come back? Is Delphine's lead one worth following?"

"Maybe." He whispered and took her hand in his, and led her from the room. Nothing had been resolved; new questions had been raised tonight. But Giuliana felt a new, tiny glimmer of hope in the heart of the man beside her; a question mark where dread had once lived, and the freedom of having faced a long-avoided demon.

13

STARTING OVER

Nicolas and Giuliana arrived at the Villa late on Christmas Eve through an early, faltering snow. From the canal, the pink marble facade of the Renaissance palace was barely visible through the tangled grounds, an oasis of complete isolation in the very heart of Venice. Giuliana's elaborate gardens engulfed the island around the Villa, spreading all the way to the surrounding canals; acres of winding paths and woods, coaxed into controlled wilderness through centuries of artful neglect.

They were home, finally. Christmas, then Carnevale in Venice. For the first time in the two months since the tragedy at the opening, she felt the normal rhythm of her life restored. Tensions were growing worse. Electra had been bold enough to accost Francois, and Nicolas had arrived only just in time to prevent his harm. In retribution, Giuliana destroyed several of Electra's brood at the cemetery of San Michele. Electra was determined to have her war.

But Giuliana was animated and happy as she greeted Maria, the tiny, bird-like woman who had served as their household manager for many years. Even Nicolas seemed happy in those first moments of homecoming, and strangely nostalgic. But when she looked up again, he was gone.

She found him already seated behind the oak desk in his darkened second-floor office, talking on the phone. He beckoned her in, and she wandered idly toward the wall of windows behind him, which offered the Villa's best view of the grounds. The snow clung to the gridwork of glittering branches, and the ground was hoary with ice. Giuliana could not look at the gardens without recalling the year the Villa was constructed. It had been completely wild then. Nothing existed here except an untamed wilderness bent on consuming the crumbling ruins of the original palace, and the hidden crypt into which Nicolas sometimes retreated for decades at a time.

She and Nicolas had walked here every night, planning these gardens, noting each new stone that had been lifted into place that day while they slept. That was 1495, the year she had been transformed, and they had not missed a single winter in the Villa since, slowly taming the wilderness into the intricate landscape that existed today. She dragged her eyes from the soothing vista and turned.

"I don't know," Nicolas was saying. "The palazzo had long been in ruins even when the Villa was built. The tower has a long, unsavory history. I don't remember it all, myself." A lie: she sensed it. "Francois, just make sure there is nothing of value there. Then the tower comes down."

Nicolas put the phone down, a look of vexation flickered on his face for a moment and then he pulled her from the desktop onto his lap. "Are you happy to be home, Giuliana?"

"Yes," she sighed. "Yes." She twisted the rose gold ring on her finger. Nicolas had given it to her earlier in the day, as a symbol of their endurance. "I love this. It seems old. The roses are exquisite."

"It came to me during my mortal life, and it was old even then. It was supposed to have protective qualities." He lifted her fingers to

130

his lips, then turned the ring from side to side. He studied her face. "You're the empath. Can you sense its power?" He chuckled and then kissed her deeply.

Her fingers trailed down his chest. "The fact that you gave it to me is powerful enough for me." She pulled back and studied his face.

"I heard you on the phone with Francois. You're going to have the tower torn down?"

"It's time. It's nothing but an eyesore. I should think you'd be glad to have your gardens rid of it."

"Nicky," she chided. "That tower has stood for more than a thousand years. You walked its rooms in the daylight, as a mortal man. Isn't that reason enough to preserve it?"

"That's another good reason to destroy it. Our homes are props, Giuli. They support—the illusion of sanctuary." He bent to kiss her and for a long moment, she was lost in the power of his mysterious pain and the pleasure of his mouth meeting hers. He grasped her waist and lifted her to her feet. "It's time for Christmas, Beloved."

She laughed. "Christmas?"

Almost happy again, he ushered her back to the oval-shaped library. The tumbling blaze in the fireplace provided the only light in the room. Hundreds of faces stared from the walls; all the masks from their Carnevales past, animated by the shimmering golden-red light of the fire. Nicolas took one down as it caught his eye and ran his fingers across the gold stars painted on her porcelain cheeks. She came to stand beside him and took the mask from his hands. "1863. You wore a huge red cloak and gave gold Etruscan coins to everyone at the banquet. Do you remember?"

He glanced at her and smiled. "What I remember is the ballroom going completely silent when you arrived at the top of the staircase in that gown. What was it? Gold foil and clouds of red voile." He smiled at her then trailed off for a moment, lost in thought. "Verdi fell in love with you that night. And so did I, all over again. Could it have been so long ago?"

His arms wrapped around her, and he clung to her as if she might vanish. "I've loved our life here, Giuliana."

The indecisive tempest she had found in his eyes so often lately was replaced by grim resolution. "It's time to move forward with Francois's scheme, isn't it?"

"Yes. Very soon. The new opera, Cry of Innocence, will premiere in the spring. Francois is arranging an explosion in the Portinari building after the gala that evening. He will ensure that we are presumed dead. We'll have new names, new identities. It will be an adventure." He smiled at her and pulled her toward the roaring fire. "I have another gift for you, Giuliana." He smiled and removed a small package wrapped in paper the color of moonlight from the breast pocket of his vest.

She carefully unwrapped a black velvet box. Its lid and sides were ornamented in a rich, gold pattern of coiling grapevines clustered with grapes. Resting inside was a heavy, iron key. Its head was a mass of elaborate gold scrollwork which formed the initials 'GD'.

"The Palacio Delacroix awaits her mistress, Senora Delacroix. Merry Christmas, Beloved."

She stared at him, stunned. The new names they had chosen as an idle, surreal joke during their long sojourn down the Nile sounded ominous and final under this roof. A peculiar misgiving possessed her. "Palacio?"

He caught the hint of her weak smile and returned it spontaneously. "Yes, in Andalusia. After we've mulled over it for so many decades, Francois has finally found the right one, and at the most opportune time." He lifted his eyes from the box in her hand to meet hers. "I can't bear Paris, anymore, Giuli."

She blinked slowly, resisting the urge to cry. "It's just outside Granada. Near your mortal home. The gardens are among the most beautiful in Spain. Let me take you to see it. I want this to be real for you."

In the moment she opened her mouth to surrender, he smiled,

and his form wavered and disappeared in her arms, his words still echoing in the room. "Come with me." The sudden emptiness made her stomach pitch. She had no choice but to cast her intention toward his and let her body melt after him. The awareness of his destination burned like a bright spot for a moment before her, and then she was there with him.

They descended on Palacio Delacroix as a mist through the air. The silvery gray structure, built on a spit of land projecting into a wide river, appeared to float on water in the light of the full moon. First Nicolas, then Giuliana, materialized at the end of an isolated path that cut through the heavily wooded grounds and led to the main entrance. Nicolas embraced her and then turned her to face the estate. Its towers, domes, and dormers rendered a symphony of granite floating in the night mist.

Giuliana followed behind him, as they crossed into a courtyard formed where the gray granite wings of the house met. In the center stood a marble fountain. Its resonant splashing filled the night air with the sound of torrential rain.

Nicolas unlocked the massive oak door and pushed it open with a touch. Cerulean moonlight washed into the room from the giant dormer windows overhead. Rising in front of them like a great blue reef was an ornately carved marble staircase. Cool moonlight poured down the succession of cascading stairs and landings, drenching the room in a submarine light. The marble floors of the foyer and adjacent ballroom glowed in the darkness.

"A ballroom, Nicolas?" she asked, cautiously. "For a summer house?"

"You don't think either of us could do without one, do you?" He smiled at her. With only the moon for illumination, they ascended several floors and stepped through a door into the chemin de ronde; a broad, covered walkway cut through at regular intervals by large openings.

"This goes completely around the roof. It once made this place impregnable. Now it provides a full view of the grounds." Stretching before them was a series of formal flower gardens crisscrossed by paths and punctuated by giant arbors of chestnut and elm trees.

"Acres and acres of garden, Giuliana, enough for an eternity of evening walks." She closed her eyes and focused on the urgency in his voice. Something vital hinged on her acceptance of this place. "The gardens are bordered all around by grape orchards and orange groves. The stables breed some of the finest horses in Andalusia. They continue all the way to the foothills there in the distance. Beyond those hills stands the last virgin forest in all of Spain."

"Nicolas, it's beautiful." She proceeded carefully, testing what felt like unstable ground. "Spring in Granada, winters in Venice. We could fashion a much worse life for ourselves." She reached to lay her hand over his, but he withdrew it, sighed, and pushed his hand back through his hair.

"Giuliana, it is not just for the spring." He turned to face her and this time he reached for her hand and held it in both his own. His obvious misery held her motionless. "We must give up the Villa, Giuliana."

She jerked her hand away. "What do you mean? "

He folded his arms around his waist and said evenly, "We must give up the Villa along with the rest of our assets. The dissolution of the Portinari fortune will draw enormous attention. To keep possession of such a high-profile landmark so readily associated with our names jeopardizes the entire plan."

Her dread took form. Finally, there was something concrete to fight against. Her frustration, contained for months, exploded into her protest. "Nicolas, it's ours, every stone and pane of glass, and has been from the day it was built! I can't tolerate the thought of someone else living there! Surely there's something you could do? Tangle up the title so that no one can take possession?"

"And draw attention to the distribution of my assets? And for how long? How long would you have it stand vacant?" She paced an angry distance away and then turned to face him. The starlight flooding in through the embrasure bathed his face in a cold, pale light. He stared at the grounds beyond, his expression blank. His voice came to her in a growl, low and strained. "Would you rather I destroyed it, Giuli? Because, I've thought of that, too."

She froze. "What?"

"A fire. An explosion. It would be a simple matter to see that no one ever enters the Villa again."

"I don't want that, Nicky. I can't believe you do, either."

He sighed suddenly, faced her, and spoke quietly. "We have no choice. Please. Please, don't make this feel more like a betrayal than it already does."

She moaned and closed her eyes, rubbing her arms as if she would freeze. "Giuliana?" His voice was tortured and anxious. She half turned her head to acknowledge him, but she couldn't meet his eyes. Not yet.

"This is why you're destroying your grandfather's tower—to keep someone else from owning it."

"I have to destroy it, Giuliana. Why should I suffer its hold on me?"

"But where will it end? At the point where you resent everything you love, for the pain it causes you when you are forced to give it up?"

"I am not giving up anything I love."

She scanned the surrounding woods which stretched as far as she could see and tried to think of them as a sanctuary. The grounds were magnificent. It was just the sort of place they might have chosen together to spend some long interlude of their lives. If only they had chosen it.

She looked up at Nicolas leaning against the wall, the wind tugging at his hair. He stood in the shadow of the chemin de ronde. He loved the gardens, orchards, and forests as she did, but they would not sustain him as they sustained her. He needed a city. He needed libraries and theatres and concert halls, the brilliant lights, and the buzz of activity. The world itself was enough for Giuliana, but Nicolas needed the world of humans—the accomplishments of humankind—to challenge and inspire him. What city could he walk free in after news of his death had spread worldwide?

"Nicolas, what will you do here?"

"I'll compose, Beloved, as I always have. I'll spend my nights with you." She thought of his music, written but never performed save for her, as it had been in the first days she had known him. She looked away to the orchards beyond. He did not see that it was not a gift to want to spend time with her now when she could not possibly be enough to satisfy him. She lifted a hand and brushed the backs of her fingers gently along his cheek. He turned his head to see her. "Can you give up the marches of Italy for the forests of Spain, Beloved? Can you be happy here?"

He was desperate for her assent—to have her happiness to cling to, if not his own. He could have picked no more perfect setting for her than this. It was as if, knowing his own satisfaction to be impossible, he had focused wholly on hers.

She gave him the answer he wanted; one she already knew to be the truth. "Yes. It has everything I need, beloved. It has forests and gardens and solitude. It has a quiet place for my work. Elegance and character. It has you."

She glanced at him. One thousand years he had claimed as home the tiny island on which he had been born into the world. Now to leave it, perhaps forever. And even if not forever, for centuries, centuries in which it would change and evolve in ways that would make him a foreigner were he ever to return to it.

"Can you be happy here?"

She almost wished he kept up the subterfuge. That she hadn't seen the sadness and frustration replace the dark anger in his expression or the haunted, gaunt look on his face when he turned to her. "I don't know, Giuliana. I don't know."

14

FOLKLORE AND FANTASY?

Snow fell in a gently sifting powder across the curving balcony surrounding the tower that was La Tour D'Argent. From his table nestled in an alcove on the upper floor of the restaurant, Paul Dendera had an unobstructed view of the heart of Paris. A palpable sense of expectation surrounded him; a timorous feeling which was echoed in the way the steely Seine coiled warily through the heart of the city in a question mark.

Paul had been at Portinari Enterprises for six years now, hired by Portinari himself fresh from Sorbonne University. The challenge of establishing a state-of-the-art research department for the Entertainment Division of Portinari Enterprises had been a dream come true.

Initially, he and Francois had been drawn together by their mutual admiration of one another's talent. Their friendship flourished in the highly charged atmosphere of Portinari Enterprises. They became lovers almost as an afterthought. Almost a year to the date after their relationship had begun, Paul found himself completely, unabashedly in love with Francois. What started out as a mutual flirtation developed into a relationship around which Paul had begun to shape his life.

But now, Nicolas's interest in some medieval ruins on his Venetian property consumed all of Paul's time. Likewise, Francois was fully engaged in a different project for Portinari; one that, for some reason, required an inventory of all the company's tangled assets. Like planets captured by the gravitational field of some great sun, Francois seemed trapped in a powerful orbital tide between Paul and Nicolas. The Maestro had become a silent partner in their relationship. Each time they attained a margin of stability, Portinari entered the picture again to throw things off balance with a new opera or a new business venture which only Francois could oversee.

Paul sighed and reopened the file on the tabletop. A photo of the crumbling stone tower, Ca' Portinari, was clipped to the inside of the folder. He pulled it off and looked at it again. He'd been working at the site for nearly a week now, sent by Francois to oversee the dispersal of the tower's contents and its eventual demolition.

The square, gray structure rose out of the moldering ruins of the original palace that once stood on the island Nicolas Portinari called home. This tower, one of two that flanked the old palace, was the only structure that had not long ago sunk into the lagoon or crumbled into ruin. It seemed unjust somehow for it to have survived the elements, invasions, and wars for a thousand years, only to be pulled down at the whim of a man, even if that man was Nicolas Portinari.

The tower's demolition was the least of his concerns now. While exploring the site, workers discovered a sealed room full of paintings and manuscripts. This hoard, which to Paul's deft eye appeared to be authentic works from periods stretching back to the Middle Ages, had somehow survived the dank conditions of the disintegrating tower for hundreds of years. Their discovery turned a simple survey job into something much more complicated.

The top page of a thick sheaf of papers was an email from

Banetti, the anthropologist who conducted the excavation of the tower.

To: Paul Dendera
From: Alexander Banetti
RE: Villa Giuliana manuscripts

Paul,

As per your instructions, I have left the paintings discovered at Ca' Portinari in situ and resealed the tower chamber. The manuscript collection found there has been safely removed to the research and preservation lab in the Portinari Building in Paris.

Preliminary examination indicates the manuscripts from Venice consist mostly of household records and inventory lists for Ca' Portinari, the earliest of which date back to AD 1015. It is frankly astounding that they survived at all given the fire which destroyed the palace appears to have started in the chamber above the room where they were found. Even more remarkably, the intensity of the conflagration was such that it fused the decorative mosaic tiles on the interior walls into glass.

Of the texts I have examined thus far, the most interesting is a manuscript claiming to be a journal written by Portia Del Cenzio. Based on what I've translated thus far (see attached), it is clearly a work of fiction or the ramblings of a mad woman. Much is missing, presumably destroyed in the fire. The surviving part is rife with fantastic descriptions of witchcraft, and spirit possession.

From what I've been able to cull from the material, Portia Del Cenzio lived and was married to an ancestor, and perhaps namesake, of the present-day Nicolas Portinari around the year 1042.

There is evidence to suggest they were both in residence at Ca' Porti-
nari for several years between 1042-1046. Though information
about Portia herself is sparse, there are frequent references to the Del
Cenzio family and to the Portinaris scattered throughout these
materials. I am continuing my work translating the manuscripts
and will forward subsequent material to your Paris office.

Alex

Paul flipped through the papers. He had read it all several times
now. It didn't surprise him that the materials left more unanswered
questions than answered ones. Portinari was like that. The Del
Cenzio manuscript was just another mystery surrounding his enigmatic employer. In tracking down the property title for the
Venetian Villa Giuliana, Paul turned up several anomalies of his
own. For as far back as records existed, into the 13th century, Isola
Portinari had been held off and on by a Nicolas Portinari—all of
whom seem to have been musically inclined with a keen sense for
business.

And that was nothing compared to the swirl of gossip, innuendo,
and rumor surrounding Villa Giuliana. The night-time existence of
the Villa's occupants was the stuff of local legend. Some of the things
he had seen made even the ridiculous accusations against Nicolas
being trumpeted in the press lately seem tame. Paul was not one to
pay much attention to idle gossip. Still, even he recognized that
there was something peculiar about Portinari.

He brought the materials tonight to turn them over to Francois.
He could deal with them. All Paul wanted to do was hire a conservator and someone to demolish the tower. Then he would be
finished with this damned project and could get back to his life.

"I'm sorry I'm late, Paul, something came up." Francois appeared
out of nowhere behind Paul's chair and glanced over his shoulder at
the file he was perusing. "Anything interesting?"

Paul looked up, annoyed. "Not unless you're interested in witches or how to resurrect disembodied spirits."

Francois removed his coat; a puzzled expression broke across his face. "What?" He squeezed Paul's shoulder, then sat at the table. Paul gestured for the waiter who whisked plates onto the table and filled their wine glasses before vanishing.

"Never mind. Where the hell have you been? I've been waiting an hour." His voice sounded more irritated than he felt.

"I told you I got hung up." Francois sipped his wine cautiously. "People were injured in front of the Opera House. A group was protesting auditions for the new production."

"Portinari really can't make a move in private anymore, can he?" Paul said, almost feeling pity for a moment.

Francois sighed. "No. No he can't. He pointed to the files on the table. "What's all that?"

"It's the site survey report from the anthropologist who did the excavation at Ca' Portinari last week. I brought it for you."

"How's that going? Is the tower down, yet?" He looked up over his coffee.

"You didn't read the report I sent you last week from Venice?" He set his coffee cup down impatiently and reached for the pile of folders.

"The tower is sitting in a fucking lake to begin with; the runoff from a shoddy job of filling a nearby canal. It took days to clear the mud and brush and find a way in. When we entered the tower, we found a room that survived the fire that burned the rest of the palace down a thousand years ago. Full of old paintings, some manuscripts, and a letter or two."

"What sort of paintings?"

"Unusual ones. Oil and tempera, as would be expected. The subjects were pretty common, mostly portraits, mythical figures, and a few religious subjects. But stylistically, they're a real mystery. They just don't conform to the Romanesque style of painting being done during that period. I'm looking for a conservator now to help me extract them. They were in remarkable condition. Same with the manuscripts."

"What were they?" He cupped his coffee cup in his hands, savoring the warmth.

"Mostly they were inventory lists and various household records for Ca' Portinari. But there is one which claims to be a journal. It's the most bizarre thing."

"Bizarre, how?" Intrigue sparkled in Francois's eyes.

"It's supposed to be the journal of someone named Portia del Cenzio, who was married to one of Portinari's ancestors, another Nicolas Portinari, back in 1042."

"Supposed to be? What do you mean? Is it not authentic?" Francois leaned forward, intrigued.

"Oh, it's authentic all right. But, based on the story it tells, it must be a work of fiction; something written to vilify the Portinari name."

"Vilify? What does it say?" Francois set his cup down sharply on the table.

"It's just your usual schoolgirl diary," Paul said wryly. "Electra del Cenzio, who calls herself a priestess of the cult of an Egyptian God, Sokaris, falls in love with her sister's husband, one Nicolas Portinari. According to the manuscript, Electra summons up the ancient spirit, Sokaris, and commands him to make Portinari fall in love with her. In the process, she loses control of him and by a rather sordid set of complications, almost everyone involved ends up dead or missing." He stopped talking, amused by the stunned look which filled Francois's eyes. "I told you it was bizarre. It's like a fucking supernatural soap opera."

"You have this manuscript in your possession?"

"Just the translation of the part which survived. It's incomplete, though there may be more mixed in with the rest of the manuscripts. The folio itself is in the lab. Why?"

"Does anyone else know about this? Has anyone else seen it?" A sudden urgency filled Francois's voice and he looked nervously around the crowded restaurant.

"No, just Banetti; he translated it. Why?" Paul leaned forward uneasily.

"Think about it, Paul. Can you imagine the stir this manuscript would cause in the media if its contents were revealed? It would be a nightmare. It's imperative no one else knows about it."

"Oh God, I actually hadn't considered that." He leaned back in his chair. "Francois, no one would take this seriously. There are similar tales to be told about almost every old villa in Venice. Surely people would realize it's just folklore and fantasy."

"People will believe what suits them, Paul," Francois said sharply.

"If one were suspicious, a lot could be made of the fact that we're being asked to destroy this tower at this particular moment. Why is Portinari so eager to have it down now?"

"I don't know, Paul. There's no accounting for a man's relationship with his family history."

"And no accounting for Portinari."

15

NOCTURNE

Giuliana emerged from the Villa onto the terrace at dusk. She paused at the balustrade and battled a sudden burst of wind to pull a short cape of blood-red wool around her shoulders. She had exited from the Villa ballroom, which flowed outside through a bank of French doors to include the terrace of silver and pale pink ceramic tiles laid in star-shaped patterns. The nocturnal owners had chosen their pearlescent hues to catch and reflect even the scant moonlight likely to filter through the cold mist of a Venetian winter night.

She was on her way to the site of Ca' Portinari, the Byzantine palace erected over a millennium ago by Nicolas's grandfather. Among all the many paths winding through the Villa Giuliana grounds, none lead directly to the ruins of the original structure. Nicolas erected the Villa on the center of its island, facing it away from the rotting tower and the sea, toward Canale Della Giudecca and the heart of the city.

The rain had stopped falling, but it saturated the air, and a fine sheen glistened over the slick tile and stone. Tonight, no light from the city pierced the cottony fog. The gas torches in the gardens were not yet lit. The only artificial light challenging the haze was the unnatural glare illuminating the scaffolding caging the tower of Ca' Portinari. It was here Giuliana's solemn gaze finally rested, her eyes as gray and turbulent as winter.

Here at the rear of the palace, an intentional break had been left in the balustrade to set off the view of the crumbling tower of Ca' Portinari above the forested buffer between the old palace and the new. Nicolas had built a gulf between himself and his past and then framed it to watch it decay. Giuliana scrutinized the tower often from this vantage point. She watched Nicky contemplating it, too, and he had looked on those ruins with such a brooding countenance that Giuliana could not imagine intruding with a question. He never invited her there or gave her leave to go. Until last night, when he asked her to do what he, inexplicably, could not. "Do this for me, Giuliana. Find out what remains there." His eyes begged her not to question him, and so she had not.

She shook off the memory and set off toward the forest and the tower. The fog carried with it the canal's pungency and the redolence of peat from the marsh's brew of decaying rushes and water lilies. The narrow strip of manicured space quickly gave way to a cultivated wilderness. She walked a quarter-hour through a carpet of frosty fallen leaves and thistle before the forest broke away suddenly to a close view of the tower. Floodlights erupted in a blistering blight over the tranquil grounds.

The remains of the old structure rose out of a still, black pond that seeped into a bog at its perimeter. A lone bittern stalked the murky edge near a canvas canopy erected as a temporary equipment shelter. Beneath the fluttering eaves, several workers in yellow parkas huddled around electric heaters, preparing to leave for the night.

Heads turned toward her, the group shifted, and she caught her first glimpse of the man at its center, the man she took to be Paul Dendera. Assessing her curiously, he held up a hand to signal that she wait. He turned to finish delivering instructions to the crew. Dendera was lively, animated, and well-received by the men. Giuliana recognized the exquisite cut of his coat and the quality of the buttery leather as the mark of Francois's preferred Parisian designer. But she suspected Francois would not have approved of the snug jeans and fisherman's sweater beneath it. A wool driving cap was doing a poor job of keeping the mist out of his eyes. He squinted at her as he approached the shadows where she stood.

"Mr. Dendera? I'm the conservator, Giuliana de Cordova." She stepped into the light to offer her hand, and he thrust his forward to meet it. The abrupt motion spooked the bittern, which let out a raucous bark and beat its spotted wings furiously to take to the air. The sudden noise unnerved Dendera. His confident air vaporized; he whirled reflexively toward the bog and the threatening noise and abruptly lost his footing in the sludge. His face registered bewilderment as his feet cartwheeled from beneath him.

Giuliana gasped into her hand to avoid laughing at the bewildered expression he made as he lost his balance and fell into the water. He landed, with a furious splash of slime, on one hip and an elbow.

"Fuck," he blurted. Giuliana hid her grin and took a few steps forward, offering her hands to help lift him back to his feet. He accepted grudgingly and came up muttering curses with awe-inspiring ardor.

Giuliana bent to retrieve his cap from the mud bank, then watched quietly as he dragged the cashmere scarf from his neck and vainly attempted to brush the mud away from his coat with a few agitated swipes. He was a full inch shorter than she, but powerfully built, and he glared up at her between sodden strands of honey-colored hair through eyes a startling shade of green. She handed him his cap.

"I'm afraid it's ruined," she said solemnly. At the same moment, he said an ironic, "Thanks."

She laughed. "Are you alright?"

"I'll be better when I leave this godforsaken mausoleum behind me." He gestured toward the tower as if it had been shadowing him for years. "So, you're the conservator? I didn't catch your name."

"I am. It's Giuli..."

He cut her off. "Glad to meet you, Giuli."

She liked his intelligent, appraising eyes. There was no evidence that he had grasped her connection to Nicolas. The fall had put him in a foul mood. He extended his hand. "Paul Dendera, Research Division, on temporary assignment to hell."

She gingerly took the man's hand, which was muddy and as cold to the touch as hers. "I'm sure hell is not nearly so damp, Mr. Dendera."

"Nor probably so dark. But it's very likely operated by the same management." He brushed the damp hair from his face with the back of his other forearm.

She laughed and released his hand, discreetly wiping hers on her cape. "You're not the first to compare Portinari to Lucifer, you know. There's a veritable flock of disillusioned prima donnas who would join you in that opinion. Does your employer know you hold him in such high esteem?"

"There's actually very little my employer doesn't know in the end. I'm glad you're here. We've been expecting you most of the day."

"I'm sorry. I thought Monsieur Durand would have explained that I am unavailable during the day and would come in the evening."

"Mademoiselle, you forget where you are. No one explains anything to the damned." "Really? Well, Francois spoke readily enough of you. He's made you out to be quite formidable."

He closed his eyes for a moment, collecting himself. "You'll have to forgive me. I'm not handling my exile well." He wiped his hands and shoved the cap and filthy scarf into his pocket. "I only meant to say that I'm out of my element, and we really need some expert advice."

He jerked his head toward the tower, and Giuliana fell in to walk by his side along the muddy perimeter of the lagoon between the canopy and the ruins.

"Tell me, Giuli, who did you piss off to earn deportation to the swamp?"

"Rescuing an invaluable collection of artifacts sounds like an adventure to me, not a demotion Mr. Dendera." She smiled and leaned toward him confidentially. "And this swamp is my home."

"Oh, don't get me wrong. I'm sure Venice, on the whole, is a beautiful city." He seemed determined to misunderstand her, but she could find no polite way to press the point of her identity, and she was enjoying his candor. "Have you worked for Portinari long?"

For a moment, she couldn't find words. "Our association goes back a few years, yes. But worked for him? No, not exactly. You see..."

"Well, let me fill you in. It's a different ball game up close. Stay alert. No matter what you think your job is, it's always something else. It's amazing how easily Portinari's whims manifest themselves in the career paths of others."

"Isn't that the nature of working for someone else, Mr. Dendera? Why didn't you refuse the assignment?"

Paul laughed. "You really don't know him, do you?"

She couldn't resist. "I take it you're not fond of Portinari?"

"Fond?" he sputtered. He pushed his hand back through his hair and glanced at her impatiently. "Well, no. Fond is not the word that springs immediately to mind. No, definitely not fond."

"Then why work for him?"

He frowned, surprised as if she'd introduced a question he'd never considered. "Because Portinari Productions is the best. And he's a genius. A bastard, but a genius. Have you ever met him?"

"Well, yes. I..." She smiled at him sympathetically. "Well, the truth is, Mr. Dendera, I live with him."

His cheeks and forehead flushed red. "Excuse me?"

Giuli shrugged. Paul gaped at her while she smiled absently and looked past him at the tower, "I'm sorry. I tried to tell you before. I'm Giuliana de Cordova."

"Giuliana de Cordova," he repeated as if the words failed to make sense. Then his eyes widened. "His... I mean, the Giuliana...?" He glared up at the sky. "Great. That's... that's just... typical." He rolled his eyes and sighed. "So how many apologies do I owe you?"

She laughed and looked back at him. "None. You owe no apologies. I was enjoying the conversation."

"Yeah, I'll bet you were." Surprisingly, there was no resentment in his voice. He studied her face intently, and she pushed back her hood and shook out her hair. "So, if you're Giuliana de Cordova, why am I under instructions to give you the grand tour?"

"Simple enough, Mr. Dendera. I've never been here."

"Never been here. Of course. This way then."

Giuliana followed him, her attention drawn to the tower. It had been one of the square twin towers flanking the palace. Most of the roof was gone, and the walls in one corner of the upper story had crumbled away. The waterside facade on each of three floors was pierced by a series of large, arched windows. They were studded with crosses and medallions deeply carved from exotic marbles and gouged in eerie chiaroscuro beneath the harsh artificial lighting. Moss and vines invaded every gap and niche in the red Venetian brick. The lower courses of smooth white Istrian stone were blackened and almost completely submerged in the brackish lagoon on the landside.

Dendera beckoned her forward. "Well, welcome to your backyard."

She tried to absorb the history of the place. She had crossed into a state of mind somewhere on her way from the Villa that made the archaic tower seem perfectly fitting, and Giuliana and her fiery mortal guide the anachronisms. Nicolas may have conquered time, but it had gnawed this stately edifice to its bones.

Somewhere inside this gutted space, he had been born into the world to live his mortal life. He had fallen in love here and seen the birth of his own children within these walls. From this perspective, the tower didn't seem brittle or broken but a marker of his history.

There was a peculiar stillness to the night. The obscene bath of floodlights intruded on a millennium of privacy. The site had only been disturbed once in a thousand years, during the Austrian occupation early in the eighteenth century, when the two canals crossing the Portinari property had been ordered filled, making one island from four. Since then, the lagoon had slowly expanded and spread over the sunken strip of land where the canals had once crossed.

The strange quiet seemed to affect Dendera, too. He walked beside her, silent and calmer now. She was aware of the discreet way he constantly appraised her and her interest in the ruin. They circled toward the dry rise of land where the tower had connected to the main palace. Only a few short segments of the main structure's walls remained standing. From the tower jutted a corner, the walls a full meter thick on this lower floor. It supported the remnants of an old, hooded cooking fireplace, its chimney, and a water trough. On the outside surface of the same lichen-green wall was still attached what remained of a stone staircase. It rose from the rubble in a few hopeful steps before it disintegrated in mid-air.

Ancient oaks grew close around the tower. Their gnarled roots heaved up jagged slabs of brick, Istrian stone, and red-veined marble. Giuliana continued her circle, with Dendera beside her, walking directly into the heart of the grass-covered ruins where the main structure had once stood. The tower on this side was singed black, the visible evidence of a catastrophic fire. Here, the foundation had already been excavated, revealing pieces of the surviving terrazzo floor.

She stood in the rubble of the great entrance hall and gazed out toward the filled canal. There was no ceiling here, and the floor was formed of huge slabs of black and white stone in a checkerboard pattern. Looking down at it, she became dizzy and was struck by a vivid impression of a mortal Nicky disembarking here from a gondola at noon on the narrow strip of shore separating the palazzo from the canal. She imagined him soaked by sunshine as he entered the dazzling ocean of light that spilled into the hall from the windows above. She tried to shake free of the sense of déjà vu, but the images persisted and intensified. Nicky, standing before the fireplace. Nicky, his human skin flushed, a mortal anger in his eyes. Nicky, walking through a similar grove of oaks, the grandfathers of these ancient giants, with a child on his shoulders.

Distraught, she stepped closer to Dendera beside the crumbled wall to look out over the pond. It encroached on the remains of the arcaded gallery along the facade. Stumps of marble erupted from the still surface of the lagoon. Giuliana reached for the stone to steady herself.

There was an air of despair here, a sense of misery and violence. She looked at Dendera, and he looked disquieted, as if he sensed it, too. Branches above them moved cautiously in a sluggish wind, stifling with the unwholesome scent of moldering brick and stagnant water.

"The paintings are inside." He pointed up towards the tower they stood in front of. "Ready?" he said.

She turned away from the lagoon and caught his eyes, unbalanced by the magnetic pull of that other century. He left her side to rifle in a plastic toolbox left by the door. Coming up with a flashlight, he pointed to the scaffolding. "We'll have to go up and in through the windows, then."

He pointed up the scaffolding and followed closely behind as she began her ascent. The frigid metal bit into her hands, and she felt a faint, queasy anticipation. His presence behind her was as solid and reliable as the steel girding.

The first-floor windows had been bricked in. But, as they came to the second floor, the unsealed opening revealed a stagnant darkness unsettled by sparks of glimmering blue eddies. It left her head whirling with vertigo. She paused.

"Not there," Paul cautioned. "There's no floor. One more story up."

She continued up the metal latticework to step through the third-floor window. It was an empty room, a complete open space, with one corner entirely chewed away. The walls were burned black. The fire and the years after had devoured whatever had existed in this room. Giuliana went to stand in the gaping void, where there was no roof or walls and the building opened to the sky. "There's no fog up here, at all. Amazing."

Paul came up beside her. Giuliana felt relief to suddenly see the lights of Venice again in the distance. She had thought they might have disappeared into another age. The Villa glowed in all its pink glory, surrounded by its dark fringe of forest. The gaslights on the grounds were lit now and saturated the gardens with a golden, comforting glow. "Well, you were right. There doesn't seem to be much to salvage up here."

"Only the view." He leaned against the broken wall on his forearms. She watched him shamelessly for a moment, fascinated with the soft movement of his hair, rippling with light and wind, until she found herself instinctively focused on the thrumming rhythm of his heart. She pulled her cape more snugly around her shoulders and tossed her hair back to feel the astringent effect of the freezing wind on her face. "I thought you hated it here, Mr. Dendera."

"I'm only bitter, Madame, not dead," he said softly, searching her face as if he was surprised—and perhaps pleased—by what he found there. "Say. Did you call me a prima donna down there?" He jerked his head toward the canopy by the lagoon where they had met and grinned.

Her eyes danced. "Indirectly, I suppose."

"I deserved it. I'm sorry I've been such a bore."

"It's refreshing to occasionally meet a man who is very sure about things."

He didn't raise his head, only cocked it toward her in its bowed position. "You're very gracious to describe my irascibility that way, Ms. DeCordova."

"Oh." She was truly disappointed. "I liked Giuli so much better. And I didn't say it was a pleasure to meet such a man often."

She looked at him askance, and he laughed, suddenly and whole-heartedly. She liked the way his eyes reflected every change of mood. They were an effervescent green, a beguiling combination of smoki-ness and sparkle.

"Well, then, it's Paul, in that case." He lifted his head and then turned to lean with his back against the wall, facing her. "So, why haven't you been here before?"

"This place and its history belong absolutely to Nicolas. I'm only an invited guest here, with a job to do, just like you." She hesitated, then folded her arms across her waist and looked out at the view. When she looked back, his eyes were on her and called for the truth. "And like you, I'm feeling a little out of my element."

His eyes narrowed slightly as he took measure of her sincerity. "I've read about you. Your charm is legendary. You're not using that..." he twitched the fingers of both hands as if sprinkling faery dust, "... Giuliana de Cordova charisma on me, are you?"

Giuliana was taken aback. Then he smiled. It was intoxicating, Paul Dendera's smile. "Dear man, if I had a desire to bewitch you, I certainly would never be sloppy enough to allow you to wonder about it."

He cleared his throat and stood erect, thrusting his hands in his coat pockets. "Well, that certainly puts me at ease."

She laughed softly. "Will you show me the paintings now?"

"I would love to show you the paintings." He met her eyes soberly and went silent. She had the impression she had glimpsed the real man for the first time this evening. "We have to go back down for that."

On the ground, she waited outside the doorway on the land side of the tower for him to fiddle with the temporary air-tight plastic fitted over the opening.

"There was no inside entrance to this room from what we can tell. And this doorway was sealed shut, then bricked in."

"Sealed?"

He nodded. "You'll have to see it to believe it." He lifted the flap, and she stepped inside while he shined the flashlight along the walls. Ripples of light glanced back in a dazzling array of blues as if reflecting from mirrors, or crystal, or the smooth surface of a calm sea.

"It is a mosaic fused into glass. This whole room. I guess it formed a protective space for the paintings—which were obviously stowed in here after whatever holocaust caused this, or they'd be reduced to cinders." He coughed and poked the flashlight's beam here and there in the corners of the room. The air was thin and dusty and incredibly dry. "Here we go."

A generator rumbled, and bright lights switched on. Giuliana marveled at what she saw. The light rebounded from the walls and afforded as much illumination as a bank of chandeliers. The second floor had been removed, and the ceiling vaulted. The chamber was intimate but ornately decorated.

"It was a chapel," Paul offered. "It must have been a Christian chapel, but there are some incongruities."

"Yes, I can see... I guessed... that much," she said, the dizzy familiarity she had experienced outside returning.

The room was square, taking up the whole area of the tower. The ceiling was vaulted, rising so the room encompassed both the ground and second floors. The old windows had been converted into niches for painted wooden panels. Flowing around them, encompassing the horizontal center third of every wall, was a mosaic, glittering every possible shade of blue. It was broken only at the door they had come through.

"We had an engineer out here this morning who left completely baffled. He said it was the strangest thing he'd ever seen, and he's been involved with the renovation of these old island palaces for nearly thirty years.

"The heat necessary to do this kind of damage would have been far beyond the ability of anyone living in the eleventh century to produce. It was incredibly intense and brief—a flash, like an explosion—but of heat, not force. See how the mosaic never really melted or ran. It just fused so that the design is still perfectly in place."

The wavering light, along with a frightening sense of familiarity, caused her another nauseating wave of vertigo. "So, the explosion caused the fire?"

"No. That's the odd thing. We thought so at first, but now we think the fire started up there, on the top floor above us and traveled through the palace." She looked up where the light swirled at the murky darkness in the vaulted ceiling. She ached to think that she would never see this room in daylight, nor the miracle this mosaic would seem, touched by the morning sun. She imagined the glass sea would toss and foam under the probing fingers of light. The galleys would seem to move over the shifting waves. Flesh would come to life with a luminous glow.

She stepped closer to the mosaic softly, afraid that any jarring step would shatter the illusion. Paul followed her and squinted at the brilliant reflections wavering against the reflective surface. "I can't quite make out what it is. It doesn't represent any religious subject I know."

She smiled. "Well, ostensibly it does. It's the voyage of Rustico and Buono, the two merchants credited with bringing St. Mark's remains back to Venice from Alexandria."

"Leave it to a Portinari to manage to sanctify a business venture."

She smiled and reached to drag her fingers over the smooth glass, speaking absently. "It was a fuzzy line for everyone. For a long time, merchants were required to bring religious artifacts back from their journeys abroad, for the glory of Venice and her churches."

"I'll bet a Portinari changed that law when he couldn't figure out how to invoice God for the shipping." He raised the torch again to the mosaic opposite. This one, too, was fashioned of many shades of blue. Brilliant white and blue clouds began the section. These shifted to denser forms in a brilliant blue, filled with light. Next, a naked man emerged from the clouds, his hands outstretched.

"And then there's this, "Paul said, shaking his head. "Maybe you can explain how Horus ended up in this parade."

The light revealed a falcon-headed deity wearing the double crown of Upper and Lower Egypt. A priestess lay prostrate at his feet, one hand raised to offer a ring. Giuliana caught her breath, recalling Nicolas's obsession with Egypt. Beyond it was a series of undulating lines giving the impression of a sandstorm, followed by multiple images of the Amenta, the Egyptian symbol of the underworld.

Paul turned and swept the flashlight around the room so that the light glanced off the bricked-in windows above. Only one of them gaped in a black void, the one she had looked into from the ladder. "We opened that one to try to enter before we forced the door."

He indicated the window niches. "Most of the icons are still in place. It's remarkable how well preserved it is, considering the age—and the bizarre situation."

When her gaze finally took in the panels in the lower windows, she gasped. Paul chuckled and set the torch into a stand on the floor. "The trefoils above the panels were stained glass. When they melted, they sealed the windows. And the paintings." It was true. The panels were covered in a brittle, multicolored film.

"The paintings are over here. Eight of them stuffed inside what we think was the altar. This, at least, was the altar stone." He crouched and laid one broad, capable hand confidently on a square of charred, striated marble. His fingers rubbed gently at the stone as he examined the metallic hulk, which rose higher than his head.

The altar had been a silver affair and was now melted solidly to the marble floor and slumped in a shapeless shell over a stack of panel paintings. Giuli knelt beside him. The painted wood panels were jumbled inside like logs on a fire. Reason told her not to touch them, but still, she flung off her cape and pulled the first loose panel gently from the center of the stack. It was cracked, but the paint seemed to be intact beneath it.

"This one almost looks as if the damage was intentional." Paul had already pulled the next painting in the stack forward. "It's been partially painted over. It wasn't finished. And look, there are gouges here in the wood, as if someone slashed it with a knife."

"Why would they be stored beneath the altar?" Giuliana mused under her breath. "Or left here to ruin?"

Paul slipped another painting out onto the floor. It was much larger than the others, and she had an eerie feeling, looking at it. This one, she would not touch. The only discernible portion of the right-hand side of the panel was half a woman's face, captured with a remarkable realism for an age where too much attention to the human form was considered unseemly.

A mass of auburn curls slipped over the shoulder of a rich Byzantine-style robe. One eye peered back at Giuli from an erupted field of craquelure with an oddly intense expression. Giuliana felt a shock of recognition, almost like an electrical jolt. A strange feeling came over her as her fingers passed along the edge of the painting.

Paul's voice dragged her back before she made the connection her mind was struggling to make. "Jesus, these don't look at all like the ones in the windows. Could someone have left them here later?"

"No, all the elements.... the technique... are 11th or 12th century. It's just the realism in this one piece that's striking..."

"You mean someone was painting ahead of his time."

"It looks that way."

"Won't that add to their value?" Giuliana nodded. Paul laid the panel aside and propped his arm on his knee to look at her. "Are you all right? You seem uneasy."

"I guess I am." She stood and drew her cape back around her shoulders. "Will you bring the crew in tomorrow afternoon and have them remove that large one? I'd like for that to come to the Villa first. I'll send someone in the morning to take some atmospheric readings so that we can prepare the Villa workshop for it." He looked up at her, and she knew the excitement shone in her eyes. She was surprised to find a little of it reflecting back from his. "Are we ready to move them?"

He smiled. "I thought you might say that. Yes, we can certainly begin in the morning. We'll be transporting them to Paris. Francois has already arranged for a lab."

"Good. We'll have to act quickly now that the atmosphere here has been disturbed."

"Yeah. That's unfortunate. We didn't know they were here until the room was already open. It's not the crew's fault. These guys thought they were just here for a demolition. If they hadn't been curious..."

She shuddered, remembering that the chapel was to be destroyed. "It's all right. I understand. Hopefully, these haven't been exposed enough to have done much more damage. The gentleman I'll put you in contact with will supervise the building of crates for them. All except that one." She pointed to the large panel. Every instinct told her that one was important.

Paul answered, still distracted by the paintings. "That one goes to the Villa. Gotcha. Hey, look at this one," he said softly. "It looks as if it's been deliberately destroyed, too. Do you think that could have been the intention for all of them?" He frowned and looked up at her again. Giuliana felt a strange uneasiness.

How much did Nicky really know about this place? She had watched him countless times through the centuries pay exorbitant prices and go to extravagant lengths to salvage much more insignificant pieces than these. How could he have doted on that collection with such loving attention, knowing what lay moldering here? She recalled his brooding countenance as he stood in the evenings at the top of the Villa tower gazing toward this one, and her heart sank.

She sighed and looked up at the window. An image like a memory brushed her mind. The bricks seemed to vanish, and early morning light poured into the room again, glistening like holy water over the dazzling mural. She heard a woman's low chant rising exultantly around them, spiraling up to meet the misty light.

"Giuliana?"

She forced herself back to the present; to focus on him. "I'm just imagining it the way it must have been." She laughed softly, mocking herself. He rose slowly beside her and reached to touch her hand, briefly. "It seems a tragedy that such beauty had to decay to this."

"Why? Why did he let it decay? Why, in all the generations of Portinaris who owned this property, none of them were curious enough about this part of their heritage to enter this room?"

"I don't know, Paul. I wish I did."

16

FUGUE

Giuliana woke while the sunset still held the lagoon in a deep teal spell and lingered in wisps of shell-pink clouds. A tantalizing puzzle awaited her: the paintings from Ca' Portinari. A true mystery, at her age, was a rare, seductive commodity.

Her windowless studio was equipped with the essentials for her restoration work. Two long, metal tables set at right angles dominated the center of the room. Several easels and rows of shelving lined the gently curving perimeter. Banks of instruments measuring humidity and temperature were the only other breaks along the wall's sterile surface.

She stopped at one of the tables. Paul Dendera had delivered the painting from the tower as promised. Accompanying it was a report from the conservator she had recommended he contact. She lifted the thin sheet and read what she had already observed. Nine paintings had been found, suffering varying degrees of damage, most of which had been natural deterioration due to age and environment. All but this one had been transported to Paris.

This one, as she suspected, required no structural repairs. The report verified the only damage to the wooden panel was due to neglect and age. Paul had taken the piece to the conservators for a woodworm treatment. The invoice was attached. Paul's signature, an undecipherable tangle of loops and angular slashes, was scrawled on the invoice. He had appended a note advising her of the atmospheric settings the conservator had recommended for the workshop.

She freed the work gently from the crate to lay it on the long metal table. The artist had chosen his support carefully. It was sound hardwood, and the sections were joined masterfully. Whatever else she might discover about the artist, she knew already that he had been fastidious in the choice of his materials.

Giuliana noted her findings meticulously in a small bound journal as she worked, carefully cataloguing each form of deterioration and its remedy. She swiveled a microscope toward her and switched on its high-intensity light. Beneath a dull, gray film of dust, the varnish over most of the painting had taken on a cloudy, blue bloom. The damage seemed to be confined to the varnish layer.

Satisfied, she pushed the microscope away and stepped back to inspect the whole painting. The bloom obscured the central third with a milky glow. The varnish elsewhere had mellowed into a honey brown. Barely perceptible beneath the darkened varnish and bloom was a portrait of a woman standing behind a seated man. The background was a garden of quince and other fruit trees. On the left, the woman's dress emerged from the bloom and flowed down along the edge of the composition in a beautiful lapis lazuli blue, its radiance dulled by the damaged varnish. Both faces were clouded. The man had raven dark hair, which evoked a sense of softness and movement uncharacteristic of Medieval art. A white garment trailed in folds along the bottom edge of the painting at the center, where the wood was splitting, and the paint blistered. The man wore red. Above his head, raised edges of pentimento showed through the fading paint, where something had been painted over.

Giuliana puzzled over the double layers for a moment. The bottom layer was too obscured to make out, casting only a faint uneven edge all around the upper torso of both figures. She dubiously dismissed it as a cloud painted in the background, then covered with the figure. She made a mental note to take special care cleaning this section, so as not to reveal enough of the underpaint to distract from the subject.

She wiped her hands on a towel while reviewing her notes. She felt out of tempo, floating in time, much as she had in the tower. The villa was silent. Giuliana felt a chill. She wondered uneasily why she had chosen this painting to begin with. She couldn't help the discomfiting feeling that she had been the one chosen.

"You're a fool, Giuliana," she muttered as she attached the painting to an easel adjacent to the worktable. Drawing a tray of brushes and solvents close beside her, she sat on a stool to begin.

The dusting process began with a soft, dry cloth repeatedly drawn over the painted area. She set to it with preternatural speed. The rhythmic contact with the surface was soothing, nearly hypnotic. Giuliana often formed an emotional attachment to art as she worked with it, and this piece had special value. It was part of Nicolas's mortal life and there was an intriguing mystery in the fact that it had endured. All told, it would take several months of work to correct the damage. But she had often spent longer on a project.

When the loose dust had been removed, she repeated the process, this time with a cotton pad moistened with a mixture of water and a few drops of ammonia. The grease and dirt responded with rewarding ease. She undertook the delicate work instinctively. Her mind went blank, aware of nothing but the energy between her fingertips and the paint.

Even as a mortal child, she had sensed a metaphysical window that opened as she painted, to the space where an artist's intention is transformed into art. That perception was her means of accessing the creative energy that lay bound in every painting. The phenomenon had become even more pronounced to her as a preternatural. It gave her confidence in her reading of a broad variety of artwork, and in her decisions about the restorations she undertook. She became a medium for the restatement of the artist's own vision, which she recreated with inhuman objectivity.

The cotton pads were coming away white; the surface of the painting was much cleaner. She stood and stepped away, shaking her head to dispel its curious hypnotic effect. Every painting exuded an energy of its own, but this one was gripping. The dirt had been plentiful, and its removal was brightening the hues of the reds and blues and making the white robe glow. But the bulk of the work was still hidden behind the damaged protective overcoats. Giuliana looked at the clock. It was just past two; still early. She closed her eyes and focused her preternatural senses to search the house. It was vacant, but for the breathing of a few sleeping mortals. Nicolas had not yet arrived.

She turned back to the painting, concentrating on the condition of the varnish. She moistened a small brush with a minuscule amount of alcohol, then touched it gingerly to the wood, analyzing the result. The varnish had been laid on in several coats, and the top one came off easily under her brush, leaving the desirable patina intact. This small success gave her the confidence to go on.

The cloudy varnish vaporized slowly, unveiling the scene below it. Creamy skin and a tumble of red-brown curls were revealed. Eyes appeared. Startling, chestnut colored, and as full of light as crystals. Wonder and fear rippled through the still depths of Giuliana's concentration as she recognized two impossible facts unfolding before her. The realism in the young woman's portrait was unheard of for its era. And, even more disturbing, the woman's finely detailed features seemed familiar. But when she closed her eyes, she didn't see the woman in the painting. She saw Electra.

Then she remembered. When the recollection came, it was not

comforting but a blow. Trembling, she laid her brush warily on the table and backed carefully away from the panel. The memory came in a wave, not as a subtle sense of timelessness anymore, but with the complete disorientation of finding oneself replanted abruptly into another age.

It had been 1495, the year Nicolas had brought her from Egypt to Venice. It was a sorrowful voyage. Her husband and youngest son were recently dead. Her older boy was eaten alive with a vicious hatred for her. She had sought solace then, in the act of painting, on the upper deck of the galley. One day she had been so numb with grief, and so hypnotized by the beguiling image on her canvas, that she had failed to notice a shift in the weather. A sudden storm had engulfed them, threatening to snap the masts and drag the entire ship under. It was only after Nicolas and her son had both nearly been swept into the sea in their attempts to save her and the ship that she had come back to herself.

During the storm, the painting had been ripped from the easel; it spun away on the wind and fell into the sea. She was struck again with the image that had stayed with her through all the years since; the last glint of chestnut eyes as the canvas had disappeared into the waves.

She faced the half-revealed figure in the painting. The painting she had been driven to create that day five hundred years ago, by an impulse she didn't understand, had been a portrait of Nicolas and a woman with eyes very similar to those of the woman in this damaged painting before her. A painting that had, against all odds, endured a millennium of destructive forces to appear here on her easel, by her own promise to care for it.

Afraid where that train of thought might lead, she picked up her brush again and focused on the subtle layers of varnish. It was delicate work; remove too little and the painting would appear dull, too much and the fragile patina would be spoiled. She shifted her focus to the figure on the right, her mind floating free as she speculated about the artist.

The painter's talents were obvious with every revealed brush stroke. His skills were advanced for his day, and he had a talent for dramatic interpretations. He had been privileged, evidenced by his use of the lavish, imported lapis lazuli in the gown. The artist was likely Venetian; he had borrowed heavily from the Byzantines, in the jewel-rich colors, the carefully balanced elements and the elongated figures. Yet, there was an unaccountable sense of rhythm and motion in the gravely noble figures and their garments. She let go of the detail again, to draw back and examine the painting.

She couldn't free her mind of images of Electra. Her heartbeat quickened. She was snared by a sequence of emotions; fear, anger, and desperation. They emanated from the board and pigment with a frightening urgency, and she knew she was feeling what the artist had felt the last time a brush had touched the panel. She was compelled to lean forward and begin her work again, trailing her brush across the seated figure's robe. But the vermilion folds of the garment spread in a sanguine flood before her eyes, and she was pulled back to the woman in blue.

The atmosphere around Giuliana abruptly took on an altered, thickened quality. She shuddered as she became aware that a brooding presence had invaded the studio. An undulating glow emitted from the panel. An almost invisible tendril of smoke curled expectantly beneath her brush.

One more stroke and the air trembled. She gasped. The brush fell. A cold breath of wind blew suddenly around the semi-circular perimeter of the windowless room. The pages of her notebook fluttered and turned fitfully. A sudden breeze carried the pages of the conservator's report up from the table. It spiraled illogically in mid-air, then drifted downward to fall beneath her easel.

She looked up uneasily as a cloud of light crossed her vision, moving from the painting toward the ceiling. She was chilled by a caress, like a lover's fingers drifting across her face.

She reached out and from a great distance, she sensed Nicolas, finally turning his thoughts from Francois and Paris, on his way home. Her effort to reach him rebounded, caught fast in the sparkling web around her. The connection between them dissolved. The cloud spiraled around her, condensing into an almost solid mass. It passed over her skin, beneath her dress, circling her limbs as if it would consume her. She struggled, but it felt as though her resistance only strengthened the force's hold on her. She had the sensation of rising as if she had become part of the mist. A pulsing energy smoothed through her deteriorating thoughts. A name came to her. It was ludicrous; couldn't possibly be real. "Sokaris?" she murmured.

The sound of her own name kept her from succumbing completely.

"Giuliana?" Footsteps ran up the stairs. The lab door flew open, and Nicolas stepped through the archway into the room. Bewilderment, then alarm, quickly replaced the smile on his face.

He moved cautiously; his eyes locked on hers. The cloud filling the room flared with an intense light and moved ominously toward him. He crouched. His eyes narrowed and shifted as they tried to find purchase on the nebulous form. A low, instinctual growl began in his throat.

There was a moment's silent pause while Giuliana had the sensation of having swung on a line out over a deep chasm to wait breathlessly while gravity struggled with momentum. The cloud contracted hesitantly. She shouted again, exactly as she had shouted in the face of the storm aboard the Khamsin five hundred years before, "Go away! You are not wanted here!"

The voice, as then, was not hers. It was deep, ancient, and rasping and drew its strength from a point in the earth far beneath her feet, then erupted from her body with a molten heat. The miasma flickered and spread thin, retreating up toward the ceiling where the high-intensity lighting burned a steaming, white-hot aura through its center. She stood firm, electrified, until the mass receded, sucking away with a bloodcurdling howl. It hissed into a glimmering mist around the perimeter of the room and then abruptly dissolved into the walls and vanished. As it was absorbed, she was overcome with another impression; grief.

There was a sudden, thick silence. She breathed a deep sigh of relief as she and Nicolas sat heavily against the counter.

"Giuliana, what happened?"

"I don't know." She laid her head on his shoulder, and the panel caught her eye, still attached to the easel. The girl's eyes stared out into the room, ruthless, beautiful, and still. A chill ran through Giuliana.

"It came from the painting, Nicolas. Exactly like it did... It was like..." She couldn't bring herself to verbalize the connection to the incident on the ship, so long ago, or to speak of what they hadn't spoken of since. For the first time, he looked directly at the painting. "Do you remember it?" she asked.

"Yes." His mouth clamped closed stubbornly. He looked away from the painting, then his hands closed in her hair. "I should never have sent you to that accursed tower."

"Whatever that was, it seemed alive. I think it came from the painting. That portrait feels like the fulcrum of some strange energy I can't read. For that matter, so does the tower itself. There's a deep sorrow there, Nicolas."

"I know. Electra corrupted that space for her own evil motives. And I made terrible choices that destroyed my mortal life there. It's the scene of unspeakable tragedy. I should have torn it down centuries ago." He stood and took her by the shoulders. "I don't want you to go back there. Once it's torn down, all the pain and misery connected to it will finally be over."

"That image seems to have something to say to us. It keeps coming back."

"I hope it doesn't come back again for another five hundred years," he said dryly. As her eyes passed anxiously over the painting and the ragged edge of pentimento, she relived the sensation of desperation that passed from the painting to her and suspected that they would not have nearly so long to wait.

17

ABSOLUTION

Distressing visions still haunted Nicolas. The clatter of pearls on marble at the opera. The betrayals of both Khali and Carlos. Giuli's distress as she absorbed the reality of losing the Villa. The eerie painting that had been retrieved from the tower. His guilt and anger were maddening and so he sought comfort in walking through the neighborhoods of Venice.

His mind and pace slowed as he passed beneath the storied palace arcades. He found a comforting rhythm following the winding sidewalks and crossing over the occasional footbridge. The sanctuary of la Pieta drew him in with memories of conducting his own string symphonies there, alongside Vivaldi. Decades of performances echoed in his memory, sweeping him along toward the part of the city that lived on only in his own immortal mind. A narrow network of alleys shot in thin veins through the district from its crystallized heart. It was toward the Arsenale he was drawn once again.

An enormous marble lion stood guard at the entrance to the Arsenale. Its fierce snarl dared one to go further. Nicolas reached out to touch the frigid stone and murmured sadly, "Hello, old friend."

With the touch came music. Music held him still. *Andante con moto... slowly, with motion.* Nicolas's fingers traced the pattern carved into the lion's shoulder and a theme heavy with longing and melancholy bloomed in his mind.

"Do you miss the harbor at Piraeus as much as I will miss you?" He walked slowly around the statue, his hands cataloging textures; the coils of its mane, its sharp teeth, the gouges carved into its body by time.

"Morosoni was wrong to bring you here." He exhaled deeply, recalling the arrogant commander who had ripped the statue from its perch overlooking the harbor at Athens. "I told him so." He exhaled deeply. For 1500 years it had stood guard there until brought to Venice as plunder.

"Everything is plunder now." Nicolas closed his eyes and leaned against the stone beast, absorbing its music through his skin. He had struggled to convince Giuliana to forsake the Villa but wondered now if he could abandon the city when she had given him, still gave him, so much? There was an unexpected echo of footsteps and laughter from within the Arsenale gates. Garish flashes of unnaturally white faces startled him, passing through the wide alleys between the abandoned warehouses. Revenants. Nicolas clutched the stone and growled at the desecration. Revenants had no place here. The drone of an approaching vaporetto drove him from the gates. He was too restless to be among humans.

The passengers disembarked and moved on. He stepped from the shadows. There was a woman standing in the fog at the station. She called to mind some lanky water bird; clumsy and slow on land, but with the potential for great grace. Nicolas's heart sank as they recognized one another.

It was Lenora Lucci, one of his Venetian proteges, and an extraordinary cellist. She had been a captivating student; brilliant, talented and devoted to her art. He had brought her into his small cadre of promising musicians. There, her potential was developed through exposure to the finest music teachers available, including sessions with Nicolas himself. She had left Nicolas's tutelage four years ago when she had turned sixteen. Since then, she toured, performing with various orchestras. Her career looked to be as successful as it had promised to be. He had to pass her or give up the idea of sanctuary this evening. And if he was right about the sounds coming from the Arsenale, she was in grave danger here.

"Maestro is that you?" Her voice broke the silence between them.

"Yes, Lenora, it's me. I'm sorry I can't stop and talk. I'm late for an appointment. You should leave this place; it's dangerous for you to be here." He would have walked on, but she blocked his path. He brushed too close and was struck with a scent he could not quite identify. It was heavy like musk and sweet, like vanilla, and somehow evoked sadness, but his mind could not make the connection.

He turned and began to walk in the opposite direction, but she hurried along beside him, chattering. "May I walk with you? I've been planning to call you. With all the talk, I've been thinking about what it was like to work with you. There was always a haunting quality particular to you and to your music. It always seemed intense, like it was about more than the music. But there was nothing malevolent in it. I don't understand why the public has begun to attack you."

She grasped his arm and pulled him to a stop to search his face. "I've heard that you aren't taking students anymore. Is that true?" Her gaze met his. "You seem so melancholy."

Was he that transparent? Her perception cut to the heart of his turmoil and fueled his escape. He resumed his pace, but she trotted alongside him until her heels slipped on the slimy embankment where the lagoon threatened to flood the walk. He reached reflexively for her elbow to buoy her up. She never lost speed, taking three steps for each of his long strides. Exasperated, he finally took her hand and forced her firmly into a darkened loggia, amongst a line of broken, plastic-covered statuary. The covering fluttered and sighed.

"If you have read the news lately you should know that it is my public who have given up on me. Half of them, at least, want to see me burn. The other half are convinced I can help them transcend their mortal lives."

"That's good. You do see that, don't you? How remarkable it is that they can't listen to your music or watch you in the world and remain numb?"

Nicolas drew in a sharp breath and bowed his head. Shrouds of plastic snapped around him. She laid a tentative hand on his arm and continued softly. "You strip the pall of apathy away. Maestro Portinari, there is something exotic and beautiful in you, and in your music. When people encounter anything so wild, perfect, and strange, with so much light and dark together, they are naturally frightened by it." She tilted her head, birdlike, waiting for confirmation.

Nicolas sighed. "Ms. Lucci, you're attributing too much to me and to my music. People are just frightened by what they don't understand." He found himself suddenly paralyzed by the woman's unexpected validation.

"No, no, listen. I gave up, too, so I understand, but I have never regretted anything more. When I was working in your studio, I was at my absolute best. But I convinced myself the price was too high. The impossible standards, the endless rehearsals, the focus only on the music as if it was the very source of all life. But I've come to understand that there is no price too high for a glimpse of my life and my music fully realized."

The distance he had always kept between this young woman and himself was hopelessly fractured now by the vulnerability in her voice. He took off his hat and unwound his scarf. She searched his eyes, like people often did, trying to understand all he was in the space of this brief meeting. Even the ones who loved his work never understood that everything there was to know of him they had already heard in the music.

"You seem to have it all figured out." He smiled. "My price *was* too high. I do ask too much of my students. You must find your own path; name the price you are willing to pay for what you want and go the rest of the way on your own."

Her eyes shone brightly, but dark shadows stained her face in pools beneath them. Her luminescent skin gave off a vague aura of decay. Nicolas's heart sank. "We should get you home. We can speak of my demonization some other time."

She gave her head a curt toss and considered. "I've been facing the question of what truly gives a life meaning." Some quality in her voice made a connection in his mind; her frailty, the dark circles beneath her eyes, the sweet, sorrowful scent of her.

"Because you're dying."

She was startled at his bluntness and stammered. "Well, not quite yet. But yes." She smiled. "But then we all are, aren't we?" She dismissed the subject with a toss of her head. "Listen, charisma and talent and soul do not make a demon. What you express is neither demonic nor sacred. It is exquisitely human. It is the promise of hope and the power to choose."

She looked up at him as if she had stumbled on the thing she was trying to say. "You give me hope. I just wanted to tell you that. In case they're beginning to make you doubt that anyone has ever understood a bit of what you were trying to say." She looked relieved.

Nicolas turned toward her. His brow furrowed. He tilted his head and asked, "I give you hope?"

If he had expected her to come so close, he would have prevented it. But he was distracted and did not react before she stepped close and grasped his hands. "Of course, you do. That shouldn't surprise you."

She moved to step back, but he willed her to remain in that tight circle close to him where his influence was greatest. It was an act of instinct, but once he had her there, where he had never allowed her before, he could not let her go. The invitation she radiated was one he was not prepared to refuse tonight.

"Lenora..." Without thought, he reached to touch her hair where a glint of light shined through it. He caught himself before he finished the gesture. His hand paused in mid-air; his fingers curled in a beckoning motion. She stood still, her eyes on him, then caught his hand and brought it up to her cheek. Her skin was unnaturally smooth, almost luminous, with a faint marbling of blue veins beneath it. Her whole body responded to that slight touch: a flush, a flick of her tongue over lips gone dry, an accelerated pulse throbbing beneath his fingers.

She seemed fragile as a sparrow, warm and trembling in his palm. The first flicker of the inevitable doubt danced across her face as she became aware of his unnatural strength. She suppressed her fear and lifted her hands to his face, but he averted her touch.

He spoke to her, thinking he might still repel her, though he knew their contract had been made the moment they had stepped into the alcove. "You know, you should not have come here this evening, Ms. Lucci."

He could see the poisonous decay clinging to her skin. He smiled grimly to think the music contrived by his predatory heart had given this dying woman hope. He let his gaze linger, pulling her into his eyes, his will consuming hers as his desire snared her.

He held her with the care he would attend to a delicate instrument and ran his hand down the length of her spine, bringing it to rest at her waist. He drew a trembling breath and looked away toward the lagoon, searching the wan lights of San Michel for strength. But the first note was struck, and he knew there was no power to help either of them to escape. He waited for the inevitable moment when the force of his hunger would exceed his will to control it. Her image swam before him as if a veil had been drawn over his eyes, and all he could see was the luminous network of veins beneath her skin. The rhythm of her pulse sounded in his head, and the rushing song of blood filled his mind.

He flinched as his transformation began. Emerging fangs pricked his tongue. Veins constricted in famished anticipation. His heart fluttered as her body undulated against his tightening grasp. He snarled at even this small show of resistance, and his fangs closed on her throat, releasing the first coppery beads of blood against his tongue. She bucked back against him sharply, sparking a primordial urge to crush the life from her, but he forced himself to attend to her gently.

He sank into the ensuing shudder of pleasure and surrendered to his instinct for seduction. He distracted her with cool hands along her thighs as he sliced more fully into the vessel. His arms released her, but now she clung to him, with her arms tangled round his neck.

Through the blood link, he felt her disorientation, her mind searching for an anchor. He gave her one in the strains of a melody that he spun around her, and she was comforted. The sharp taste of her disease, harmless to him but deadly to her, filled his senses. A gasp escaped her as he swirled the first chords of the symphony he had plucked from Venice that night into her florid consciousness. She swooned against him, caught in the bitter, metallic melody. The blood gushed into his mouth along with a rush of images from the deepest part of her subconscious. Biting down on his own lip, he released a single drop of preternatural blood and kissed her deeply. Aroused at the taste of the healing elixir, she pulled greedily at his mouth.

He gasped and let her go. He folded his arms across his chest, bowing his head, struggling for control. She swooned against the wall beside him, leaning a distracted head on his shoulder, hardly noticing how he recoiled.

She peered through the gap in the wall. "I can see so clearly, all the way to Murano. My god, look how the lights shine. Have you ever seen the water so blue at night?" She laughed softly, renewed, and stepped toward the gap, delight, and power shining in her eyes.

Now a dose of truth. Reluctantly, Nicolas raised his head. Her smile faded as she caught sight of his face, which he knew had changed into a mask of pure, preternatural craving.

"What are you doing to me, Maestro?" Her voice invited him to lie. She attempted another laugh which shattered weakly against his implacable expression. The shared blood permitted him to feel the machinations of her terrified mind as it fought to make sense of what she saw.

"Listen to your instincts. What do they tell you?"

Fear grew in her eyes, and he knew what she was feeling, a conflict old as humanity. She craved him, and she loathed him. They stood staring at one another across the empty space, both gripped by a nature they abhorred. There was only one natural way for this to end, but Nicolas fought it, even as the fear in her eyes wounded and enraged him.

His voice was grim. "Don't despair. I've made sure you won't remember it later. Or remembering, you won't believe it—it is a clever defense of the human mind to effectively deny our existence." Her fingers drifted up to the wound at her neck. She recoiled and stared at the blood smeared on them, trembling. "Mother of God, what are you?"

"I am the maker of music," he answered bitterly. "I'm what you crave, no?" A discordant rage crashed in his head. "The one who will lay you bare and show you what your life means?"

He backed away, feeling the ugliness of the killer in his manner. Language left her, sacrificed to the need for ambiguity, to leave space for denial. Her fear enraged him. Her vulnerability and fragility enraged him. It enraged him that he was able to take so easily what he wanted, that there was no obstacle in the world big enough to save him from his need. The lack of justice made him reel. She should be terrified. He should be seen for what he was. Seen, as he had seen her.

"This is the price for my music." he roared, all suffocating connections breaking with a satisfying snap. Hunger left him, and his fangs retracted, his countenance transformed, and his nature retreated behind its thin facade.

"Price?" she murmured and touched his cheek with her palm. Her face clouded as the memory of their encounter began to fade. "I could see it for a moment—the suffering there, on your face. You pay a terrible price, don't you?" Sadness filled her eyes.

"Me?" Nicolas drew back incredulously. "No! Not me! It's those who come close to me who pay. You misunderstand." But the spell of denial was spun.

She looked around, confused by her surroundings, and smiled weakly. "I'm sorry to have kept you. I should go. Thank you, Nicolas. For the music. For leading me to myself. I hope you give your public another chance."

He walked her back to the sidewalk and waited until she reached the streetlights. She lifted her hand to wave, but it fell against her neck where the puncture of his kiss was already healed. She turned and looked at him with soft, questioning eyes, but he knew she had already forgotten her terrifying encounter with the truth.

18

ILLUSIONS OF POWER

It was early morning on the last day of Carnevale. Giuliana should have been finalizing preparations for the night's celebration before sleeping, but she hadn't been able to shake the memory of the strange chapel in the tower since she had seen it with Paul. Nor could she forget Electra's defiant assertion that she believed Sokaris was real but bound, or the fog oozing from the painting to surround her in the lab. The random thoughts picked at her until she relented and made her way through the woods to the darkened tower.

She brought the LED light stand inside and carefully focused it on the mural where the solid image of the god transformed out of a bank of clouds. The tesserae here were white glass interspersed with a ragged topaz blue. She took her camera from her bag and thoughtfully captured the image, a safeguard in case she failed to convince Nicolas, and the tower was destroyed after all. She stepped back for a better perspective. Even with the limitation of the imprecise piecing together of the mosaic, she could not deny the similarity between the event depicted in the mural and her experience with the fog emerging from the painting in the lab. The fear, anger, and desperation that had emanated from the painting threatened to take over again. She moved slowly, dragging her fingers along the mosaic. The top border appeared to be rose petals. Her own love for roses had grown from Nicolas's. What had he told her about the significance of the rose in ancient Egypt? She could only remember a vague idea of pure love. She rubbed at the obscured bottom border with the hem of her sleeve. A gasp escaped her lips as she recognized a band of falcon symbols, exact matches for the sigil used by the cult of Sokaris. This was no coincidence.

She turned her attention to the ruined altar, trying to imagine how it had looked originally. From the rubble, she picked out four stout columns of green marble that had held up the silver canopy. The silver had melted and was partially slumped over the altar, a simple waist-high block of the same stone as the columns. Giuliana pushed piles of rubble off the surface of the altar. Greek crosses which had once adorned its corners, were badly scraped as if someone had attempted to remove them. In their place was a border of walking falcons. This space may have originated as a Catholic chapel, but it had morphed into something darker by the time of its destruction.

Giuliana was still crouched behind the melted altar taking photographs when she heard Electra enter the tower from outside. A flush of anger burned in Giuliana's face as she stood to confront her. Electra started at the sight of her, then snarled.

"What gall you have, to think you can trespass here." Giuliana placed her palms flat against the cold stone and leaned across the altar toward her. "Where is your notorious sense of self-preservation?"

Electra waved a hand in the air. "Retract your claws, kitten. I'm just feeling nostalgic. This used to be my home. Or was Nicolas remiss in sharing our history here with you?"

"Your mark is all over this disaster, literally and figuratively." She pointed to the hawks carved into the altar and scowled. "Either say why you're here or get out."

"I'm following an instinct. Like I said plainly at that misbegotten convocation, I believe Sokaris is nearby and about to take form. I'm looking for evidence to push those elder imbeciles into recognizing where the next threat really lies. It's a mission of mercy, really. Doddering old fools," she grumbled.

Electra's trademark saunter was galling as she moved around the space, possessively touching things. Giuliana bit back her anger. "Why would you seek out a creature that caused nothing but misery?"

A cruel little smile played across Electra's lips. "So, you believe he's real? A little wedge of dissension then, between the princess and her prince? Does he know you've dared think for yourself?"

"I don't underestimate your capacity to scorch the earth in pursuit of any scrap of power, or any opportunity to plague Nicolas. You are dangerous because you believe Sokaris exists, whether he does or not. My question is, why compound this mess by seeking to introduce a new element that is sure to infuriate Nicolas and the Council?"

"Because Sokaris is a great source of power. Someone will eventually command him. I'd rather it be me."

"That, I believe," Giuliana scoffed. She brushed the remaining detritus from the altar to take more photos of its surface. In the center of the altar was carved an image of Sokaris standing on the back of a feathered, winged serpent. Above its wings, its body divided into three arching necks, each held by a leash in Sokaris's hand. Each head wore a crown of fire. The mouths were lined with sharp teeth.

"Mm," Electra purred, watching Giuliana's expression. "It calls to you, doesn't it?"

"It's a beautiful piece of art." Giuliana allowed. "Why is it here? What is this place?"

Electra hesitated, picking at a glob of silver melted on the altar top over the tail of the serpent. "You wouldn't understand. People only scoff at the beliefs of the ancient Egyptians now. But they were insightful. And this place is sacred. You're the sensitive one. Can't you feel it?"

"Yes," Giuliana admitted, moving toward the mosaic. "Are you the priestess represented in the mural?"

Electra remained where she was, with one hand on the melted canopy. "Yes, I was priestess when the mural was commissioned. The Sisters converted the Christian chapel into what you see now. But I was only one in a long dynasty. Before I was fully an adult, I ruled over a cult of thousands of Sokaris worshipers from here to Egypt. With Sokaris under my control, nothing was beyond me."

Giuliana sighed. "So, your lust for power began in the cradle."

"Again, you think you understand more than you do," Electra snapped. She let go of the canopy and turned to examine the mosaic. "That power was thrust on me by someone who didn't want it, exactly as Nicolas has forced me into seeking power in Venice."

"Spare me, Electra. No one has to force you to seek power."

"Once you have held such power in your hands, you're never again satisfied with anything ordinary," she responded reflectively, in little more than a whisper. Then she chuckled and turned back to Giuliana. "I don't suppose Nicolas ever told you who burned this place down, did he?"

"He didn't have to tell me; I see it in his eyes every time he speaks of the place." She sighed. "So, was this place meant as a fulcrum for controlling Sokaris?"

"What does it matter? You don't believe me, remember?" She turned away quickly, and her hawkish eyes scoured her surroundings. Giuliana watched closely to see where they would light.

Keeping the altar between them, Electra moved casually to the opposite side. She glanced sideways into the sepulcher where the paintings had been discovered, then looked away. "Why are you plundering through this rubble tonight?"

"Nicolas is planning to tear it down."

A look of surprise played across Electra's face as her eyes darted back to Giuliana. "Tear it down? That would be tragic!"

"As it happens, I agree with you. But it belongs to him, and he wants it gone."

"But why? When?" Electra was sincerely alarmed.

"You'd have to ask him, but soon. Demolition has been paused while we examine the contents. He asked me to look for anything of value. Is there anything of value? Is that why you're here?" Giuliana stepped around beside Electra and tilted her head to peer into the sepulcher. She looked back at Electra and raised her brows in a question.

"You fools don't know what you're playing with! You must convince him to leave the tower alone. Who knows what Sokaris will do if he's bound here, and the place is destroyed? I need time to find him, to bring him under control!"

Giuliana busied herself examining the rose petal border of the mural. "So you say. But Nicolas believes you are delusional. And looking at this, it all looks like a myth, like a thousand others of that time." She turned back to look at Electra but could read nothing on her face. "He was never real, was he, Electra? Just a lie you've invented to make yourself feel powerful?"

"Both Nicolas and Delphine told you about the lore. Who invented that?" Electra spat.

"Khaldun apparently," Giuliana said, shrugging.

"Delphine was closer to the truth than you imagine. Khaldun knows that Sokaris exists." Electra's voice had risen to a near shout.

"Does he?" Giuliana gave her a purposeful look. "How would you know that, Electra?"

Electra threw her hands up in frustration. "Alright, Giuliana. You caught me. I've been in touch with Nicolas's dead archenemy, and he personally validated Sokaris's existence. Is that what you want to hear?" She laughed unconvincingly and moved around to examine the mosaic, though her attention was clearly elsewhere.

"What I'd like to hear is the truth. You're fixated on finding a way —any way—to manipulate Nicolas again. Why would I doubt you'd try to find Khaldun? You've used LeCourbe and revenants. You've tried to force him to take power he doesn't want. Now you're attempting to bring Sokaris back. But why? Why do you need to control him? Don't you see what you're doing to us all? Would you really consider dragging a hostile ancient into this without any knowledge of what it might mean for the rest of us?"

"Us? There is no 'us.' I am clearly standing alone, so I'll drag anyone into it who will stand by me. The illusion of power needs to be stripped from Nicolas. The others need to see him for what he is: a has-been, afraid of his own potential. He is a liability to all of us." Electra's rage grew with every word.

"What you mean, Electra," Giuliana said quietly, "is that Nicolas won't support you in your vile objectives and you are useless without him. You had your chance to convince the Elders, but all you managed was to confirm your potential for sowing chaos. You will never have real power because you are reckless, you revel in making powerful enemies and you respect no one's will but your own."

Electra shot back, "You are all so arrogant and sure you've got it right. I will tell you once again, it's not all me. But I am not weak. I have more powerful allies than you know. Don't make me count you as enemies."

With that, she exited through the plastic covering the tower door. Giuliana sat heavily on the platform that supported the altar feeling severely disquieted. She couldn't try to protect him anymore. Nicolas would have to be warned. But after tonight. Let there be one more Carnevale in Venice.

19

THE HUNT

It was Shrove Tuesday, the last night of Carnevale, and though they hadn't missed a last night in five hundred years, Nicolas was loathe to go into the city.

He sighed, "I don't know, Giuli, won't the city just remind us that we're leaving? There are feral vampires everywhere. People who will want to talk."

"That's what the masks are for."

A smile teased his lips. "You're sure we're ready for this?"

They had settled in the Villa library, as they always did on this night. A wall of arched windows opened the space to the city outside, where shouts and laughter already filtered in from gondolas on the canal. Dozens of their favorite masks from past years decorated the walls and were displayed in cabinets around the perimeter of the room. Heat from the fire stirred feathers and ribbons attached to the masks in movement lighter than breath.

Giuliana gestured toward the wall of masks and nodded. "I am sure. I want to have this night to remember should things grow dark. Our problems will wait until tomorrow, won't they?"

He inhaled deeply then shook his head to clear it. "Of course, you're right. I would regret not having gone the first hour I missed."

"Thank you," she said and placed a gift in his hand. "Maybe this will help?"

He kissed her forehead, then unwrapped the box. "Gold?" Nicolas questioned, raising an eyebrow, as he folded the tissue away.

Giuliana lifted the mask from the box and held it up for him to see. It was the burnished color of Egyptian sand with two narrow triangles of dark green painted across the eyes. He examined it more closely as if his eyes had deceived him.

"Emeralds," she provided. "A mask of emeralds upon a mask of gold."

She watched him take the mask to the fire, to examine it there. The costume he wore was a brocaded robe in a geometric design of gold thread stitched on teal green. Around the hem paced a line of winged men and women, each naked form offering a stylized sun in their outstretched hands. The sleeveless robe lay open over a wide-sleeved tunic spun of luminescent gold silk that rustled like wind over sand when he moved.

Giuliana picked up a headpiece from the last box. He stooped and she laid it over his hair, a simple twisted circlet of green brocade, metallic gold, and black net.

"And now your turn," he said, as he laid a large, ribboned box before her. She slipped the silver ribbon off and lifted the lid. The costume inside shimmered, velvet and liquid; the color of blood and night. It seemed alive within its cloud of black tissue.

When she finished dressing, she wore a voluminous hooded cloak of jet-black silk and lace, which fell in soft folds to her waist. Beneath it, a blood-red cape cascaded down over her shoulders in layers, like the petals of a flower. Her arms were covered in a pair of white lace gloves heavily encrusted with opalescent seed pearls. Under the cape, showed a cassock of purest white satin, embroidered with glistening chevrons of gold thread.

188

Giuliana opened a smaller box containing a luminescent mask of eggshell white porcelain. It was simple and completely unadorned; the only color was found in the ruby-red lips.

"Nicky, it's a miracle. It's so thin." The quavering amber light of the fire could be seen through it. She secured it over her face. Her blue eyes sparkled like sapphires embedded in the cold mask.

When they were dressed, Nicolas stepped back and bowed deeply. "Madame, your gondola awaits."

The night hit them, cold and still, as they started down the path from the Villa through the garden to the dock beyond. The noise from the canal was louder now. Around the last bend, the sky exploded into the light of dozens of torches. Giuliana gasped.

The wooden planking of the dock glittered with frost and reflected torch light. The rail was braided with silver garland and festoons of white silk and white lights. The canal beyond it teemed with gondolas and motor craft, lighted and decked out in colorful decorations. Music assailed them from several directions, and there were shouts of appreciation from the boats beyond, directed at the commotion around the dock. It took a moment for their eyes to focus on the shimmering shape of their old gondola.

White roses covered it, silver in the torchlight, and a layer of them covered the floor of the craft. The arms of a teak Diana embraced the main bench. It was draped with a canopy of silver silk. The gondoliers stood ready in their cloaks of creamy white wool and gold braid. One stepped forward to assist, but Nicolas waved him away, boarding the craft with one effortless step. He bowed and offered his hand to Giuliana. They sat on the bench beneath the canopy and the vessel moved forward, slipping silently into the crowd of boats already headed toward San Marco. The palazzos along the shore glowed and dazzled with the lights and music of masquerade balls.

He squeezed her hand as they disembarked at the Piazza San Marco and when she turned again, he was gone, and she was alone in the press of people in San Marco. He had gone to fulfill the first part of their tradition. Early in the evening, they would each separately seek out the perfect mortal offering to tempt the other's appetite and passion.

She lifted her eyes dizzily to an explosion of early fireworks bursting across the sky. They trailed brilliant, fizzling streamers behind the winged lion of St. Mark which soared over the square atop its pillar of red Egyptian granite. The next moment the crowd pulled her forward into the current's swirling vortex.

For nearly two splendid centuries—from Napoleon's no-nonsense decree banning Carnevale in 1797 until 1980 when the public celebration was officially revived—Nicolas and Giuliana had preserved the tradition privately with annual galas in the Villa gardens.

During a long span of decades when such celebrations fell out of favor, and even some when they were declared illegal, the fantasy balls at Villa Giuliana were legendary affairs. It was for this purpose the luminous shell-pink terrace had been added to the Villa's original design. An image of flickering torches along the winding garden paths leading to that otherworldly, coral-colored dance floor was to many, the quintessential portrait of a Venetian winter.

Nothing, however, could match the exuberance that infused Piazza San Marco on the last night of Carnevale. Laughter roared sporadically across the plaza from audiences gathered around stages where actors recreated the classics of the Commedia dell'Arte. Crowds flocked to cafes lining the arcades, drawn by the music of jazz bands and string quartets.

Giuliana was pulled along the facade of the Library San Marco, toward the Campanile by the crowd. Nicolas was gone; veiled, body and mind. He had succumbed to the same solitary prowling instinct that tempted Giuliana toward the shadowy alleys and darkened rows of gondolas moored in the back canals. The perfume of erotic passion permeating these trysting places was nearly irresistible, yet she kept to the main square resolutely. It was far too early to sacrifice the edge of hunger. The tension of the evening was intensified by the possibility that she might raise her eyes at any moment and find Nicolas again This night, which was the anniversary of her birth into darkness, was theirs, together, and every chance meeting was an opportunity to fall in love again.

Giuliana entered the plaza. Her scorching hunger burned through the press of mortals and left a trail of uneasiness in her wake. Once or twice someone especially aware would identify her as the source of their arousal. Their eyes would brim with a question that on any other night, she would have extinguished with a gentle touch to their fevered minds. Tonight, she met their eyes and let them feel what she was; a hunter set free in a field of prey.

Occasionally, she met another preternatural watching her cautiously from the crowd. The city was full of them tonight and no mask could hide their burning eyes. These young ones presented no danger to Giuliana, but each encounter left her with a prickling suspicion of menace.

At length, her path was blocked by a satin cord marking off a large dance floor in the corner of the square. The cord demarcated the dance floor and there was a flurry of activity while performers came and went between dances. As she watched, a tarantella began. Violins sang and from somewhere under the arcade, a piano answered, and the dance began in earnest.

She stopped to watch, and the best of the dancers captured her attention at once. He was tall and lean, wearing the traditional costume of black pants and a white shirt, with a red sash in honor of the dance. His black hair had begun to gray. He effortlessly guided a series of less experienced partners into a graceful interpretation of the intricate dance.

His eyes dimmed when the music began again: a slow, sultry piece called the Underwater Waltz. The crowd gathered behind her, but she did not move and in a moment, his eyes found hers.

It was casual at first but grew in intensity each time he danced by her. His brazen stare was met and returned by Giuliana. As the dance progressed, his expression became more alive, changing from boredom to a question, then desire. His discontent propelled him toward her enticing aura of possibility.

Finally, as the dance ended, he wove his way to her through the shifting crowd, until he stood in front of her. Silently, he lifted her cloak from her shoulders and, folding it over one arm, released the cord to invite her into the square. Giuliana hardly noticed the rush of activity as the dancers changed around them. The hunt had begun.

The music poured over the square, washing the dancers into the rhythm of a waltz. Couples swirled around them. She removed one glove and offered him her hand. He dropped the glove and cloak over the satin cord and took her hand in his. Blood boiled to the tips of his fingers, and through the arm which circled her waist. He sighed as they began to move.

Whirling along the border of the dance floor, she remembered to search the crowd for the green and gold. Nicky was not to be found. Yet. Her heart beat a bit faster.

The pattern of the dance was repeated in a whirlwind of milky stars high in the velvet sky. As they twirled, fingers of wind lifted fabric and snow in illogical patterns around them. She let the beguiling man spin her weightlessly through the crowded dance floor, pushing from her mind the strange name that had come back to her in a whisper. *Sokaris.*

They danced another. Then again, something slow, modern. Then a rhumba, seething with sexuality and longing. The snowfall grew heavier, still dissolving quickly as it kissed their clothes. Her hand at his chest measured the tempo of his heart and then moved to caress the bare skin of his neck over the pulse.

At the cool touch of her fingers, he drew in his breath and looked down at her, suddenly. His eyes narrowed in a treacherous misunderstanding of the gesture. He mumbled a muffled expression of need into her hair. Intoxicated by the movement and his nearness, she nodded. When the music ended, he gathered her against him, and they were away down the arcade with the applause and shouts of the crowd receding unnoticed behind them.

He led her with great familiarity through a narrow passage to the rear of the Doge's palace. Up a guarded staircase, which was opened to him with a single nod. Past a scattering of musicians coming and going from some warm reception room off the second-floor arcade. Around a corner.

Miraculously, they were above the square where they had only just danced, in a protected part of the loggia. The music and noise of the crowd wafted around them. The distant din insulated them, and somehow enhanced the illusion that they were utterly alone. A smile fluttered over her lips, because now, finally, she knew without a shadow of a doubt that they were not. A gold and green chimera shimmered in the deepest black shadows behind them.

Another dance began below them. The dancer pulled her into his arms, but his elegance was lost to the impatience of his hunger. She let her hands find the marble behind her, drawing patience from the cold stone. He lifted the mask from her face uncertainly, as if fearful of what he might find.

The mask came away and his expression revealed nothing, but his lips parted slightly, and he lifted a finger to trace the fragile line of her jaw. He made one small sigh of approval, then lifted her into him while his hand gathered the silk upward along her thigh.

The mask dangled from his fingers behind her waist. His blood boiled at the suggestive arch of her body against his chest. She pressed her parted lips to his. With a barely noticeable abrasion of fangs on tender flesh, she infused his stunned perception with a wave of music and orgasmic sensation. In the moment of unguarded ecstasy his mind opened to her, and she knew his thoughts more deeply than any human could in a lifetime.

She pulled away and his mouth followed hers, like a man fighting wakefulness to hold on to a dream. She smiled, and something he saw in her eyes jolted him awake. He drew back. "Who are you?"

"Maybe a miracle. Maybe one who sees precisely who you are."

He stared down at her through hollow, vulnerable eyes. The depth of his need was raw and sobering. The wind ruffled gently through his unkempt curls. His eyes glistened with a distant hope even as his mouth hardened into a thin, cold line. "And you will show me this miracle, no doubt."

Her tongue transformed his doubt into a shuddering groan, flicking over the salty and surprisingly delicate hollow of his neck. The mask slipped from his fingers, but somehow did not clatter to the floor.

He moaned, laid bare. She felt his body surrender while his mind still resisted. He was tangled in suspicion, as if every previous journey here had ended in a burnt wasteland. "There is a price, of course," he said flatly.

"No price that you cannot easily afford; a gift as simple and natural as a dance." She entangled him once more in the melody. "Trust the music. It will never mislead you."

She drew his wrist to her lips, leaning back against the pillar and he leaned into her. Her lips trailed along his forearm as his trailed across her cheek. He was halted by a voice sounding quietly from the shadows.

"You would begin without me, Beloved?"

Her dancer emitted a possessive, growling threat. He was enraged to find Nicolas leaning casually on the railing, only a few feet away. Giuliana's forgotten cloak and glove were draped over his arm and her mask dangled from his fingers.

"Who the hell are you?" the dancer demanded in a voice that allowed for no intrusion.

She turned, still tangled in his arms. Nicolas removed his mask and smiled vaguely, pushing his hand through his hair. His eyes played over the crowd below before he brought his attention back to face the man's challenge. "A man without a name... or at least I am soon to be."

Giuliana cringed at the bitterness in Nicolas's voice as his eyes passed slowly over the dancer's tall, attractive frame. She imagined how Nicolas saw the dancer, his hard grace and determination, his aggressive masculine hunger. The mortal was waging a war with time, his heart pulsed with a need to experience something transcendent. She knew she had chosen well.

The mortal noted her lack of surprise at Nicky's abrupt appearance, and he turned to face her, a question in his eyes. Left to his own imagination, he quickly arrived at the wrong conclusion. He looked past her, and she watched his eyes flicker with a new possibility as his gaze traveled languorously over Nicolas in a barely disguised appraisal. His eyes came back to Giuliana, and he sighed his reluctant acquiescence to whatever game they would choose.

Giuliana flattened her hands against his shoulders and pushed him gently backward. She traced the top edge of his belt. Her fingers fluttered delicately around the front of his shirt until it was opened and pushed aside with barely a touch. She cast a web of pleasure around him and laid her head against his shoulder. He recoiled at her sudden, sharp bite and then melted in surprised surrender against the wall, succumbing to the music which flowed up and around and through them with the blood. His hands slid up her sides and he pulled her completely against him.

She felt Nicky's cool fingers at the nape of her neck the moment her fangs pierced the skin and the man moved to embrace her. The shock of pleasure at Nicolas's jealous touch mingled with the explosion of brilliant warmth over her teeth and tongue. Nicky turned her face toward him into a starving kiss. He took the blood back from her lips and tongue, blood that had been meant for Nicolas from the moment she had first noticed the man's strangely erotic relationship with the sultry Underwater Waltz Nicolas had written for her more than a hundred years before.

"You were almost too late..." she teased, but her smile faded as the blood passed between them, hers joining it as, stung by the playful chastisement, his fangs bit her lips. She gasped and surrendered; it always surprised her that she could hurt him. She held the mortal fast to the wall, her head pressed against his shoulder while she was lost in her dark father's possessive kiss.

"For me?" Nicky demanded, his voice gravelly, his lips still pressed relentlessly against hers. The man cursed and struggled, outraged. Nicky stilled him with a thought and one broad hand positioned expertly at his throat. Nicolas remained motionless, waiting for her reply.

"For you, Beloved."

Nicky drew away from her and gazed into the man's face. Giuliana fell back against the wall beside the dancer, breathless, pressing the length of her body against his warmth. He glared at Nicolas, trapped and furious, but he relented, and Nicolas's hand relaxed at his throat. The vampire's eyes remained fixed on the dancer, his ancient magic working quickly until the man reached suddenly for Nicolas with both hands and pulled him into a brutal, deep kiss.

Nicky uttered a husky, satisfied laugh against the man's ravenous lips and Giuliana unclenched one of the dancer's hands from Nicolas's shirt and, gently spreading the fingers open, brought his palm to her mouth. He looked up sharply as her teeth sank into his wrist, but he did not pull away. He wrapped Giuliana in his arm and sank further into euphoria, while she gently pulled the intoxicating elixir from his veins. The man's smokey gaze met Nicky's.

"What are you?" he moaned.

Nicolas slid his long fingers around the man's neck and turned his face toward Giuliana. She held the man's arm to her lips with both hands. Her hair fell around her shoulders in a veil of trapped moonlight. Her face glowed, and she wore an expression of pure rapture as she drew hungrily at the vein in tempo with his pulse. "Does it matter?"

The man gasped at the sight of her and shook his head slowly. He was weakened and confused now as the loss of blood made him light-headed, and his legs gave way beneath him. Nicky caught him before he could fall, dragging the enraptured man into his arms.

"We mean you no harm." Nicolas's hair hung around the dancer's face. The man's eyes grew bright.

Giuliana released the dancer's arm as Nicolas leaned and in one motion buried his fangs in his throat. The man arched his back as the vampire's spell wrapped around him.

Nicolas fed feverishly and Giuliana pressed her face against his chest to hear his heart, her fingers twining in his hair, her breath whispering in his ear, thrilled by the sight of his hunger. The dancer succumbed to the vampire's embrace. When the mortal's conscious-ness began to fade, Nicolas broke their connection, releasing the man's bruised senses to a revelation of music and light. He lay back against Nicky's arm, hypnotized by the vision which danced in the still, bright surfaces of his eyes.

Nicolas brushed his fingers soothingly against the man's face, then laid him down to gather Giuliana into his arms. He pressed her back against the wall where she stood and kissed her, his lips still pliant and warm from the feed. He dragged hands, now hot as a human's, over her skin in the exact path the dancer's had taken, as if he remembered vividly exactly where the man had touched her. "Your prowess is incomparable. Each year, I swear you won't, and still, you amaze me again and again. How will I equal such a gift?"

"I could think of ways, Maestro, if your imagination fails you." Giuliana raised her eyes delicately to his and smiled.

An appreciative sigh escaped him as he ran his thumb along her cheekbone. His eyes softened. "You are as dazzling and deadly as winter. How I love Carnevale with you."

He bent as if to kiss her, but drew back at the last moment when their lips had hardly met. "But it's my turn now." She opened her eyes, which had closed in anticipation of the kiss and growled at him.

"Now, Beloved, I only wish to ensure that I will return to find you with an appetite." He smiled at her wickedly, straightened his mask, then vaulted over the balustrade to vanish into the unsuspecting crowd below.

She wrapped her arms around the pillar to resist following him to take back the gift, which would be a thousand times sweeter now, mixed with his own ancient blood. Instead, she sank to the marble floor beside the dancer and brushed the hair idly from his face. At her touch, he stirred and wrapped his arm around her waist, pressing himself against her in a groggy offering. Only centuries of discipline silenced the instinct which pulled at them both equally, crying for his death. She unwound herself from his arms and touched a few drops of her healing preternatural blood to the wounds at his neck and wrist, then leaned against the wall beside him.

A gust of warm wind blew long tendrils of Giuliana's hair gently against the dancer's shoulder and chest, then buffeted past them down the loggia. She shivered and frowned, suddenly ill-at-ease.

His face looked drained and gaunt, but exultant. Though the deep punctures had healed at once, the dancer still smelled of death. She turned her face into the wind, toward the square and the crowd below, and inhaled. They all did, these mortals. They all smelled faintly of some distant death.

She slipped away from him and stood restlessly, leaning out over the balustrade to inhale the clear, cold air. The snow had stopped, and the sky was gray with hovering clouds. Dark shadows churned behind the haze; silhouettes lurking behind frosted glass. Giuliana shuddered again, and turned back to the dancer, feeling a vague urge to escape the claustrophobic loggia.

His eyes were fluttering open. She took her cape from the balustrade where Nicolas had left it and draped it over him then knelt and kissed him deeply with a commanding thought: *Forget.*

She took the beaded glove, as an idle afterthought, a bit of vanity, and slipped it into his shirt pocket with another kiss. He sighed and closed his eyes. She took leave of the Doge's Palace, through the long corridor, down the steps, and out into the loggia.

The warmth of the dancer, still burning at her lips and palms, felt unusually sad and final as the brisk winter wind struck her. She stepped back into the square and replaced her mask, oblivious to the steaming fog rolling in a menacing wave down the second-floor loggia toward the sleeping dancer above her.

20

THE HUNTED

The crowds had become more reckless as the night grew older. A sensation of being watched had gripped her since leaving the dancer, compelling her to keep moving.

A warm wind sighed suddenly past her, disturbing the cold momentarily and inspiring an irrational feeling of dread. She pushed through the crowd disembarking from gondolas and let the stream of people determine her path. It deposited her before the Royal Gardens, beneath a latticework of ice-laden branches. A sheen of frost glistened over the ironwork of the old gates. The sounds of passion and the rhythm of swiftly beating hearts spoke of lovers huddled in the shadows of greenery. The scent of blood shocked through the night air; a vampire absorbed in seduction. No. This was not where she should be.

She turned and exited the garden, following an urge to find Nicolas. She reached out but couldn't sense him. He was close to her while he hunted. She had the sensation of being watched again and fought back an unfamiliar panic. Snow whispered down. Raw instinct drew her down the rimy steps to stare at the flotilla of revelers on the Grand Canal. Frost glittered from an army of mooring posts and the decorated vessels which bobbed and swayed against them. Standing at the water's edge, she looked across the canal to scan the unearthly white lights of the domes across the black barrier of water.

Of course. She felt a rush of relief and suddenly knew exactly where he was, the Basilica across the way, Santa Maria Della Salute. The pull was undeniable, and she knew she would find him there. The Ponte dell Accademia pedestrian bridge was nearby, but she had no patience for the walk. Instead, finding a deserted cove near the canal, she took to the air.

She materialized silently in the shadow of the great basilica. Its twin domes rose majestically above her. Two soaring towers flanked the domes and were surrounded by a chorus of Baroque statuary. The main entrance bordered the Grand Canal and three staircases cascaded down its front and sides in a sweeping stone fan. The immense portico, built to resemble a triumphant arch, glowed beneath the brilliant bath of illuminating spotlights. It was strangely deserted—except for Nicolas.

He stood, hidden at the top of the side stairs in the glow of an alcove formed by the main entrance and one of the basilica's side chapels. He did not see Giuliana. He was watching someone who was hidden from her view by the building.

His lean body was as motionless as the marble statues perched around the radiating chapels. The hunt had honed his hunger to a ravenous edge. He was oblivious to his surroundings, focused only on the unseen prey that had captivated him. He uttered the low, familiar growl of resistance that always unconsciously preceded his final moment of surrender. Giuliana's pulse quickened. Her lust, as always, rose to meet his. She walked through the square until she could see the side of the courtyard he was fixed on, curious to see what stirred him so.

It was a woman, tall, covered in a sweeping cloak of black lace. Giuliana shook off a frisson of anxiety. The woman made her way to the stairs at the front entrance. Her hood was drawn closely about her face. Nicolas slipped from the alcove to follow her progress. She hesitated at the bottom of the stairs and then slowly began to climb them. His plan was clear now, to take her at the doors of the church. The setting was masterfully contrived, a pearly stage against the backdrop of the most majestic building in Venice.

Giuliana struggled with a half-formed sense of recognition as his quarry moved slowly up the stairs toward the portico. Her sense of unease returned, then the premonition of something amiss hit her like a slap. The woman lifted her arms slightly to lift her cloak. On one hand was an elegant glove. One familiar glove encrusted with seed pearls.

Giuliana glanced down at the single, pearl-encrusted glove on her own hand. There was no mistaking it. The glove and cloak the woman wore were the ones Nicolas had given Giuliana. Nicolas believed he was stalking Giuliana.

She shook her head in disbelief as the hoax became clear. Even with the acuity of a vampire more than a thousand years old, Nicolas believed this imposter to be Giuliana. What power could contrive such a deception; and more ominously, why? The hair rose slowly on the back of her neck as she backed slowly between the square half-pillars abutting the stairs.

This was no human, nor any preternatural form Giuliana had ever encountered. She watched the being carefully as it progressed slowly up the shallow stairs. For a moment, it shimmered and there were two women moving up the steps. Something real and a shadow, like the image on a double-exposed picture. It was an illusion cast in perfect detail.

A spell wrapped the human form like a lead shield; no energy escaped, and she could not pierce the barrier. She steadied herself against the wall, no longer sure what she saw. She was afraid to speak—afraid the woman would lift her head and reveal Giuliana's own eyes shining back at her.

She thought of her journey to the basilica tonight and realized that something had lured her here; had likely lured them both here for a purpose she couldn't fathom.

The cloaked figure reached the top stairs, stepped into the portico, and turned her face into the moonlight toward Nicolas. Too late, Giuliana remembered where she had last seen her cloak and glove. The figure flickered before her eyes and for a moment, she saw a mane of her own golden hair and the glint of her own icy, blue eyes.

And then the spell dissolved and so did the figure of the woman. She looked in disbelief as the illusion of the false Giuliana evaporated and was replaced by a macabre version of the virile dancer she had left just an hour ago. Giuliana gasped. With the illusion dispelled, Giuliana felt her vampiric perception return.

The man's bruised face was a jaundiced mask of ochre and plum. Terror and pain filled his eyes and blood oozed from his lips. His mouth gaped open as if to scream, but only a ghastly, gurgling moan escaped him. She reached out automatically to offer a soothing touch to his mind, but there was nothing of the man's essence left. He was a shell, containing a force of energy so powerful and chaotic, the sense of it made Giuliana's mind swim with vertigo.

She was struck with the sudden, intense scent of stale blood. She ripped her mask away and covered her mouth. A gruesome trail of gore smeared over the steps from the direction the dancer had come. His pants and shirt were dark with it. Freed of the illusion, she could see that the lithe body which had moved with such elegance a few hours ago, now moved in jerking, halting steps. The monstrosity limped slowly toward Nicolas who stood stone still. He, too, was battling his senses, fighting the illusion, which still had command of him.

A malevolent stare crept over Giuliana's back, raising chilblains on her skin. She whirled and looked up to finally find the source of her constant discomfort this evening. A tall vampire stood on the rampart above them. He wore layers of frayed robes and a hooded cloak. From the floodlights illuminating the dome, what could be seen of his face was dark and withered like old leather. An ancient. To one side, hovering in the shadows stood three others, sisters by all appearances, their faces nearly identical. They all wore decayed linen robes. One wore a golden jeweled belt and collar, and a crown with a falcon crest.

The ancient raised his hand and the figure climbing the stairs toward Nicolas halted. "Nicky!" Giuliana dropped her mask, which shattered on the marble floor, and pointed to the figure.

Nicolas turned and looked up. A low growl escaped him. He removed his own mask and rubbed his eyes, struggling with what he saw as the fading illusion released him. The ancient fixed glowing, copper-colored eyes on Nicolas and pushed back its hood to reveal himself. He was clean-shaven, his skin parched from long-term starvation. Dark braids fell to his shoulders. His hawkish expression was full of malice, and it was focused on Nicolas.

"Khaldun?" Nicolas's voice echoed his shocked disbelief through the square. Light glinted from the gold embroidery of his robe and the circlet on his head, the celebratory costume incongruous with the heavy seriousness of his voice. He gaped at the ancient as if seeing a ghost.

Khaldun stared down, as hatred and recognition grew in Nicolas's eyes. A bitter laugh twisted the ancient's face. "Did you truly believe one fledgling could destroy me and all my coven? Did you think you would never pay for what you've done? Your ego is astounding,"

Nicolas fought for composure while Giuliana moved close to his side. She cursed herself for waiting to warn him that Electra had hinted at a living Khaldun. Giuliana had scoffed and now he was here. Her easy rejection of a story she had not wanted to believe had put them both at risk.

Nicolas's gaze met hers, then he looked at the dancer who had paused on the stairs below them. Simultaneously, they both looked back up to Khaldun: the connection was clear now.

Nicolas found his voice and looked up to Khaldun. "I'm not surprised you survived. After all, you fled and let others die in your place. It was common knowledge that you made your escape to Egypt and buried yourself in the sand at Thebes. I *am* surprised you had the audacity to come back to Venice." He pointed toward the ancient, "There is nothing here for you, go back to your sand dune."

The three companions hissed and whispered from the shadows. Khaldun glowered at him, "I don't think so, Nicolas. I've been told of events that indicate it is time for me to return. The world has need of my foot on your neck again."

"Though your foot on my neck was never as secure as you thought, was it, Father?"

"Secure enough to drive you to burn down the Council to remove it. You would have done better to focus on me." He paced along the rampart, his hands clasped behind his back, "But, sadly, now it's too late. I have decided your time in the world is done, my son. I've come back to extract some revenge of my own."

"Just say what you want."

"A fool woke me and reminded me that while I slept, you still walked the earth in brazen defiance of the consequences you should have suffered a thousand years ago. An imbalance like that must be corrected."

He began to pace again on the rampart above them as if he could not resist the sense of movement after his long confinement. "Do you know how long it took for me to recover from that night? I spent years suffering beneath the sand while my skin bubbled and bled, with no progeny left to bring me sustenance." The three sisters moaned.

"But even that wasn't the worst of it. The worst was that you upended our world." He stabbed his hand toward Nicolas, "You shattered the authority of the Council of Elders, and let all that power slip through your fingers, as though it were worthless."

"It was worthless, Khaldun. The power was an illusion. It didn't save you or your Council. You turned it into a means of imposing your deranged will on everyone around you. For reshaping the world into your ghastly image. You had to be stopped."

Khaldun laughed. His companions shifted and tittered. "I was deranged? You revealed yourself to be a freakish aberration that night. I can still hear the screams of your brethren as you incinerated them into ashes with not even a bit of remorse."

Khaldun raised one hand in a bored motion and the poor dancer capered and spun along the stairs, legs, and arms flailing in a grotesque display.

"Stop it," Giuliana demanded. "Is this who you are? Torturing the innocent to prove your dominance?"

"A small demonstration my dear. An inkling of things to come. I watched you with the man earlier. I was stirred, really, and tempted to join you in your kill. But when you were not able to embrace your natures even to consummate an act of passion, I thought the man deserved to see the truth of what we are."

"Or you thought to intimidate us. Well, think again."

Giuliana snarled, but Nicolas caught her wrist. He looked away from the dancer in disgust. "I'm not afraid of parlor tricks, Khaldun. You overreached and you paid for it. You've become nothing more than a cautionary tale."

Khaldun chortled and his eyes shifted to Giuliana, leaving her with the same cold dread she had felt all evening. Her eyes flicked from Khaldun to the sisters, identifying options for escape. She found none. "And you, Giuliana. Have you seen the true nature of the serpent you consort with?"

Giuliana's jaw set and she stepped toward the dome, "I know that Nicolas's rage the night you left has become a legend among preternaturals. Even now, they live in fear of provoking it. Like you, they huddle in their crypts and secret places and recount how a mere fledgling took on the oldest and strongest vampire among them. Nicolas shattered your power and utterly destroyed your hold in the vampire realm. What more is there to know?"

Khaldun huffed. "Do you think he had control of what happened that night? He didn't." His attention shifted to Nicolas; his ragged robes shifting in the wind. "You were stupefied and confused by the power that flowed from you," He sneered. "The disbelief in your eyes was almost comical as you incinerated your brethren one after another," he cackled.

"I don't remember merriment. Just you, scrambling over the ashes of your kin to save yourself."

Khaldun waved his words away. "No matter. I am back now. And you should have spent the time I was gone trying to understand the source of that power, how to master it. It would have served you better. Because I *am* a master." He pointed toward the dancer. "As it turns out, such power can be manifested through other means than an accident of birth, if one knows where to look."

"You are as mad as you ever were. Leave tonight and I won't look for you. Come, Giuliana." Nicolas grasped her hand and turned toward the stairs.

"Look closer!" Khaldun shouted. "I wield a power now that will drain you of your will, and when I command it, relieve you of your life." He beckoned the cloaked figure on the stairs forward, and it moved toward them, blocking their way. "You may remember my friend, Sokaris? Or maybe not? You were not wholly yourself then."

"What are you babbling about, Khaldun?" Nicolas replied, but he pulled Giuliana back a step.

Smoke boiled through the surface of the dancer's skin; something exited his body. The man was a gruesome, pulpy mass. He fell from under the control of the creature and slumped to the ground. Giuliana reached again toward the mind of the tortured man. The human synapses overloaded and exploded at the vampire's mental touch. The dancer stopped shuddering and relaxed into death, clutching the crimson-stained glove to his ravaged chest.

What was left was a glittering cloud. Giuliana recognized the creature from the tower mosaic and her studio at once.

The atmosphere around Nicolas and Giuliana quivered with energy. The cloud stewed as if it would churn physicality from thin air. Nicolas shifted uneasily on the stairs.

Khaldun raised his arms and shouted, "Come forth, Nicolas, the vampire! What became of that hellish demon who annihilated a whole coven with just a thought? When did you become a mincing fool, playing at a human life? Where is the awesome Nicolas Portinari who destroyed his whole blood family, save me?"

The being of fog and electricity rose and wrapped itself in loops around Khaldun's arms. He drew his hands back then pushed them forward, and the creature sped toward Nicolas but stopped and hovered just before them. Nicolas spoke to the creature before him in a calming voice, edged with bewilderment. "Sokaris. So, it seems you do exist. And still a slave?"

The cloud went still except for a single arm of smoke that slipped silently around Nicolas's waist. Giuliana went rigid, her hand still on his arm.

"You can't charm him, Nicolas, he is nothing but a tool," Khaldun responded, the movement of the creature echoing the rolling movement of his hands as the thing drew more tightly around Nicolas's waist. "We are all slaves to something, Nicolas-- if only to what we crave. You know craving, don't you?" the ancient hissed.

Then he said more softly, toying with Nicolas, "Such as your obsession for the del Cenzio witch? The one you burned your life to satisfy?" The crones turned their faces to one another, then back to Nicolas, and their voices raised in a sibilant buzz.

Giuliana's heart dropped as the expression drained from Nicolas's face, and Khaldun chuckled. "Yes, I've been talking to another old friend of yours. It seems there isn't much she wouldn't do to destroy you."

"You're in league with Electra? I should have known that she was the snake whispering in your ear. You deserve one another."

"Her greed for power over Sokaris was easy enough to manipulate. Tragically for you, she has done my bidding and released him back to me. It was easy to convince the scheming egomaniac I'd turn him over to her."

Khaldun leapt suddenly from the dome and landed somewhat heavily before Nicolas and Giuliana. His voice, when he spoke, was cold and steely, "You're a pariah, Nicolas. You've embraced your exile and called it strength. You could have consolidated your power over the houses. Instead, you dismantled it and made enemies of everyone who could have helped you.

His voice became venomous, "With Sokaris, I will destroy you and make every human whose life you have touched dance just as this fool danced." He kicked the dancer's body and the corpse tumbled down the steps.

Nicolas's eyes narrowed. "We've clashed before, Khaldun. Do you recall how that turned out?"

Khaldun let loose a roar, "Sokaris, occidere eos!"

The creature began to move toward them. Giuliana felt flashes of painful memory, a baffling, brutal lust Nicolas had not been able to resist, years of self-loathing, and despair.

A flashing tendril of blue light flared from Sokaris's nebulous form. It lashed out at Nicolas, who cried out with pain. And yet, he still goaded Khaldun. "I don't fear you, Khaldun, or the misused creature. Your connection to Electra has betrayed you. You are subject to all her weaknesses: arrogance, recklessness, greed." Nicolas clinched his teeth as the creature seethed and coiled tighter around them.

The cloud enveloping them smoothed cold and electric over their bodies. A wave of fury took Giuliana. Without a thought, a fierce pulse of energy exploded from her fingertips, striking the epicenter of the creature. Sokaris contracted sharply, releasing them both, flinging Giuliana against a pillar where she sank to her knees. The air crackled while the creature hesitated. Then it expanded, gathering mass, as though preparing to attack them again.

Before it could strike again, Giuliana did. A howling, feral scream escaped her as another blast of energy shot from her hands. Lightning engulfed Sokaris. His form flickered and a long, wavering wail escaped him to echo from the domes and towers of Santa Maria Della Salute.

Another wave of anger shot through Giuliana followed by another burst of electric flame, then another. Each jolt was more powerful than the preceding one and they all found their mark exploding deep in the cloud that was Sokaris. Each wave illuminated the cupola in an explosion of unnatural blue light. But Sokaris remained. She had done her worst with little impact. Anger turned to desperation then frenzy.

Nicolas reached Giuliana just as her scream formed into words from some hidden place deep within her,

"Sokaris, mitto te ad tenebras!"

The three sisters screamed. The creature roared in anger and pain and with a flash of light it suddenly disappeared, its departure marked by a moaning wail. Nicolas and Giuliana both gasped in bewilderment.

Khaldun watched the cloud vanish, wide-eyed, then stared at Giuliana, his expression contorted in rage. His face twitched, but no words came. Then, without a word, he, too, vanished into the night, with his three companions howling behind him.

Nicolas and Giuliana clutched one another, their minds still possessed by fear. Nicolas took Giuliana by her shoulder and searched her eyes. "What happened?"

"I... I don't know."

"You spoke Latin."

"Gods, Nicolas. What did I say?"

His eyes were somber. "I send you to darkness."

Giuliana was completely perplexed. "I send you to darkness. What can that mean?"

His hands fell away from her shoulders, and he wrapped her tightly in his arms. "It was the same phenomena that we saw in your lab, wasn't it? It was Sokaris then, too?" She nodded against his chest. He sighed. "I've been blind. I couldn't believe it was real. I refused to face the truth and now..." His body tensed and she recognized fear. "What if..."

"It holds no power over you now, Nicky. You know it for what it is, and you won't be drawn into its nightmare again."

"I fear we already are."

21

ENTR'ACTE

1047 A.D.

Nicolas leapt from the gondola as soon as it reached the dock, not even giving the servants time to secure it. He dashed from the pier and was swallowed by the pitch-black night. His velvet cape flapped behind him in a shadow like someone pursuing him. For a moment, the darkness was disorienting but soon a line of flickering torches pricked out a path through the ancient copse of oaks leading toward the villa.

"*Electra!*" Nicolas burst through the massive door of Ca' Portinari. It crashed open against the wall, then slammed shut. The sudden detonation of sound thundered in the cavernous interior. His shout roiled like lightning and warned of an approaching storm. He snatched a lit torch from a sconce and strode across the checkerboard-patterned floor toward the place where he knew he would find her. He held the ring clutched so tightly in his hand that it bit into the flesh of his palm, drawing blood. A sense of betrayal washed over him, and a murderous anger blinded his senses. She would pay for what she had done.

Shadows from the torch quivered and trailed around him in the murky gloom as he ran up the stairs leading to the chapel in the western tower. The cherubs forming the newel posts seemed to dance in the trembling light. His heart pounded in his ears as he flung open the door to find Electra sweeping the contents of a wooden cabinet onto the floor before her.

Ransacked. Piles of papers and books were strewn everywhere. Furniture overturned, shelves emptied, and the contents of drawers and chests were piled in great drifts of debris across the room. Electra was so distracted she didn't hear the door open.

"Is this what you're looking for Electra?" Nicolas's voice dripped acid as he opened his hand and revealed the gold ring in his palm.

She looked up, caught totally off guard. "Nicolas, where did you...how did you..." Her voice trailed off as her dark eyes fixed on the ring. The red gold roses carved on it glinted in the light from a bank of candles arranged on a table occupying the center of the room.

"Where did you get that?" she blurted.

He slammed the door closed. Electra backed away slowly as he made his way into the room.

"I got it from Portia, along with a letter warning me to keep it out of your vile grasp!" he shouted.

"Nicolas, I can explain." She stared at the closed door behind him.

"Can you?" He slipped the ring onto his finger and scowled. "Can you explain why you have ruined my life, Electra?" His voice was cold as steel.

She rose to her full height and stood defiantly in the center of the room. "It was my sister who ruined your life! She was a mouse and gave up the only thing that would have made her worthy of you."

He looked at her, puzzled, the flickering torch turning his eyes into flames. "She didn't tell you that part, did she?" Electra chuckled. "No, she had to play the devoted wife."

"She told me you used black arts to bewitch me away from her!

She warned me you were in league with a demon!" He took another aggressive step closer. "What have you done, Electra? She was your sister!"

"My dear sister," she spat, "was a coward and an apostate. She betrayed her god and her family and renounced everything she believed in to have you. Something she didn't deserve." Electra moved deeper into the room so that the table was between them. A look of fear flashed in her eyes.

"I am less than the worms that devour her body," Nicolas moaned. "I abandoned all that was good and dear to me, and for what?" His eyes fixed on Electra, as if seeing her for the first time, then snapped back to meet hers. "To be with you."

A wail of agony escaped him as the realization washed over and sickened him. His cry echoed through the room as he swung the torch and swept a mass of objects off the table and onto the terrazzo floor.

"What kind of creature are you that you would do this to me and to your sister? How could you?"

"How could I?" A tinge of anger colored her question and then broke free. She snarled. "It was Portia's fault. She forced a responsibility on me that wasn't mine!" Her arms rose to encompass the room as if the answer lay there in plain sight. "She abdicated a familial duty she'd been groomed for all her life and threw it at my feet! She broke a chain of power stretching back from time immemorial."

Her eyes stabbed daggers at him. "I despised her for that. So, I took away everything that she loved." She grimaced at Nicolas. "I took her home. I took her family. And I took you from her, too! And in the end, I took her life. Easy."

She hesitated, realizing she had revealed more than intended. Nicolas dropped the torch onto a mound of papers on the floor. He lunged and grasped her by the throat as the fire caught quickly and began to spread and they fell to the floor.

"Witch! Abomination!" He tightened his hold on her throat. She fought against him clawing his face and hands with her nails. A growing fire began to creep up the curtains. The crackling flames crept up the drapes and began to lick at the exposed oak beams of the vaulted ceiling.

"Nicky! It wasn't my doing! It was Sokaris! We were all under his spell! It was a curse!" She choked out the words as his hands tightened on her throat.

He growled, "*Liar*," and slammed her head against the floor. "You didn't need a spell or a demon to work your evil, you witch! You didn't care what it cost, as long as you got what you wanted!"

She gasped for breath and struggled beneath him while her hand searched the debris for a weapon. It closed around one of the heavy silver candlesticks. She screeched as she clubbed him with it. He groaned and fell over on his back, his hands releasing their hold.

She scrambled free and stood over him, brandishing the candlestick. "Your heart was never as virtuous as you pretended with Portia! You didn't have the courage to seize what you were really hungry for. I just gave you permission to take it. Now you're paralyzed because you have to live with the consequences? You knew what it would cost the people around you, don't pretend otherwise!"

She was right. Everything he knew as the truth; loyalty, family, reputation, morality, fidelity, honesty, all had been lost to desire in the end. No witchcraft, no curse. Something was broken inside him. It was what he had wanted. He groaned in defeat. His anger dissipated and his head fell back against the floor. Blood trickled into his eyes, and he swooned.

For one timeless moment, his awareness floated outside his body. His will to live was broken. His life was utterly empty. He was completely defeated. He moaned. His eyes focused as he tried to make sense of the rippling web of orange light that flowed over the ceiling. Finally, the room rotated back into place, and he saw the flames for what they were as they coiled sinuously through the intricate wood vaulting. Fire boiled over the entire ceiling as it consumed the ancient beams. His vision blurred. An amber rain of cinders began to shower down from the ceiling. He looked for Electra as smoke began to cloud into the room.

"Electra!" he shouted and raised himself unsteadily to his feet. The fiery holocaust filled the air with the deafening clamor of beating wings. He was lost, unsure of where he was, or whether this was real or a dream. Explosions and crashes sounded all around him as the room began to disintegrate into flames.

"Electra!" He staggered toward where he thought the door should be and stumbled over something and fell. His hand reached out and touched her face. Her groan sighed against his palm. The gold ring on his finger glowed incandescently at the touch of her breath, or was it merely a flaming reflection? She was alive. Something huge and burning crashed to the floor on the opposite wall and revealed the closed door and their path to escape. The heat was unbearable. He lifted her in his arms just as a corner of the ceiling collapsed.

The gap in the roof revealed the night sky, which was shot through with stars and flashing embers. He slammed into the door and struggled to open it. The influx of air sucked in through the cleft in the roof, sent a maelstrom of flames scorching through the room. A pillar of fire convulsed and twisted around them. He roared and crashed against the door which burst open the moment before they caught fire. The inferno followed them through the doorway, howling like a beast.

He leapt into an alcove with her still in his arms as the blaze began to consume the villa. Tapestries, furniture, curtains, and rugs ignited instantly. The draft welling up from the great staircase drove the blaze to the upper floors until they were surrounded in a sea of flames. In only moments they would be trapped. Holding her in his arms, he threw his cape around her and ran recklessly through the fire down the stairs. Objects exploded and walls tumbled around them. Bathed in heat, submerged in fire, he leapt down the stairs until he reached the bottom. A stygian blackness of night and smoke obscured the entryway. He searched desperately for the door. The possibility of asphyxiation burned in his lungs. His hand found the door and he plunged down the outer stairs into the night air just as the marble staircase collapsed behind him.

He fell into nothingness and Electra dropped from his grasp. In his last moment of consciousness, he only heard his own howl echoed by the shriek of the firestorm.

22

REVELATIONS

Nicolas left the next night before Giuliana woke and flew toward the place where he suspected Khaldun's attack at Carnevale had begun, Electra's palazzo across the canal in the San Polo district. He materialized in a flicker of motion in a courtyard at the base of a winding staircase that climbed up to the second floor of the Gothic-style palazzo.

The courtyard was empty and dark, but bright lights showed in the building and a shadow wavered across the windows upstairs. With preternatural speed, Nicolas bolted up the stairs and burst through the French doors in a hail of shattering glass. The next moment, his hands grasped the struggling vampire and slammed it against the wall. The figure grunted with the force of his impact and then, in a voice trembling with fright, called out, "Nicolas!"

Nicolas growled. "Were you going somewhere, Argus?"

The vampire struggled against him, but Nicolas held him tight, pinned to the wall. A look of terror played across his face. "Nicolas... what...why are you here?"

He wrapped his hands around Argus's neck. "Where is Electra?"

"I left her at the Coven house at Delphi a few nights ago." The vampire's voice was weary and humble; not at all the Argus he had last seen. The change was alarming. His impenetrable mental wall had been replaced by a marked vulnerability. Nicolas shoved him away.

"Last night, Giuliana and I were attacked at Carnevale. What do you know?"

Argus's face twitched, and he pushed a thick mop of curls back from his face. He had exchanged his dreary robes for modern clothes, and it transformed him. He looked sane; civilized, but distraught. His chocolate-colored eyes darted about the room, then finally settled uneasily on Nicolas. A charged sense of dread fell heavily around them.

Nicolas fixed on the vampire's face, impatient to be finished with the conversation so he could track down Electra. "Just say it," he snapped.

Argus lifted his hands in a defensive gesture. He took a shaky breath. "I've been in contact with an elder in Egypt." He paused and measured Nicolas's reaction. Nicolas waited, stone-faced. "Khaldun."

Nicolas scoffed. "It was *you*?"

Argus nodded miserably. Nicolas stared at him, exasperated, but he had no sense that the man was lying. "What business could you possibly have with him?" Argus bowed his head. A cold understanding dawned on Nicolas, who said, "He is at the heart of the terror in Venice." He cocked his head and growled at Argus. "Are you mixed up in this?"

Argus drew back from what he saw on Nicolas's face. He dropped to his knees, cowering, "I believe I may have been."

"You believe you may have been?" Nicolas's voice began to rise and intensify. "You believe you *may* have been?" He grabbed the vampire by the hair and forced him to meet his eyes. "An explanation had better come quickly, Argus."

Nicolas saw fear in Argus's eyes, but there was also guilt and contrition. He released the creature, fighting his anger. "Get up. Get up and explain why you did not share this relationship with Khaldun at the convocation when we were searching for answers."

"I couldn't." Argus slumped, still on his knees, and drew in a deep, shaky breath. "Physically, I couldn't. I can only say that I was not free to speak. My mind has not been clear for quite a while. It's hard to know where it started, but I know precisely when it ended." He kept his head bowed and his voice was strained and hollow.

"A couple of nights ago, I was taken by visions of a strange blue inferno and violent electrical storms. Cyclones of flames were all I could see before me." His breath was rapid and shallow as he was caught up in the memory. Nicolas watched him, stunned. There was no doubt that he spoke the truth.

"I was terrified and paralyzed, unable to leave the coven house. I could only cower, hostage to the scene playing out in my blind eyes, a war against men and vampires. I saw your image, and Giuliana's and Electra's, and another woman with chestnut hair. It went on for hours, but, suddenly, just before morning, the madness released me. In the blink of an eye, I was whole again. I felt a stillness and peace that had evaded me for many months."

Argus looked up for the first time. His voice became steadier. "I know now that I was released from the clutches of a spell or hypnosis that night. I know it sounds like madness, but I also know it is true."

Nicolas's mind reeled. *Blue light. Fire. Possession.* Visions of Giuliana's lab returned with a shock: an electric blue storm filling the air and engulfing the painting. The portrait of Portia and the children. The painting to which Portia believed she had bound Sokaris. Could Giuliana have inadvertently set him free?

Argus mistook Nicolas's horror for anger and pled, "You must understand, I was a scholar when I came into this life, Nicolas, and not much else since. But for the last few weeks, I have moved through my existence in a cloud, doing violence I would previously never have done, remembering nothing until I woke up that night and could remember it all. And the things I remembered." He choked on his words and turned abruptly from Nicolas, unable to look at him.

In Nicolas's mind, he was mortal again, in the moment the scales had fallen from his own eyes; it was the night in 1047 that he had learned that Portia was dead. He had been suddenly released to remember that he had abandoned all that sustained him to possess Electra. Dizzy, he sat and laid his hand on Argus's shoulder. "Tell me what you remembered."

Argus collected himself and continued. "Electra introduced me to Khaldun."

"Electra was part of this?" Nicolas felt the old enmity color his voice with rage.

"It was her obsession with the mythology of the god, Sokaris. She sought out Khaldun because of the rumors of his knowledge of old Egypt. She tracked him down near Thebes."

"She had already spoken to him before the convocation? And she lied."

"Because she is Electra, she would say that she did not lie." Argus smiled ruefully. "And she did not know the whole story and had no reason to assume a connection between the revenants and Khaldun. That happened later."

"Tell me."

"When we entered those caverns, I saw the cruelness in him and thought he would kill us both. He was fierce, in turns mad and incisive, and powerful; he could have been a god himself. He refused all questions about the old gods, so Electra turned to her other obsession. She complained to him about you and your growing popularity; her fear that you had drawn dangerous attention. She asked for his intervention, but his mind was suddenly elsewhere like she had said something that triggered him."

"My name could have been the trigger. It would have reminded him of the beginning of his exile. She hasn't said anything she hasn't said before. There seems no reason for her to lie to the Elders. So why did she?"

"I don't know. But I do know that she is eaten by fear. She sees ghosts *everywhere*. She was also obsessed with you. Always cognizant of your movements. Railing about your public life." He hesitated, then met Nicolas's eyes. Nicolas could feel his terror; of what Nicolas might do, but also of what he, himself, had done.

"Then, one day, three women of Khaldun's coven came and brought me back to Thebes to see Khaldun alone. I was terrified of him, but I was compelled. And so, I went."

His voice became urgent. "He convinced me. I heard words I knew I did not believe, yet I had no ability to stop myself from acting on them. It was as if... as if... I was under the control of something I could not see. Something inside."

Icy recognition crept through Nicolas's memory of his own inexplicably cruel actions in a distant life. "You felt as if you were being controlled by someone else's will?"

"Yes," Argus sighed, and the word was colored with disbelief and absolute truth.

"And what happened?" Nicolas asked simply, pushing down his fear of what might be said next.

"We devised a plan. Centered around you. Together we concluded that we would take control of the reputation you had made and use it to drive you out of Venice. But the power Khaldun wanted- that I seemed to want- was different than what Electra wanted. Electra wanted stability in Venice, and to rule there. But Khaldun's first step would be to raise an army of feral vampires and destabilize the city."

"And if I refused to give up Venice?"

"It didn't matter. Either way, we would make sure of your death in the end. Khaldun would not share power with anyone."

The thought of once again being manipulated sickened Nicolas. "And how were you to go about creating this army?"

"Khaldun provided one hundred revenants from Egypt, and we descended on Venice. We turned one thousand of the wretches at first. I...it... was against everything I believed. I had never turned a soul into darkness. Like you, I had sworn I never would... but I did. Over and over.

"I hated it, but I was possessed by a desire I could not quench. After the thousand were turned, we couldn't control them. They feasted on Venice, then were called by Khaldun to invade other cities where Elders were sympathetic to their human communities. Even now, the population of newborns grows without restraint."

"What part did Electra play in this?"

"None. Khaldun threatened me to keep silent. At the same time, she had become obsessed with Sokaris. With finding him, so that Khaldun could show her how to control him again. The cult became her life. She said she had to prepare for his return. She said that Sokaris had been bound for centuries, cut off from her, but she could suddenly hear him whispering again. The coven began to think her mad. She was losing influence over us. Many of us thought to take matters into our own hands. We thought-hoped- that you might intervene."

"And you were released from this madness just before the end of Carnevale?"

"Yes. I have racked my brain for a way to undo what I've done. At the convocation, I realized how far it had spread. After I came to my senses, I fled. I only came tonight to gather my things. His brood searches for me still. I feel that, if anyone can save us from this, you can and..."

He faltered on words he could not quite form. Nicolas sensed another important truth running just beneath the surface. "What?"

"... I think you may understand what's happened to me."

"Understand a plot meant to destroy me and everything I love?" Nicolas demanded.

"While I was out of my mind, I was strangely preoccupied by you.

It felt as if you had somehow done wrong by me, yet I did not know you. It was what drew me to the theater the night of the ballet. It felt like I had something to say to you. But my hatred had no basis."

Nicolas sighed. "It had more basis than you know. So, you came to the theatre to warn me," he said thoughtfully, remembering that he had been drawn to Argus, too.

"And to ask for help. I don't know. I was of two minds. In a fog."

"You're sure Electra is in Greece?"

"Truthfully, I left her last in Athens. Since the convocation, she's terrified of having hidden her encounter with Khaldun, and maybe even more terrified that you will discover what she has done. She is at the coven house. "

"Then it's there I must go. Argus, are you willing to atone for what you have done?"

"With my life."

"Then you must find Max and tell him what you have told me. Tell him we need help taking Venice back from the revenants. Tell him Sokaris exists and Khaldun is alive. Ask him to gather what friends he can."

Argus said, breathlessly, "Then you will lead them?"

"I will stand alongside them. Tell them to meet at the coven house after the premiere tomorrow night. Tell Max that there isn't much time."

"And where shall I tell him you are going?"

"Tell him I plan to destroy a god."

———

NICOLAS CAST his intention to the Delphi coven house and in a tremor of light and shadow, he arrived in the darkness of a copse of trees.

Still known as the 'new house,' the Delphi house was a walled fortress that had been erected on a tiny islet in the Aegean Sea in

1432. Its impressive central tower was surrounded by smaller connected buildings topped with terraces landscaped with pistachio and almond trees. The air was thick with the scent of Electra's brood.

She was pacing the parapet on top of the tower. He leapt upward and landed silently in the open space near where she peered out over the wall. She didn't turn to face him. "I heard you had an encounter with Khaldun. Have you come to kill me now?" Her hands grasped the edge of the stone wall.

He walked to stand beside her at the wall. His anger dissipated. He just wanted the conflict to end. "I haven't come to kill you. I need your help to fix this mess. If you refuse, then I may kill you." Her eyes jumped to his and he couldn't suppress a reluctant chuckle. "I've also spoken to Argus."

Her eyes grew wide. "Argus? Why?"

"Electra, I need you to tell me the truth about Khaldun. If you don't, I swear it won't end well for you. Khaldun told me that you visited him, and Argus confirmed it."

Electra closed her eyes and her posture stiffened. She bowed her head and her dark hair fell around her face, as she confessed. "Yes, I went to Khaldun for answers about Sokaris." She stood straight and the veil of ebony fell away from her face. Her expression was resolute. "I asked him to help me, since no one else would. He said he knew how to control Sokaris if I could find him. I heard he's unbound now?" she said tentatively.

"You know he is, Electra. If your minions reported on Khaldun, then surely, they told you about his companion."

An aspect of calculation passed into her expression. "Then, I have an ally." Her eyes narrowed. "What did Khaldun say?"

"He laughed at you. Called you a useful tool. You're not his ally; you're his patsy." Their gaze met. "He used you, to seek revenge on me. And you've given him the one tool that might help him do it."

Disappointment, then anger and finally, amusement, played across her face. "Nicolas, have you suddenly become a believer?"

"It's hard to maintain disbelief when you're about to be consumed," he snapped, and her smile faded.

Nicolas paced along the parapet. He struggled with the implications and the sea air on his skin helped him think more clearly. He turned back to her. "Argus told a tale I recognized all too well. I believe he is, or was, until recently, controlled by Sokaris. He has been working with Khaldun to overrun Venice."

"Argus!" she gasped, then her normal wily look reappeared as she struggled, no doubt, to think how Argus's story may have implicated her.

Nicolas chuckled bitterly. "I know your part in this, Electra, and it appears you may actually be innocent of this one thing."

"What the devil are you talking about, Nicolas?" Her brow crinkled in a furrow that he recognized as an expression of genuine puzzlement. Her gown and hair moved in the wind. She looked strangely vulnerable.

"You weren't in league with Khaldun last night?"

"Nicolas, I've screamed from rooftops what I know about Sokaris. He's been gaining strength for centuries. Now he's loose and he will come, probably for me. I have no power over him." Panic rose in her voice. "Was Khaldun controlling him?"

"At first, he was. But when his threats turned to an actual attack, it seemed to be Giuliana who drove him away." Understanding dawned on him. It had been the ring. Portia's ring that he had given to Giuli.

"Giuliana?" Electra sputtered. "But that makes no sense!"

"Yet, it's what happened." His eyes shifted back to Electra to find her staring at him. "What I want to know is, how do I destroy Sokaris? Without him, I am a match for Khaldun. With him, we're all at their mercy."

"You can't destroy him!" she shot back. "He's unbound! Freed, somehow. In that state, you'd need to know the method by which he was bound. You'd need to destroy the object that held him and the rose ring that controls him, together. Even if you had both, it would take something extraordinarily powerful to destroy those objects. They are imbued with magic. But, as I told you, I've lost my means of controlling him. I've lost the ring." she said simply.

Nicolas felt a moment of relief. "The ring and the object to which he was bound? That's all I would need?"

"*All* you would need?" Electra was obviously puzzled at Nicolas's relief. "Well, yes, and a force great enough to destroy charmed objects."

A plan began forming in Nicolas's mind. "Would an explosion do it?"

"I suppose if it was powerful enough. Nicolas, what are you thinking? You can't take this on alone. And the spell that bound him is a mystery!"

Could he do it? He had to try. There was so little time. "Electra, Max will call on you. Do not deny him, or I will not forgive your part in this."

"But, Nicolas, what...?" But he was already gone.

———

IT WAS TOO near dawn when Nicolas found Giuliana readying the bedroom for the day. She had secured the shutters and was drawing the heavy draperies around the bed. When the lights were extinguished, it would be pitch black in this haven.

"What's happened?" She seemed alarmed by something she saw in his expression, so he drew her into his arms. He breathed in her scent and buried his face in her hair. "I may have found a way, Giuli. A way to protect us."

She drew back and searched his eyes, "What do you mean?"

"I don't have time to explain." Her eyes were already glassing over as she fell toward the deep vampire sleep. He lifted her hand, where the rose ring glowed. "I need your ring."

She shook her head. "What? Why?"

"Please, beloved, trust me. I will explain tomorrow."

She smiled. "Tomorrow is the opening, then the gala. You'll be gone before I wake."

"Then after the gala." He kissed her deeply and slipped the ring from her finger and placed it on his own. Her arms went around his neck, and he coaxed her to the bed. She laughed softly and tugged at his coat, as if to pull him in with her, but she was asleep before he pulled the drapes closed. He felt the lure of sleep himself and knew he had to be quick.

He sped down the stairs to Giuliana's laboratory, and found the portrait crated with the others in the saferoom, to be moved to Granada tomorrow morning. As he uncrated it, he touched it for the first time and recoiled at the shock of power it contained, somehow invoking Giuliana and Portia together. He moved the painting back to the lab, which was to be the center of the explosion. There would be time to place the ring here tomorrow night. He closed his eyes and said a silent apology to Portia for not destroying the thing a thousand years ago, as she had asked.

Slipping from the lab, he took the elevator to the safety of their penthouse bedroom. He slipped into Giuliana's arms.

"Where have you been, beloved?" she murmured as he wrapped his arms around her and pulled her close.

"Taking back our future."

23

A LETTER FROM THE PAST

An electronic buzz shot through the room as a new e-mail arrived. Paul's laptop flashed on the desk amid a pile of open books, scraps of paper, and the translation of Portia's letter. Reluctantly he walked to the desk. He tapped the keyboard and a file popped open. A new e-mail from the clipping service. Intrigued, he slipped into the chair and opened the index of articles matching the new search criteria he had sent to the librarian in New York. The Portinari family had a bedeviling history.

He rubbed his unshaven face, hesitated, then paged through the results. He felt like a fool. Against his better judgement, he had added new criteria, anything about the Sokaris cult, and then he had added a more general search on reports of paranormal activity in and around Venice.

He let the cursor race down the list, idly scanning the list of articles—ghostly sightings commonly resolved as illusions caused by the heavy Venetian fog over the lagoon. A new series of dates caught his eye. A rash of sightings at Carnevale this year. One had a photo attachment. He clicked on the icon and opened the image on his screen.

"Shit."

He stared at the grainy photo for a long moment, then hit print. He jerked the sheet off the printer and stared at it, disbelief washing over him. The printed version was foggy; it was a poor photograph and a poor print. Still, the similarity was unmistakable. He pulled out the envelope of photographs taken at Ca' Portinari. The image captured in the photo was identical to the image in the mosaic on the wall. Paul knew with an uneasy certainty that it was not the fog.

His eyes fell on the letter. He lifted the translation and read it once more.

To my beloved husband, Nicolas Portinari, from his still devoted wife, Portia Del Cenzio Portinari,

Despite our estrangement, I care for you, and I write to you out of fear that great harm will come to you if I do not. Some will say that what I will reveal here is born of pettiness or spite, or worse, are the ramblings of a mad woman. Do not believe them. Please, heed me; your life is in danger from those closest to you.

For generations, the women in my family have held a wraith in their control. This creature, Sokaris, is a monster from antiquity. He has been described in many ways over the ages, as a demon, the devourer, God of the underworld, soul-eater.

The Sisters of Sokaris once worshipped this creature as a god, but at some point, a priestess discovered a weakness and used it against him. She bound him as a slave to their will, using a series of symbols she found engraved on an ancient gold ring. This changed the creature's nature and turned it into something base and malevolent. The burden of safekeeping this secret has been passed down from mother to eldest daughter in my family from time immemorial. This creature, when properly controlled by The Sisters, is incapable of acting in the world. But it is held in check only by the will and sorcery of the del Cenzio women and our ability to manipulate the symbols which bind spiritual matter to the physical plane.

By use of this spirit, the Del Cenzios secured for themselves unplumbed depths of power. They can control men's hearts and the forces of nature. Mad as that must sound, I swear it is the truth. Out of either wisdom or fear, our line put away use of the demon and our purpose turned to preventing its release into the world. And so it has been for many centuries.

I rejected the old gods and my role in this cult long ago. I thought I had put it all behind me when we married, and I was baptized into the church of the one true God. But now it rises as a menace to all that I love.

Beware of my sister, Nicolas. She seeks power and has reconstructed a temple of Sokaris at Ca' Portinari. I believe she has already used Sokaris to lure you to her. Electra is young. She tampers with a force she does not understand. She believes she can control it, but she cannot for long, as it is ancient and cunning. It is not her fault she came into this awful power, but my own. If I had not forsaken my duty, this evil would not have taken hold of her. Do not blame Electra; blame only me. But do what you must to protect yourself.

As the creature is manipulated, it will struggle against its bonds. It will free itself from her control, and it will churn and transform until it is able to enter the physical plane. When it does, our lore says the monster will be unbound and take physical form. The event will be marked by a tremendous explosion of fire and heat and brilliant blue light. I cannot let that happen. I have taken the ring back from Electra, and I am struggling now with the symbols to bind Sokaris in a way such that it can finally be destroyed.

I have embedded binding sigils into the portrait I gifted you our last year together. The painting was created with a charm of protection then, and my love for you and our children will help to keep you safe now. If Sokaris does gather the potency to become corporeal, the spell will create a vortex that will pull Sokaris to the painting the moment he passes back into this realm. When he comes into our world, I will use the symbols to take life from him and bind him to the painting. When it is over, I will destroy the painting. Remove that temple from your home, or it will always hold temptation for Electra. In case something evil befalls me, I leave our children safe in the care of my family at Casa del Cenzio. Do not forsake them. They are your blood, Nicolas, and grow more like you with each passing day.

I always have, and always shall, love you.

Your Portia.

A frisson tickled the back of Paul's neck. Clearly, Portia had wanted the tower torn down and now, dozens of generations later, her husband's namesake seemed hellbent on doing it. He slipped the letter back in its notebook. His fingers tapped its surface nervously, a new dark possibility bubbling up through the foundation of everything he believed. Cracks were forming, gaps where paranoid suspicions took on a reasonable shape.

He shook off his fear and tried to recount what he knew. Sure, Portinari made him uneasy, but that had been true since the day they met. Did that make him a monster? Probably not. There were lots of possible explanations for that, including simple jealousy.

The public who studied Portinari was convinced he was super-human. But the obsession of fanatics was not proof of anything. What did he know himself, firsthand? Only what he had seen in the tower and read in the documents found there. And there was no proof that any of it was true.

Except that the omen Portia had warned of had apparently been photographed recently in Venice, along with Portinari's unreasonable determination to destroy a landmark associated with the obscure legends. Was it a coincidence that the sightings of this thing had resumed in the year paintings from the tower had been unearthed? The paintings and the situation where they had been discovered had certainly been unusual, but were they unnatural? Did any of them even match the description Portia had left?

Paul sighed and pushed the papers on the desk into his satchel, then pulled on his coat and gloves. He knew where to find the truth and it was time to face it, no matter how uncomfortable it was.

24

THE PORTRAIT

The guard at the dark gray marble desk took little notice of Paul as he entered the lab. He was surprised to find it brightly lit. The glaring fluorescent lights spilled through the glass wall from the work area.

It took a moment to realize that the tall blond woman working there was Giuliana de Cordova. She sat on a high stool in front of one of the paintings he had helped her drag from the rubble at Ca' Portinari. A garment bag partially covering an elaborate costume lay over a nearby divan. He had almost forgotten the *Cry of Innocence* opening and gala were tomorrow night. But it was obvious that her concentration was fully focused on the tiny patch of canvas beneath her brush. Rows of sterile steel shelving towered above her.

Paul doubted if anyone would recognize this woman as the Giuliana De Cordova so often featured in the arts and culture news. In fact, the first time they had met at Ca' Portinari, he had not recognized her. Since then, nothing he had read about her rang true. Try as they might to dissect her under the focused lens of media attention, her true nature eluded them. Her hair was caught up in a clip and tumbled in an unruly mass around her face. She wore a pristine white lab coat unbuttoned over a casual knit dress. She focused intently on the painting where the tiny brush in her hand met the canvas. She seemed exhausted.

Giuliana laid the brush aside and looked up as he pushed open the glass door. She was startled, not at seeing Paul, but as if startled to find herself planted in the modern world again.

"Paul." Her greeting was welcoming; almost relieved. "Why on earth are you here at this hour?"

He smiled and gestured back at her. "We're two of a kind, aren't we? Do you think anyone appreciates us?"

She laughed softly and her eyes wandered back to the painting. "Oh, is it appreciation we're after? I thought we did it for our own selfish reasons."

"That's what I like about you, Giuliana. You don't allow anyone their delusions."

She pulled herself away from the canvas. "What brings you here?"

"What else? The artifacts from Ca' Portinari. I thought I might find some clues in the paintings."

"Can I help?"

"Maybe. I received the translations of the documents in the tower, and I've found some information about the mosaics. The cloud and the figure emerging from it represent an Egyptian god, Sokaris. A cult of his worshippers existed here in Venice at the time of the paintings. The cult was well-known and feared. It seems the sanctuary in the Portinari tower is a temple of Sokaris."

"So, how did such a cult get tangled up with the Portinaris?"

"The Nicolas Portinari alive in 1047 married Portia Del Cenzio, the daughter of the cult's high priestess. It was a marriage between two very powerful families."

"So, she is accused of consorting with demons?"

"Yes, the whole Del Cenzio family is accused of consorting with demons according to the translations of the documents we took from the tower. Portia's sister, Electra, was especially notorious and was accused of having some sort of unnatural alliance with the creature." Paul hesitated. Giuliana's reaction had been subtle, but that name reached her. Odd. "She supposedly kept him bound by means of a series of symbols engraved on a gold ring."

She lowered her eyes and said nothing, so he continued. "I've also found a potential explanation for the explosion that sealed the tower at Ca' Portinari."

"Have you?"

"There are several references in the city records that year to a powerful blue explosion. No official reports ventured an explanation. But Portia del Cenzio did."

"And what was her theory?"

"That the explosion happens, just as the mosaic illustrates, when Sokaris takes human form. The journals talk about a creature that could be the same as the one illustrated on the mosaics. And then there's this." He pulled the printed photograph from his pack. "Have you seen what happened in Venice during Carnevale?"

She studied the blurry photo of Santa Maria del Saluta engulfed in a blue cloud. He tried to read her face, but her expression was inscrutable. Her liquid eyes fell on him. She seemed to choose her words carefully. "No, I had not seen this."

"But you realize what it is."

"Yes, I know what you're thinking, Paul. What can I say? It's a remarkable coincidence, but surely you don't believe this is the creature represented in the mosaics at Ca' Portinari?"

"A remarkable coincidence though."

"Where did you get this?"

"Honestly, I stumbled on it. I was originally only interested in the tower."

"Frankly, it's a lot of energy for you to put into something you were just asked to tear down. Why are you pursuing it?"

"I think it's a crime to destroy it, and I suspect you do, too," he snapped, then drew a deep breath. "Sorry. There is another reason. I couldn't shake the feeling that it was more than coincidence that Portinari wants it destroyed now."

"Because of the rumors about Nicolas's nature?" He stared at her without comment, unwilling to admit she'd guessed the truth. But she knew. "Paul, you can't become unsettled by gossip and conspiracy theories."

"But I am unsettled. So, I dug into the tower's history. I uncovered a long tradition of paranormal phenomenon connected with the Portinaris and Venice. Things reported in small papers- stuff too weird for the legit press. Then I got this photo of an unexplained blue cloud seen in Venice the last night of Carnevale. Giuliana, you should be careful." He paused and inhaled deeply. "I'm worried about Francois, too. There's something off in all this."

She laughed without conviction. "What do you mean?"

"This may seem an odd question, but how well do you know Portinari?" He paced around the room a moment, gathering courage, then stopped and faced her. "Has it ever occurred to you that there might be something to all the rumors and gossip surrounding him?"

Her face clouded with impatience. "I don't put much faith in gossip, Paul. What are you talking about?"

He measured his next words, then went ahead gingerly. "Just consider that these documents came from the tower he's awfully anxious to destroy. There was a frenzied letter from Portia to that other supposed ancestor, Nicolas Portinari, pleading with him to destroy that tower."

She tilted her head, a fleck of interest reappearing. "There was?"

"Yes, there was. People have wanted it destroyed for a very long time, yet it has remained standing until now. I can't stop thinking of that old saw about history repeating itself. Something has been gnawing at me since the night of the suicide, telling me that I may not be living in the world I imagined. Something hinging on Portinari. That's why I'm here. The translations may describe one of the paintings. It made me curious to see it. A portrait. One that Portia was convinced she had imbued with power to entrap some force or being."

He was alerted by a glimmer of alarm in her eyes, but her voice remained neutral. "And what did it say about this portrait? Is there any information about the artist? That would be remarkable!"

He narrowed his eyes, surprised by her obvious attempt to change the subject. "It was painted by Portia del Cenzio Portinari, the wife of Nicolas Portinari and author of said letter."

"Indeed," she said. He couldn't tell if she was giving him the cold shoulder, or simply in shock. Then it occurred to him. "You want me to leave this alone. Why?"

"The ones who know the answers to your questions have been buried for a thousand years."

"Have they?" he said quietly.

She turned her head quickly to face Paul. "Surely, you don't think these fantasies are true?"

"I'm not as sure of anything as I was a couple of weeks ago. The Nicolas Portinari alive at that time was just as notorious as the one alive today," he said. "And if I'm not mistaken, there is a portrait of him among these paintings."

Paul walked around to see the painting she had been working on. He hadn't seen it since it had been cleaned. Since then, she had uncovered a great deal of the female figure, but that wasn't what made him gasp.

"Dear god. It's him." The obscuring bloom still covered one side of the face, but it was the perfect image of Nicolas Portinari peering at him across centuries.

Giuliana tossed the covering down over the painting. "Paul."

He couldn't help shouting. "It's him. You know it's him."

"Paul, you know that's impossible." Her calm expression was belied by a small tremor in her voice.

"I know it's impossible, but it's him!" Paul clutched his reeling head with both hands and stared at her. "What is he, Giuliana? How old is he? He's unnatural. I've always felt it! Tell me that he is no danger to Francois!"

"Nicolas loves Francois. He would never harm him."

"Why does everyone around this bastard protect him?" Paul strode forward and ripped the covering from the painting.

It was him. It wasn't just the physical likeness that convinced him, it was the quality in his eyes.

"I can't let this go, Giuliana." He turned to leave, then turned once more to search her face. She looked very small as if something inside her had collapsed. There was something else she wasn't saying. He looked around with a sudden uneasy feeling. "Giuliana, where are the rest of the paintings from the tower?" He rummaged through a few canvases on a nearby rack.

"They're not here, they've been moved to a more secure storage facility."

He stared at her, bewildered, a slow rage rising in his chest. She looked away. "Oh, Jesus, not you, too? Now you're going to start covering things up? Why were they moved?"

"I don't know what you mean," she said. She stood and walked to the metal table where she began to wipe her brushes clean.

Paul couldn't recall feeling quite so disappointed. "You're no better liar than Francois, you know. Look around you, Giuliana. This lab has been completely cleared of the artwork I had delivered here. Nicolas has been quietly disposing of his property for the last year. His next opera throws the public's biggest criticism of him right back in their faces—not as a denial, but as confirmation. He's getting ready to disappear, isn't he?" She didn't respond and focused instead on quietly arranging bottles and tools in their trays. "You know, Giuliana, that other Nicolas, the one from the past, according to history, that's what happened to him. He disappeared."

She stored her supplies and closed the cabinet door. Then she turned, her back against the wall. "Please Paul, for your own sake, just let it go." Her voice was tired.

"You know I can't, and neither should you." His words hung in the air as he turned and stalked from the room.

25

CRY OF INNOCENCE

The chaos backstage at the Palais Garnier was deafening enough, but it was the thunderous shouts and applause rolling through the auditorium that left the opera house quaking. It seemed as if it would never end. Giuliana pressed her back against the wall in the crowded wing, waiting for Nicolas to return from his final curtain call. There was no longer any doubt that *Cry of Innocence*, a title which had caused much speculation, was indeed the success Nicolas's critics had been certain he could not possibly achieve twice in the same season.

The cast was ecstatic, milling around her, hugging and congratulating one another. They had no way of knowing that his grand coup —which they were already calling Nicolas's finest hour and a resounding counter to his critics the past months—would also be his final performance. Giuliana was already certain that each of them had played a part in a performance by which others would often be measured. Now they had everything they needed to make him a legend.

Nicolas appeared suddenly, caught up in an eddy of excitement as the principal singers rushed from the stage. They merged with a stream of tuxedos and black organdy, the musicians of the orchestra exiting the pit. A knot formed around Nicolas at its center as they pumped his hand joyously, soaring on post-performance euphoria. He was relaxed and part of things here among his colleagues, many of whom had devoted the better part of their careers to the interpretation and execution of his music. To see his glow, his unguarded smile, his eyes resting warmly on each in turn, no one would guess he had ever been called reclusive.

Giuliana also responded to the Maestro's seductive elan. He felt her hunger and looked up, his intense, onyx eyes sweeping over the crowd to anchor swiftly on hers. She smiled and sank back against the wall with her hands behind her, drawing him to her through the milling crowd. He passed absently through one handshake after another, hand over hand, pulling himself toward her, refusing to break his gaze, until suddenly he swept her into his arms and laughed a warm and willing surrender against her neck beneath a wave of her upswept hair.

"Nicky, they will say it's your best ever."

"Fitting, isn't it?" A wry, sexy smile of complicity lit his eyes. He leaned in to kiss her again.

"I need to go. It will take some time to get ready, and I promised Monique I'd help oversee the setup at the gala."

"Of course. I'll go with you," he said, his eyes drifting back to the celebrating cast.

She laughed. "No, you won't. You should be here to celebrate with them. Go say your goodbyes. Just leave in time to see Francois before the guests begin to arrive. He'll want to discuss the final plans. I'll meet you there."

She left him to be swallowed up into the crowd. Nothing would detain him for long now. He was anxious to see tonight's plan through. Still, they would barely have time to change into their costumes for the gala. She huffed in frustration as she recalled that she had left her costume at the laboratory last evening, then slipped unnoticed through the stage door to the alley outside and with a thought, cast her intention towards the Portinari building and vanished.

The suite of rooms forming the restoration lab had the cool, chemical smell of a hospital. She started toward the main lab where she had left her costume, but then thought she should locate the safe room, which had just recently been completed. Tonight, she and Nicolas were meant to leave the building undetected before the explosion happened. But Francois, ever cautious, had insisted on a refuge. In case things go wrong, he had said.

She moved through a storage area toward the inner halls. In the very center of the building, she came to the door made of a heavy metallic substance she didn't recognize. This must be it, then. This room would survive the blast in which Nicolas Portinari and Giuliana de Cordova would cease to exist.

The door swung open. The room was small, lined with lead. There was a narrow table at the side and sheaths of papers bound in leather stacked atop it. All they would need to start their new life. It felt suffocating. She slipped the door closed without going inside.

The main laboratory was flooded with a sterile, searing light. She stopped short. As Paul's keen eye had observed, the paintings that had been stored here awaiting restoration had been whisked away to Granada. They had been replaced with an assortment of worthless works, most of them new, carefully saturated with a flammable solution, which would ensure their complete destruction.

Her eyes rested on the costume she had flung over the back of a sofa. She started toward it, but then she was startled to see that the portrait she had been working on sat leaning on a tabletop easel. It had been left uncrated, an uncommon act of carelessness. Annoyed, she moved to lift it away from the table, which had been set with explosives, to take it back to the safe room. They would have to take it with them this evening. But once she looked at it, she could not look away.

Painted eyes turned like smoke in the partially revealed face. She thought, once again, of Electra. She did not know if it was the sudden music in her head or her lover's face staring at her from the canvas that left her with a premonition of disaster. Paul had been right. Though the bloom had not yet been completely removed from the painting, the image was undoubtedly Nicolas.

Paul had guessed that they planned to leave. How many others had caught on, or would tomorrow or the next day after they were gone? Nicolas's absence last evening had prevented her from talking to him about the man's suspicions, and he had left for the theater before she woke that evening. She felt heartsick. Another human connection ended in deception and disappointment. She was almost relieved it was time to set the final subterfuge in motion and perhaps emerge in a less complicated life.

She shook her head to clear it. She would be late. She determinedly lifted the panel, intending to take it to the vault. But as she did, Nicolas's black eyes in the portrait tilted up, and she felt pinioned in their bright, artificial focus. She glanced at her watch. She still had almost an hour before the gala. Then her attention was pulled back to the painting. The woman's concealed face beckoned to her.

It was a tricky thing to do, contrary to her instincts as a preservationist, to take the solvent to the delicate paint. She forced herself steady and held the cotton pad against the canvas, letting the solvent do its work. Where the cotton came away, the glow of a deep chestnut brown eye appeared. She worked in long sweeps now, exposing the lapis-colored gown, down to where the woman's hands were folded in her lap. Her fingers there were still shrouded in a cloud of bloom, but a glint of a gold ring caught Giuliana's attention where she had never seen it before, and she remembered Paul's words, *"She supposedly kept him bound by means of a series of symbols engraved on a gold ring."*

Then without another thought, she moved the painting to the

floor. She sank down on her knees into a sea of gold satin and crino-line, the hot, industrial lights burning against her bare shoulders, the brush in her hand. The costume was discarded on the sofa behind her. She worked at the painting for over an hour. Her silk gown for the gala still lay in a careless red slash across the back of a white leather couch behind her. She was already late, but she could not force herself to leave the laboratory.

She was held in place by a dawning possibility. A tenuous calm had come over her as she studied the painting with this new under-standing. As the minutes ticked by, she became more certain her suspicion was true. The explanation for the violent emotion became clear, as well as the images of Electra she saw as she touched the painting. Portia had been terrified the last time she had touched this painting. Giuliana, with her peculiar talent for psychometry absorbed that intense emotion. *A portrait. One that Portia was convinced she had altered to power a sympathetic ritual.* Portia had altered this portrait to create an object that could power a ritual meant to break Electra's power over the spirit controlling Nicolas. Paul was right. The whole sordid story was true.

Driven to understand, she began to take reckless liberties, aban-doning the tiny brush of solvent for a wad of cloth. She wiped away large areas of paint, removing the swath of nebulous cloud to reveal the face of a child sitting on Nicolas's lap. A child with black eyes and raven hair and the delicate, slender hands of a musician. "Oh, Nicolas," she whispered.

Understanding this artifact was now more important to her than preserving it. As she worked, another child's face appeared, a girl. She was about four, with hair the color of cinnamon and moody hazel eyes that seemed distracted by what others could not see. She stood beside Nicolas, who held her tiny hand in his.

Portia had the same color hair and eyes as the girl, except that her gaze was fierce rather than distracted. Her expression challenged Giuliana to see, to understand.

A buzz like a fly sounded from the laboratory across the way. The lights flickered, then returned to normal. Giuliana hardly noticed. The painting pulled her back in until she could feel Portia's intention in her brush strokes. In the violent colors, the sharp ridges of paint. The speed of the artist's brush could be measured in the wake it had smoothed through the tempera. Giuliana sensed where she had hurried and where she had obsessed for hours over a detail of color or light. The woman's strength and magic now poured from the work as Giuliana's connection with her strengthened.

Soon, the images which had set Giuliana reeling at Ca' Portinari took hold of her again. She felt herself standing at the window of the high tower when it had been whole and majestic. Below her, along the narrow riva, Nicky, in the full light of day, jumped impatiently from a gondola before the boys attending him could moor it. He strode toward the palace, his face turned up toward the tower window where she stood. Giuliana grew dizzy and caught her breath, knowing he had been away too long and was now coming to make his absence permanent. She closed her eyes quickly as if to prevent his empty eyes from picking her out from the shroud of shadows. Fearful children clutched at her legs. Her mouth was dry with panic, and she was overwhelmed with despair and anger and the bitter taste of betrayal. She could not tell if it was Portia or herself, wondering what could have made Nicolas desert his family for Electra's frail beauty; for eyes as dark and cold and empty as night.

A breeze soft and warm as a lover's breath slid across her shoulders, anchoring her again in the present. The laboratory lights flickered, and there was a sound. She had dallied too long, and now Nicolas must have come to find her. Now he would explain. She would tell him what she had learned, and he would explain.

She rose to meet him when her eyes riveted helplessly to a bead of solvent trailing down the canvas. She had no choice but to remove it before it had eaten all the way through the paint. She lifted the painting back to the counter and swept away another streak of grime and ammonia.

The swirl of paint she had identified as a cloud drew her attention. With a clean cloth, she brushed at the area around Nicolas's head and stepped back. Upon removing the creamy residue, the cloud shone through in its original color. A pale, undulating field of blue. She watched, amazed, as the last smudges disappeared, and a cord knotted in Portia's slender fingers unfurled unexpectedly out of the bloom.

She had been completely unaware of this element of the painting. Her hands trembled as she dipped the brush into the dish of solvent and made another passage across the painting, with no care for the paint that was beginning to come away. A red satin sash was revealed. It slashed chillingly across Nicolas's throat, anchored by the silk cord in Portia's left hand, knotted around the finger wearing the gold ring. A scroll of writing appeared as a decorative motif stitched into the satin. Its words were now legible, and Giuliana read them aloud, "*Sokaris, voco te e tenebris, ut facias voluntatem meam*"

"I call you out of the darkness to do my will."

A wind blew suddenly into the room as if a window to the outside had been opened. But there was no window. She looked up uneasily at the door. The space around her felt dead and quiet.

Her eyes darted down to her own hand, looking for the ring she normally wore. It wasn't there. Nicolas had taken it the night before. But she didn't need to see it to know that her ring was the ring in the painting. Older, smoother, but the rose design was identical to the one painted on Portia's hand.

The air in the room chilled and then seemed to come alive. Her heart fell at the familiar sensation as the gust swept around the room and then back around to her. She looked up at a soft noise in the doorway. Her blood chilled.

Khaldun stood there, the same ratty robes rustling around him, his copper eyes no less eerie in the bright light. The soft current of wind turned into a fog.

The vampire stepped into the room. "Sokaris, come to me." The cloud obeyed and slowly fused into a cloak of fog that curled around him.

"Get out," Giuliana leapt to her feet.

"Giuliana." His voice was deep and could have been soothing had she not known his nature. "You speak with such contempt. Why would you assume I am your enemy? I have no intention of hurting you. We've barely met."

"I know enough about you."

"Nicolas's version? I offered him great wealth and immortality. In the end, he betrayed me, even though I gave him life."

"You took his life," she interjected. "And deserved worse than you got." She set her jaw. Her voice was strong, but her mind was racing through the ways this scene could play out. None of them ended in her favor. Khaldun was thousands of years older, and Sokaris was a wild card.

"If you had been there, to see him mindlessly slaying dozens of his own, you might have a different opinion. But, if justice doesn't interest you, there are other reasons to reconsider your allegiance to Nicolas. Consider that I am ancient myself, and I control Sokaris. I could take Nicolas's mind—it's been done before—and entice him to murder you. Or I could take his body, like the dancer's and squeeze the life from him. You must accept that Nicolas must die. But you don't have to suffer the same fate."

She moved away from him a few steps, but he mirrored her motion, keeping the same distance between them. Why wasn't he attacking her? She was vulnerable on her own. Then it dawned on Giuliana that after Sokaris had fled at her command at Carnevale, he might be a wild card to Khaldun, too.

"Have you learned how to control your pet better since that night in Venice?"

"Are you prepared to find out? Consider your options. Stand against me if you must. But there is hope for you. As Nicolas's child, you are of my blood. I would welcome you to the new Rialto family. You would have great power- second only to my own."

"Yet, you bring your demon here to threaten me. Get out," she spat, though her heart clutched with doubt that she would be able to force him.

"I didn't bring him here. I felt him rise tonight, and I followed him to this place. He was drawn to you as if called. You sense that you are connected to him; have you ever asked yourself why? I know the answer. And I know that he will always come back unless you find someone who can teach you to banish or destroy him."

"Someone like you?"

He blocked the doorway. She did not know if she could take to the air. Sokaris had blocked her at Carnevale. "You have one opportunity tonight to step away from Nicolas and reclaim the life you are meant for."

"I have the life I was meant for. I will only tell you once more. Get out."

Khaldun's visage changed from false benevolence to real hatred in an instant. "Very well then." He bowed his head and held his arms to his sides. "Sokaris! Take her."

The cloud uncurled from around him and swept toward Giuliana.

She caught her breath and bit back a rush of panic, turning quickly toward the elevator, only to find her path blocked by Khaldun, with his fangs bared, his face a mask of hunger. Sokaris had become a swirling network of luminous, nerve-like connections integrating the milky cloud into a single body.

She focused her will to flee and felt the first quiver of the transformation that would sweep her safely from the room in a glitter of light and intention. But as the change began, a wave of energy escaped the creature, ensnaring her in a sparkling web. Her intention scattered, and she abruptly coalesced back into her physical form. A sense of heaviness trapped her in place. She could barely breathe with the weight of it. She fell against the counter, helpless to escape. The thing was a ravenous void, sucking in all the psychic energy around it.

Bolts of electricity spun from Sokaris to explode into the room. A long coil swirled off to detonate in a fireball against the white walls. Another flash of energy skittered off the marble floor and shattered the bottles of solvent and cleaner on the counter. Everything it touched burst into flames and charred black. The portrait had become a vortex of pure energy; the figures of Portia and Nicolas were alive with a malignant light. Giuliana's rage suddenly concentrated in her fingertips, and she was able to escape whatever force held her in place as a jolt of fire shot from her hands and hurled the creature back against the wall.

Its bewildered howl wavered through the room as it concentrated in a corner of the ceiling like a snake coiling to strike. The voice escalated into a wail. Sokaris struck out with its own powerful jolt of electricity. The force of it flung Giuliana across the room to slump behind the heavy work counter. She cried desperately, *"Sokaris, voco te e tenebris, ut facias voluntatem meam."*

But it had no effect. She looked again at the place her ring should be, then screamed as she felt Khaldun's cold hands at her neck, pushing her toward the ground.

26

PENSEROSA

Francois opened the door, flushed with excitement. "Congratulations, Maestro. You have a masterpiece on your hands. The phone hasn't stopped ringing since I got home. I've never seen the tide of public opinion turn quite so sharply."

"I can't decide if I trust public opinion less when it's with me, or when it's against me." Nicolas said as Francois closed the door behind him. "Thank you for hosting the gala for us, Francois"

"I'm happy to. Does it feel strange that it's not in Venice?"

Nicolas sighed. "No stranger than anything else these days. Is Giuliana here?" Nicolas asked.

"No, not yet; she called to say she was delayed." Francois glanced at his watch and frowned. I imagine she won't be much longer."

Nicolas ignored a frisson of alarm. Her costume was elaborate. She was likely still dressing.

They walked through the foyer and made their way to the garden in back. The grounds had been transformed into a fantasy grotto for Giuliana's gala. They stepped beneath the pavilion and looked out over the Seine. Directly across the wide expanse of the river rose the Portinari Building. It soared into the night sky; a dark tower of glass outlined against the surrounding lights of Paris. The building was dark, unlit but for a narrow band of light which wrapped around the floors where the laboratory and penthouse were located.

Nicolas reached out to Giuliana, *Beloved, I'm waiting for you.* He felt an instant of premonition, no more than a finger of a chill along his spine, but Francois's voice called him back.

"Nicolas, we should talk about what will happen tonight."

"Yes," Nicolas answered resolutely. "We'll make sure we are seen going into the building."

"The communications team has messages ready to drop, alerting the press that you'll stop and comment on your way into the building after the gala."

"We enter the lab with our keycards, leaving an electronic record to show that we were there. The explosion is set to take out the lab and the residential floor. Nicolas and Giuliana are dead. What could be simpler?" Francois looked up sharply at the bitterness in his voice.

Nicolas cleared his throat and walked closer to the water. Francois paced alongside, watching him. Nicolas couldn't bear the look of concern and empathy on his face. "What of you, Francois? What will you do next? You will have your life back. That's something that no first-born Durand could say for the last thousand years."

"That isn't the gift that you seem to think it is, Nicolas."

Nicolas flinched and looked back at him, away from the river and the Portinari Building across it. Francois would never want for anything. The Durand fortune was almost as vast as Nicolas's. Most importantly, with Nicolas gone, he would be safe from retribution from Nicolas's enemies. He would no longer have value as a pawn. The only thing Francois would lose was the thing that Nicolas struggled to believe could have value for him. Their friendship. He reached for the words he had been avoiding; how could he say goodbye and thank this man, who had given him so much?

Francois said thoughtfully, "I have avoided thinking about what comes next because I honestly can't imagine what it will be." His face was thin, pinched. Nicolas wondered how long he had avoided seeing the impact tonight would have on his friend.

"Francois, I..."

Francois held up a hand to stop him, his expression cold as he anticipated Nicolas's usual dismissal of anything personal between them. "There's no need to say more. I understand that you are doing what you must do. But I do want you to know that I have felt privileged to experience a small part of a universe to which humans are normally blind. That has meant something, Maestro. It helped shape my life."

It was painful to hear Francois embracing the connection between them that Nicolas was trying with all his might to sever. But he owed the man this. "I could not have survived these centuries and remained relevant in the world without your family's loyalty and stewardship. Thank you, Francois."

"I hope you find a replacement soon." Then came the question they had avoided so diligently these past months, and it pierced him like a knife. "Will I see you again, Nicolas?"

He was trapped by the hope in the man's eyes. His mind fixed again on the curious validation he had found in the words of Lenora Lucci, who claimed to see the power of the vampire as a reflection of human potential. A bud of possibility had gently opened when she claimed he gave her hope. In all his immortal life, Nicolas had never considered that there could be a place for him to live honestly among humans without inspiring loathing and terror.

Christ, Giuliana, can it be true, what you've said all along, that we have a right to a place among them? Before the thought could fully form, he was struck with the recollection of the vile tide of vampires bringing horror to Venice. He remembered Khali and Carlo and the suicidal woman. The nascent glimmer of hope winked out. Nicolas forced his expression to go blank and replied with no hesitation. "No, Francois. My exile will not allow me to keep you safe if it is suspected that you still have value to me. Your safety depends on a complete severance of our connection."

"I see." Francois's expression went as blank as Nicolas's, but the human could not mask his eyes, which swam with turmoil. "That should not cause a problem. I'll need to continue to complete the formalities of the asset transfers over the course of the next year, but there should be no reason for us to meet."

As Francois acceded to something he clearly did not want, Nicolas was suddenly full of doubt. A sense of dread washed over him. Francois cleared his throat, uncomfortable with the silence. "Then, I suppose tonight will be goodbye." His voice carried a thin, artificial note of indifference. He was facing away toward the void of the Seine, his eyes resting on the Portinari building.

Nicolas knew for certain that he would forever remember this moment and knew just as certainly the memory would always be steeped in regret. He allowed his gaze to linger and pick out the man's features bathed in the scant light and realized with surprise that he had committed each of Francois's expressions to memory. For a man so reserved, he had a kaleidoscope of them, and Nicolas knew every nuance. Now his face was hard, chiseled in pain. His hazel eyes were churning in a face as still as marble and Nicolas had no words to comfort him

Though he spoke to Francois as if he had been only one in a lengthy line of stewards, Francois was more to him. More than any human had ever been to him, save Giuliana. He struggled with the words to reassure the man that he would feel the loss of their friend-ship just as deeply, and would miss their connection even more profoundly because, for Nicolas, their bond was unique in all his long life.

"Francois..." he began.

But Francois had not heard him. He was looking up toward the house where a man stepped outside and walked swiftly toward them. Paul Dendera. He called out, as he came nearer, "Francois, I need to talk to you. It's important."

Francois glanced at Nicolas, who watched Dendera's approach warily trying to recall something that Giuliana had said about him. He was dragged from his thoughts by a sudden disturbing realization. He paused, staring intently over the river for a minute or two.

"Francois," Paul began as he reached them.

"Wait," Nicolas snapped. "Francois, what did Giuliana say when you spoke to her?"

"That she was going to the lab. She had left her costume there."

Nicolas cursed. He whirled toward the river. "Giuli?" he whispered hoarsely.

"Nicolas, what is it?" Bewilderment bloomed in Francois's voice.

"I don't sense her."

"Sense her?" Francois said, confused.

Francois and Paul stood still, bewildered, but terror was all Nicolas felt as he started to run toward the shadows at the riverbank.

27

ACCESO

Khaldun dug his claws deeper into Giuliana's shoulders and tilted his head to rip out her throat. His fangs were yellow and pitted, and his breath smelled like a moldering grave. Giuliana twisted and flailed but his sinewy strength overwhelmed her. Panic took hold. Familiar fire raced through her veins. Her skin heated and he ripped his hands away, leaving deep scarlet slashes from her neck down her chest. She screamed in pain. Blood spilled freely onto the torn, gold satin of her dress, leaving her dizzy. But it gave her the instant she needed to escape his grasp. She scrambled across the room to put the wide worktable between them and summoned fire.

Khaldun leaned on the steel table with both hands, shook his dusty braids, and sneered, "Bring on your flame. It can't kill me. I was forged in it."

In her fury, Giuliana barely recognized Nicolas as he materialized in the lobby and stepped into the lab. His tuxedo was disheveled, his hair windblown, and his expression worried. He gasped as he took in the charred chaos in the room. His gaze swept frantically over the disarray until he found Giuliana. His eyes flickered with a strange horror, and she knew he was trying to find something to recognize in her, as well.

"Giuliana, no!" he entreated softly. It was the shock in his voice that stopped her. She barely curbed the eruption of fire which could have consumed the laboratory and everything in it. The suppressed conflagration seared through her core. It caused Khaldun to back slightly away.

"Giuliana, beloved, you can't," Nicolas coaxed, his eyes softened with distress. "The main lab is mined with explosives." He reached his hand toward her. "We have to get out of here."

His eyes traveled down as he became aware of the wounds on her chest. "What...?" he began, astonished.

Then he saw Khaldun approach from the side. Wrath erupted and his face took on a malevolent aspect Giuliana had never seen. She took a step back. He trembled. His face went gray, and his eyes turned into the silvered black of hematite.

A repugnant smile crossed Khaldun's face. "There's my lad. There's the power of my Rialto blood."

Nicolas roared and lunged. He wrapped his arms around Khaldun and took him across the room. Giuliana barely jumped aside as they crashed through the steel worktable. They hit the ground and Nicolas smashed the elder's head against the wreckage on the floor and the scent of his rich, ancient blood filled the air. Khaldun raked his elongated fingernails across Nicolas's throat, leaving a horrendous gash, as he screamed a command at Sokaris. Nicolas slumped back against the floor.

Sokaris engulfed Nicolas, testing his skin, beginning to press through. "No!" Giuliana screamed. Nicolas's fingers dug at the wall as Khaldun retreated, letting the demon take over. Nicolas tried to stand but slipped down to one knee.

She cried, "Nicolas, I need the ring!"

She was afraid he was too dazed to understand, but he slowly took the ring from his pocket. He stared at it in his hand. "Nicolas, I need it now!" she urged. He looked up at her, disoriented and still besieged by the demon. But he threw it toward her in a clumsy motion, then dropped his head back against the wall.

Khaldun watched in horror as the ring flew across the room. "No!" he cried, lunging for Giuliana, but she was nearer. She caught the ring and slipped it on her finger. "It's impossible! That cursed ring has been lost for centuries!"

She raised her hand once more toward Sokaris, Portia's ring glinting on her finger. Electra had commanded this thing; so would she. "Heed me, demon! *Release him!*" A burst of blue shot around the ring, then up toward Sokaris.

The portrait burst into a blue flame. As it disintegrated into ashes, a blue wind spiraled up from the cinders. A bloodcurdling scream began from a great distance and seemed to converge on them from all sides. With a blinding flash, Sokaris was sucked violently toward the remains of Portia's portrait.

Khaldun shouted and his one voice broke into the sound of many. "*Praecipio tibi.* I command you! You are bound to me!"

The demon let loose a hollow shriek. It released Nicolas, who shuddered and moaned as the thing left his body. Sokaris was heavier now. He ripped along the aisles of the storage area, causing shelves to topple against one another, sending glass and metal containers crashing to the floor. Their chemical contents spread in pungent pools that filled Giuliana's mouth and lungs with an acrid smoke. Fireballs rolled from the ceiling, licking dangerously low over the flammable liquids.

"*Kill him!*" Khaldun screamed. But the ring on Giuliana's finger glowed and the cloud coiled heavily above her head.

Khaldun snarled and looked from Giuliana to Nicolas back to Sokaris. "This isn't over! You think you have the power now, but that ring is nothing but a toy; a weak reflection of something beyond your understanding. Before it's over, I will use it to destroy you both."

"Sokaris, take Khaldun!" Giuliana commanded.

But Khaldun was gone.

Giuliana ran to kneel beside Nicolas where he had slid down the wall to the floor. They huddled together against the elevator doors, aghast, their gaze fixed on Sokaris. There was a different quality about the demon now. It sank toward the floor, denser and less able to take to the air. Its body transformed into a gelatinous mass shot through with bursts of the same electric blue light which had consumed the painting. The ring burned a brilliant gold in the shadows, then dimmed and went out. A human-like form was defining itself from the cloud.

Giuliana stood and pulled Nicolas to his feet but neither of them had the strength for flight. The thing advanced on them, its movement more adept every moment. She demanded the creature leave, to no effect. The ring burned bright, scalding her hand. She wrenched it from her finger and Nicolas caught it in his palm.

———

"GIULIANA WE MUST GO." She nodded and he clung to her. Their energy shifted for flight, but they were blocked. They could not leave the room.

Nicolas's mind raced in panic. Portia had written about this in her letter. What had she said? *It will churn and transform until it is able to enter the physical plane. The event will be marked by a tremendous explosion of fire and heat and brilliant blue light.*

Instinctively, Nicolas pulled Giuliana close and whispered into her ear, "For eternity, beloved," just as a horrible implosion of electricity collapsed in on the creature. An intense, blue light radiated from Sokaris, then a fireball swept outward from the demon as an explosion ripped through the lab. The very air seemed to ignite.

Nicolas held Giuliana in his arms. Her pale eyes widened in fear then pain as gravity surrendered to the force of the explosion around them and they were hurled into the air. In the maelstrom of fire and energy, he somehow caught her outstretched hand and pulled her towards him with all his strength.

Their eyes met and she shouted, "Don't let go!" But in the next moment, she was wrenched from his grasp. Fire and an incandescent blue light engulfed her, and she screamed as Nicolas was hurled away by the force of the explosion. "Giuliana!" he screamed but it was lost in the chaos as she vanished from sight. In the next moment, there was only darkness as Nicolas lost consciousness.

The air reverberated with a horrendous crash as it seemed to ignite in a blinding explosion. A solid sheet of flame welled liquid and hot through every corridor. The force of the fusion ripped the upper stories off the building. A cloud of fire blossomed blue and iridescent in the clear Parisian night and then the blaze of light which had been the Portinari Building went completely dark.

28

CALL TO ARMS

Moonlight streamed ashen and cool through the charred interior and broke in a swell against the mound of seared rubble that had once been the Portinari laboratory. Dunes of shattered glass scintillated like sea foam in the darkness. Windows, their great panes smashed or melted, stared out over the city, as open and blank as the eyes of something dead.

The investigators, with their shovels, crowbars, and ultrasound detectors, had come and gone. For a week, they had pored over the ruins; searching for a clue, for an answer which had eluded them; an answer which still lay hidden in the depths of the wreckage.

A perimeter of flowers and mementos surrounded the building; the rain had scattered most of the throngs of supporters that had left them. A few of the stalwarts remained, drenched under umbrellas blacker than the night. For now, the press was supportive, but under the benevolence lay a current of spite that would soon explode with twisted theories and unfounded explanations.

Wind howled through the wreckage at the top of the building. A sudden shock of thunder was followed by a flash of lightning, and rain began to fall in heavy cascading sheets. The debris rumbled, a sound which could have been the rubble settling beneath the heavy cloak of rain. The building shook with each concussion of thunder.

Somewhere a wall gave way and collapsed. The storm intensified. Another brilliant stab of lightning cracked phosphorescent across the heavens. In the momentary illumination, the mass of wreckage pulsed upward. A shower of broken glass and iron beams crashed from the top of the mound as the doors of the room-sized safe erupted open from beneath the shattered masonry and fallen girders. The remaining rubble atop the room fell aside, the room so recently installed that it had not appeared on any building plan or schematic.

Another spike of lightning burst the sky open, and from within the heart of the gloom inside the safe, a pale, slender man appeared, Nicolas. With great difficulty, he pulled himself from the lead room. He wrenched the heavy metal door from its hinges and, with inhuman strength, flung it fiercely aside to crash through to the floor below. He tilted his head back and howled at the sky, then sank down on one knee, his arms around a twisted beam to support him.

The rain plastered slashes of black hair to his face and down the back of his drenched shirt. The sounds of his weeping were absorbed by the storm. Lightning cracked, and another figure emerged, leaping up the wreckage swiftly from somewhere below. Electra stopped at the sight of Nicolas and her intense features relaxed into something resembling relief.

"Nicolas," she whispered. "What in the name of the gods were you trying to do?" Her voice was desperate. She knelt beside him. "You fool," she sighed sadly, almost tenderly. "You know we do not have the luxury of dying."

His forehead pressed against the freezing beam. Her voice came from far away, through a dull ringing in his ears. He forced his eyes open to understand where he was. Her fingers dug into his flesh as she grasped his shoulders and shook him. "Wake up! We have work to do if any of us is to survive." She leaned forward and shook him, peering into his face. "And we cannot survive without you."

Nicolas stirred. Consciousness lapped against the void where he had drifted night after night.

"Giuli," he moaned, finally. Comprehension replaced the wildness in his eyes. He rolled over and pushed himself up with significant effort. She sat, exhausted, on the floor and let her head fall back against the girder. "I've been looking for you for nights."

The voice was clear now, and the woman's face came into focus. "Electra! Where is Giuliana?" he demanded. He stood and staggered a few steps through the wreckage before he recognized what was left of his surroundings. His hands flew to his aching skull. His memory was shocked with a concussion of billowing flames. "What happened?"

"What do you mean, what happened? It was an explosion, just as you planned. It was your trick to leave the world, wasn't it? I knew it the moment I read about it."

He shook his head, confused, trying to remember. "No. No. Not this. Not..." He lifted his head suddenly. "Where is Giuliana? Where is she?"

She shook her head cautiously. "She's not here, Nicolas."

"She must be!"

"But she's not. And Sokaris has disappeared as well."

He whirled on her as his memory began to function. "He came here. But Giuliana had the ring."

"What?" she choked out. "You had the ring? All this time?"

"I gave it to Giuliana. She was able to command Sokaris. But afterward, he... he changed. I think he was becoming corporeal. Then there was a terrible explosion. I attempted flight but blacked out. I only regained consciousness just now."

"I heard you when you left the vault. I've been here every night since the explosion, searching for you. I couldn't believe you were gone."

Her eyes met his, filled with pity. He grimaced, and bile rose. "Giuliana!" he shouted. He pushed blindly through the wreckage of walls through the leveled rooms until he found himself staring down the empty shaft of the elevator.

Electra followed behind him. "Stop it, Nicolas! I promise you, there is nothing alive in this building. Look at you. You've barely survived, and you're five hundred years the stronger! Everyone in Paris saw the explosion. Look around you and remember."

"No!" He stumbled through the rubble, tossing aside doors and charred furniture. "She is here! She must be here! Giuli!"

But in his heart, he knew it was not so. There was only the tremulous sound of water trickling against metal and glass. He tried to remember the end; what had happened after the blast, but he could not. He could only remember panic, pain, and desperation. A moment of hope as he tried to take flight, then rage as he was pulled back, a blinding flash of blue light, and then only the black, empty sea of unconsciousness.

He walked to the edge of the building. From his vantage, he could see all of Paris, the Opera, Francois's house on the Ile St. Louis, the spires of Notre Dame. Everything which had once defined his world was spread before him. Weary emptiness washed over him. Hunger burned in his throat, and clawed through his veins. The unfamiliar need to feed seemed insatiable.

"I've been through every inch of this rubble, Nicolas. There is no sign of her." She walked to the crumpled safe room and peered in. "I wish I had known about the safe room. It saved you. She couldn't have survived outside it. I hate to say it, Nicolas, but you must face the fact that she was killed in the explosion, along with Sokaris. You have managed to destroy him."

Nicolas moaned softly. Thunder rocked the building and somewhere below them, something gave way and crashed to the ground.

They stood in silence staring out at the night from the trembling parapet. "It's true then. She's gone. I don't sense her. The connection between us is broken."

"This changes things," she said softly, holding his gaze. "Argus told me he and Khaldun raised the revenants."

"Which was possible only because you raised the bastard from his sleep. You aimed to manipulate me, Electra. Don't think I will forget that."

She backed away from the anger in his voice but said quickly, "Yes. I did. But only to fix things. To give you back your power."

"Don't lie to me now, Electra; I will kill you where you stand."

She took another step backward. "Alright. All right. I wanted control. You're right." She gestured around her. "But not this. Never this."

"Why are you here?" Nicolas said bitterly.

Electra bowed her head. "A hunch. I knew you were planning to disappear. I thought you had succeeded. I might never have come to look for you, except..." She hesitated.

Nicolas looked up sharply. "Except what?"

"Durand," she admitted. "He's grieving. I knew that you might lie to the rest of the world, but that you couldn't lie to Durand. When I saw that he really believed you were dead..."

Nicolas felt nauseous. "I need to see Francois. I need to tell him what has happened." He felt empty, as if a limb had been severed. Alone. The echo of thunder rattled the building. The rain fell in a torrent. Lightning ricocheted with a crack across the sky.

"Nicolas, the devastation has only begun. Rumors of your death have spread like wildfire through the covens in Europe. They are cautious still. They are testing the fact of your death. The revenants have begun to turn those you've touched—"

His heart froze, and he turned on her. "Where is Francois?"

"No, not him. He is safe. But this is bigger than one mortal, Nicolas."

Lightning tore across the heavens. Her eyes darted instinctively to the place where it ripped the velvet sky. He turned suddenly, and before she could avoid it, his hand caught her throat, and he backed her against the broken wall. "The truth, Electra. Did you bring this on us? Did you send Sokaris here to kill us?"

"You fool. If I had wanted you dead, would I be here tonight?" She shook her head. "No. In the end, I could not control him. If he came here to harm you, he came of his own will. Or Khaldun's. I never intended to harm you or Giuliana. I only wanted a place, Nicolas."

Her words resonated, and his anger dissipated. He released her and backed away. He felt too heavy to move. "Go, Electra. Leave me."

"Nicolas, if you want to prevent our world toppling, we have only this chance to act. To restore order."

"I don't give a damn about order. The world can topple."

"Then, what will you do?"

"Electra, can't you see that there is nothing for me to do? My life is over as surely as if I had died in that explosion."

"The revenants have been desecrating the Arsenale all week. Khaldun's coven has taken control and they are gathering their spawn from all over the world. They've sent out a call to burn the Arsenale and Villa Giuliana to the ground."

Nicolas flinched.

"The Elders are here, in Venice. Argus summoned them when we thought you were dead. There is a unique opportunity here." A question swam in her black eyes, and he had a sense that no matter which answer he gave, it would set him on a path he could never take back,

He pushed his hand back through his hair as if wiping away the dilemma. The sunbaked warmth of the desert called to him with a promise of numbness and solitude. He could abandon this world and leave it to others to manage. After all, his choices had all led to failure. Why was it his to deal with?

It was one simple thought that goaded his decision. Leaving Giuliana's death unanswered, as if she had not mattered, not to him, not to the world, was a legacy he could not leave behind. They would remember her.

"Call them," he said.

29

REPRISAL

Nicolas materialized at Porta Magna in an instant while Electra sped through Venice, calling out the Elders. Max arrived first. They remained grimly silent as the others each arrived after him, one by one until they were all gathered. Electra came last.

"The stench of them is overwhelming," Max grimaced. They stood atop the gate's pediment, next to the statue of Santa Giustina. Below them was the winged Lion of St. Mark, holding a closed book, a symbol of war. The air was cool but fulsome with the scent of blood and decay that always clung to revenants. The heaviness in the air indicated their numbers had increased significantly.

Nicolas clutched the stone statue as other images of this place flickered before his eyes. He saw it at every stage of its existence. The original, unassuming Arsenale Vecchio, built in his human lifetime. Its expansion to the east, then further to the east, buildings rising and falling. Destruction by fire and explosions; rebuilding by sweat and blood. The rush to fortify after the fall of Constantinople. Additions of foundries and munitions shops. Through global supremacy, Austrian domination, and French imperialism. And all the attempts to restore her failing one by one until the thriving center of the most powerful city-state in the world became a house of ghosts.

And with those memories came visions of Giuliana in every age since she had come to him and the glorious creature she had become. All gone now. Like the Arsenale, like his life, his own dead heart, lost to him.

"Nicolas." Max pointed up to the tower opposite them.

There, at its crenelated top, stood Khaldun's three ancient female companions. But they had abandoned their rags for pleated linen gowns, sheer as gossamer. A gold and lapis lazuli amulet in the shape of a hawk hung around each of their necks. One of the three stepped forward. The others hung back, flanking her. She was the most adorned, with a wide collar piece made up of rows of geometric shapes in carnelian and gold. Her arms were bound in bracelets of similar design. A gold circlet rested on thick crimped waves of raven hair that fell to her waist. She tilted her head, bird-like, toward the compound walls, where wails of terror could already be heard.

Nicolas felt an ancient language penetrate his thoughts and the honied voice choking his will. *Nahkti, Nicolas, powerful son of Venice, you live still! How delightful. We thought you had perished in the explosion. Why have you called your own house to arms? It is a shame that we should be at war.*

His comprehension of the strange words startled him as they hissed into his mind. Even the name, Nahkti, called to him, urged him to obey. Sapped by grief, Nicolas struggled to dispel the compulsion to surrender to the hypnotic command running beneath the language, even deeper than thought. The three voices spoke as one. *Come to us. Rest in our protection. Rule with us.*

"Where is Khaldun?" he shouted.

"This altercation is beneath Khaldun's attention. He sent us, instead. It will be over in a few moments, and you will be forced to heed your rightful leader."

A fluttering sound called to him from far away, deep inside the Arsenale. A memory of something bound teased at the edge of his mind. Nicolas shook his head.

"No," he said aloud to force the voice out of his head. The other Elders situated themselves strategically around the plaza. Restless, Persephone had disappeared inside the structure, and cries intensified in the distance, telling him the battle had already begun.

The female vampire looked in the direction of the screams, then back to Nicolas. *Do you slaughter your own kind so easily, Nahkti?*

"It's Nicolas. And speak aloud if you want my attention. I will not be controlled. These abominations you have created are not my kind."

"Very well, then," she said aloud in a voice shimmering with magic almost as powerful as her psychic touch. "Nicolas," she said sweetly with a sweep of her graceful hands. "Surely you see the power we could have together? Khaldun is merciful; we three are his first progeny, destined to rule Rialto someday. Join us. We can unlock your past; provide answers you have not yet even thought to seek."

Nicolas snarled at her, "Until now, I have been blind to the consequences of relegating power to those like you. Tragically, that veil has been lifted. Take your brood and leave the rest of us in peace. Show me that you do not share Khaldun's madness. Tell me where he is, and retribution for his sins will not fall on your heads. Stay to fight and you make another statement—one that will cost you your lives."

She clicked her tongue as if she were scolding a child and sighed. "Khaldun is wise. You do need to be reminded that your power only exists so long as others tolerate it. One way or another, Nahkti, you will be ours."

She raised her arms and brought them down in a powerful arc

forward, and the other two females soared toward Nicolas. Argus shouted a curse and flung a boomerang, its edge razor sharp, at the second of the sisters. She lifted her hands to intercept it, and her fingers were sliced clean off at the base. She howled and retreated, clutching her ruined hands to her chest.

Argus dove away, and Nicolas intercepted the second of them, pushing her aside and down. A fountain of blood gushed from her breast as she was impaled on the iron fence below. The last of the sisters screamed in fury, and flew to assist, summoning a tide of revenants to sweep toward the complex. They emerged from the depths of canals and the web of alleys below.

Nicolas leapt from the column over the wall and into the Arsenale. "Giuliana!" he bellowed, and the others picked up the cry until her name echoed from end to end of the great complex.

He followed the scent of blood. The wide paths were clear, but revenants skulked among the columns and arches of the old docks and nearby sheds, terrified of the sounds coming from the old artillery factory. Persephone and her clan were intercepting creatures as they poured from the structure. The delicate vampire had transformed from woodland fairy to a creature mad with rage. With fangs and bare hands, she set to the horrified young ones. They fell before her, to water and to land, as she roared through them, tearing them limb from limb. The fetid water of the old bays teamed with their bodies writhing beneath the surface.

Nicolas joined one of Eoghan's progeny who had taken position at a corner outside the rope and cordage factory. She flew above the newborns with a wooden spear and plunged right and left through their fragile hearts. Nicolas dove beneath the murky canals where they fled, chasing them back to land, where he was on them before they could move. The old vampire raised her spear in a salute to Nicolas and turned back to the slaughter.

Nicolas's eyes were clouded with blood, tears, rage, and persistent visions of Giuliana still haunting him, each one a fresh reminder that she was gone. There was not enough gore, not enough blood, not enough brutality to satisfy his outrage. He needed no weapon but his bare hands; he wanted to feel the flesh tearing, bones cracking, heads shattering in his hands. A trail of vampire bodies disintegrated behind him, leaving nothing of themselves in the world as they died. He was as empty as those corpses. When he was gone, he would leave nothing behind.

He moved relentlessly through the oldest regions of the Arsenale. He drained lives, spilled blood, as if it could fill his emptiness. It was a feast of savagery that desecrated his memory of one ancient structure after another in a bloody trail of emancipation from love of the life that would not let him go.

He drew up short. Before him was the row of alabaster forms bound in plastic shrouds. He was hypnotized by the wind running through the plastic, with sounds of flame and the constant beat of a drum. Music for a war.

He stalked closer. Their forms trembled as if they would emerge in an explosion of vengeance. Reaching tentatively, he pulled the shroud from the ropes that bound the first of them. It was a mediocre reproduction of a sixteenth-century masterwork. He moved from one to another, ripping away the plastic. The wind took the winding sheets from his hands, and they spiraled away, leaving the freed forms glowing in the darkness. They were copies of great statues, and student renderings, with all the form, but none of the life spark of the originals. The sense of life had come only from the wind disturbing the shroud.

Nicolas, what's wrong?

He froze. Her remembered voice came to him unbidden and stirred him from his impasse just in time to feel the wake of wind behind a sword taking a revenant's head. That revenant had been about to plunge a knife into Nicolas's neck.

"Nicolas, you whoreson, wake up and fight!"

Nicolas whirled to find Eoghan, who grasped the ivory hilt of an iron, leaf-shaped sword. He relished plunging it into the throat of revenant after revenant as they fled past him. A few stood and fought, but their strength was only in the swarm of numbers, and Eoghan welcomed the swarm. Spinning and thrusting at lightning speed into the mob that threatened every moment to overwhelm him, he bellowed an ear-shattering war cry. "Giuliana!"

Nicolas, disoriented, leapt up to the outer wall and leaned against the parapet to survey the struggle below. Eoghan was nearest, still chasing down every shadowy target. He could pick out Electra several bays away, fighting side by side with Argus and others of Delphi. As he watched, a wave of the rogues pushed them back, but they rallied and regained the ground. There was no sign of the sisters.

When he looked away and closed his eyes, he heard her voice again. *Nicolas, what's wrong?*

He drifted, and let his mind go blank, so his lips could form the answer he had not been able to see then. "Doubt," he whispered, feeling pieces slip into place.

All the time, he had doubted their place while she had been so sure. He had decimated their ruling structure, and now the consequences of that decision ravaged the city he loved. He had thought no vampire should wield such power. Now the worst of his kind had destroyed the best. The half-measures he had taken by leaving Khaldun alive and letting Electra keep her mysteries had destroyed Giuliana. Every attempt to avoid having an impact had proven destructive. Perhaps it was time to try a different tack.

He turned and looked out toward the Villa, listening as the sounds raging behind him began to calm, to move to a distance, as the others finished the work he had begun. Venice would be free from revenants, at least for a while. Nicolas looked up to find the grim faces of Delphine and Eoghan, as they joined him on the wall.

"If any survive, they'll not forget her name," said Eoghan. "And neither will we, brother."

Friends? Was it possible among vampires? They had come to his aid, perhaps out of selfish motivation, but still, they had come at the risk of their lives. "Thank you," Nicolas said, "I did not deserve your aid, but I would not have survived this night without it."

He fell back against the tower wall and listened to the sounds of terror dying out over Venice. Sobs exploded from his lungs, and sanguine tears poured from his eyes as he heard her name still emerge occasionally above the din.

"Nicolas," Delphine said, "We aren't finished. They have reached Villa Giuliana. Khaldun may be with them."

––––––

PATCHES OF FLAME licked at brush covering the Villa grounds as Nicolas materialized on the coral terrace. He strode into the ballroom. He was dismayed to find furniture and drapery aflame. Burning logs had been tumbled from the fireplace. Revenants shrieked in glee as they clamored through the house, bent on desecration and pointless destruction. Nicolas turned his head away from the sight of the exsanguinated bodies of several human employees.

He stumbled, bracing himself with a hand on the mantlepiece. *If I think of her, or of this as our home, I will not make it through the night.*

He took in a breath through clenched teeth, screwed up his courage, and let out a roar. He looked up at the mob before him, fire reflecting in his eyes. The revenants pushed back, away from Nicolas, instinctively fearful.

"Where is Khaldun?" he bellowed.

Above the fireplace, among the masks, his eyes lit on a pair of crossed long swords. On one was engraved, *in commercia pace,* in trade lies peace. It had belonged to his father. The second unadorned sword had been his brother, Michael's. He strode to the fireplace and plucked them from the wall. They felt familiar, solid, and powerful in his hands.

"Where is Khaldun?" he shouted again, brandishing the swords.

"Wait! Hold your ground!" An older vampire shouted from the foyer leading into the ballroom. "He is alone! We are many!"

Some of the fleeing creatures hesitated, then turned and edged back toward the ballroom. Their eyes shifted nervously. Fingers curled and twitched in anticipation. With a sudden howl, Nicolas raised the swords and spun them in an arc over his head as he pivoted into the midst of them. He bloodied the floor with several of their corpses but was soon engulfed in flailing nails and teeth and pummeled with random candlesticks and other makeshift weapons. His heart pounded, the swords became difficult to wield in the press of bodies, but something feral in him relished the fight. He felt himself giving ground and being pushed to the floor. The older one closed his hands around Nicolas's neck, pounding his head against the tile, the vampire's fingers beginning to press through Nicolas's skin.

Then suddenly the creature's head was gone, spattering Nicolas in a spray of blood, and a beefy fist was punching through the crowd and offering Nicolas a hand up. He gratefully accepted and was jerked to his feet. Eoghan was there.

"Let's not make this a habit," Nicolas said grimly. He heard Delphine and Argus arrive outside and begin cutting down the miscreants trying to escape through the gardens.

"We've got this, brother. Go find Khaldun." Nicolas gave him a grateful nod and ran up the stairs to search the house.

The rooms on the upper floors were untouched; no revenants had made it so far. He held the swords at his sides. He found himself in his office, looking out toward the gardens. Khaldun would not miss the opportunity to gloat should Nicolas fall, but he would not risk involvement until his victory was ensured. Where would he go to bide his time?

A flicker of movement caught his eye atop the distant tower. A finger of recognition traced up his spine, and he knew. Of course. Back to the beginning, to a place that represented a time when Khaldun was at the height of his power.

He moved quickly down the stairs, back across the terrace, and through the woods. He emerged from the trees and crept silently toward the tower. As he drew near, the silhouette of the vampire became clearer. Nicolas's heart pounded. Uncertainty clutched him.

It was Khaldun standing in the broken wall on the topmost floor. He was as still as stone, staring back out toward the Dorsoduro district of the city. Nicolas only had a moment of advantage before the ancient realized he was there. Nicolas leapt up soundlessly behind him, swords still trailing in his hands. He raised the blades, but Khaldun spoke. Nicolas stumbled and hesitated at the sound of the mesmerizing voice.

"My palazzo was there, directly across from your father's." His raised hand indicated the spot across the canal where his home had long since fallen to ruin. "I would stand in my own tower during the evening and consider new ways to bend him to my will. I knew this place would someday be mine, and now, here we are." He turned around to face Nicolas.

Khaldun's voice was stronger than the last time they had spoken. He was recovering from his long time asleep. *If I cannot destroy him now, I never will.*

Nicolas's grip tightened on the weapons in his hands, but then, caught in an instant of clarity, he lowered the blades slightly, and said, "That was always the force compelling you, wasn't it? I was in awe of you then and thought you had designs beyond my understanding, but it was only petty jealousy and a small man's spite. A way of forcing entry in a community to which you could never claim membership."

Khaldun frowned. "Petty? Small? The host I planted here is

enough to take back Venice. Your death will set the vampire world reeling, and I will be here to pick up the pieces."

"Your horde is being routed even as we speak."

"Routed?" Khaldun's brow knitted with a trace of concern, but he recovered, waving to the fire across the villa grounds and the smoky air above the Arsenale. "It's unlikely you could take them all yourself. And even were it true, there would still be the problem of me. What to do with me, Nicolas?"

"You?" Nicolas scoffed. "You've murdered Giuliana." His face turned to stone, and he raised the swords, tips crossed, their intersection hovering before Khaldun's neck. "There is no hope for you."

But in the blink of an eye, Khaldun was behind him, whispering in his ear. "You well know you bear more guilt for her death than I do."

Nicolas jerked away, panic knotting momentarily in his chest. He whirled around and trained the swords back on Khaldun, who continued in a snakelike hiss. "*You* filled that building with explosives. *You* allowed Sokaris to become fixated on you. *You* created a way of life that supported your ego but left her vulnerable because you had not built the community that could have protected her." Khaldun scanned Nicolas's face.

A familiar feeling rushed over Nicolas as Khaldun waited for his reaction. Why does he watch me and not strike? Why does his next action depend on what I do next? Then it dawned on him. He hesitated, just as Nicolas had hesitated when Khaldun had first spoken. *This is it. This is the point where I turn aside as if I've no right to claim justice. That, more than my death, is what he desires. Turn aside, and he would kill me and be done with it.*

Nicolas was possessed by a cold calm, finally utterly certain of how this must end.

Khaldun shifted as an errant wind brushed by them. An instant of uncertainty. He thrust his chin toward Nicolas. "Where is the unbridled rage? That fierce destructive force that turns everything to ash?"

Nicolas's eyes narrowed. He took a few small steps forward. Now only the length of the blades separated them. "You took my life, and you made me a vampire. My rage has found focus. No need to decimate the innocent."

Khaldun made a clumsy step backward, but he snarled. "Do you think I fear you?"

"No, you don't fear me. You despise the injustice of being sent into the sand by a fledgling wielding strength he never should have had. You must hate me with everything you are."

Khaldun took another step back toward the broken wall, and Nicolas matched it, pushing him closer toward the edge. "That arrogance will be your undoing, Nicolas. You don't know when you're about to be beaten."

"You won't beat me, Khaldun. You made a mistake thinking Electra could give you all you needed to understand me. You won't break me with doubt. You would destroy my public life? Prove me a traitor to my kind? Take back the power you think I stole from you? You've miscalculated. The Elders are fighting with me, Khaldun, and you've lost control of Sokaris. I'm one thousand years older than I was then, and your hatred makes you weak. If only I could have seen it."

Resentment exploded in the old one's eyes. He snarled and trembled as if the earth was shaking. Then, as if suddenly unchained, he lurched forward and charged toward Nicolas, arms outstretched. His hands clawed toward Nicolas's chest; his rabid copper eyes fixed only on Nicolas's steely face. The ancient need for revenge possessed him.

Nicolas stood his ground and in the blink of an eye raised the points of the crossed blades. Khaldun's momentum carried him forward into the sharp Damascene metal. Nicolas snapped his arms apart and the blades uncrossed, slicing through Khaldun's neck. A look of surprise flashed briefly across the wizened face as the patterned metal severed head from neck. The grasping claws savaged Nicolas's chest as he tumbled to the side. Khaldun's body fell past him and crashed against the partial wall and down into the marsh below, A hiss of steam rose from the bog as bricks fell from the crumbling wall into the bubbling stew of vegetation.

30

WHERE THE FUTURE LIES

Nicolas arrived back at the Rialto house courtyard a few hours before dawn. He could not bear to go back to the villa, where his memories of Giuliana were the strongest, and he knew that this was the place the Elders would gather. He paced for a few moments, resisting entry. When he finally laid his hand on the gate, he was surprised to find that it swung sturdily from its hinges once again. Puzzled, he stepped through it, and a new wave of grief overtook him.

The gardens were manicured and bare branches pruned. Flower beds were newly prepared for spring planting, paths were cleared, and benches and the central fountain repaired. He had barely given it a thought, but of course, Giuliana would not have been able to bear seeing the courtyard in decline. How like her to make it right without a word. It would be glorious in spring, a spring that Giuliana would never see.

He lingered for a while in the small garden until he heard movement along the tiny alley. Electra appeared cautiously at the gate, closing it behind her as she entered. "Thank the stars," she said in relief as she saw Nicolas. "No one knew where you had gone." She sat down beside him, and they were silent for a while. Her dress was torn, and her face was splattered in blood and worse. Finally, she prompted, "What are you thinking about?"

"Electra, what happened to Sokaris?

"Nicolas, I know what you're hoping for, but don't deceive yourself. It will only compound your grief."

Nicolas stood and fell to pacing. "The ring and the object that bound him were in the lab. They were there, Electra."

"How did you find...what object?" He shook his head. She sighed at the lack of trust. "Then ... it was enough. He must have been destroyed."

"He's here," came from the gate. "Max, Nicolas is here." Argus and Max pushed through the gate. Max's face was badly damaged. Argus was covered with blood, and a deep diagonal gash cut across his chest.

Max embraced Nicolas. "Argus is weak. Let's get him inside. Sounds like most of us are here. The rest should be soon."

They moved inside. The portego had been cleaned and its furniture repaired. Newly reupholstered benches lined the hallway. The mosaic floors had been polished and shone beautifully in a hypnotic glow. Voices wafted in from the central meeting room. Somehow Giuliana had made the place live again.

Nicolas flinched, in no way ready for a public appearance. He looked down at his clothes, ruined and bloody from the explosion, the battle, and the days beneath the rubble. He felt exposed...vulnerable. "Max, I can't do this." He brought his hand to his forehead, tired beyond measure. "I have no anchor, no reason to care what happens next. None of it means anything anymore."

"They came here for you, of their own accord, for the first time in a thousand years. They've sensed leadership and responded. That means something," Max reassured him. "You owe them an appearance, at least, to let them know you survived." Nicolas sighed deeply, then nodded reluctantly. They stepped through the open door.

Nicolas was taken aback to see how many had really come. He looked at the group of vampires scattered around the meeting room. It was daunting; he would have escaped, but heads had already turned as Electra closed the door behind them.

The voices formed a cacophony of stunned exclamations and excited questions. They were talking about the future. They quieted as he took the steps down toward the group slowly, one at a time.

"Will you tell us what happened?" Max's voice was quiet and full of sorrow.

Nicolas pulled himself together and said thoughtfully, "I'm not entirely sure. I had set explosives as a trap for Sokaris. But something else happened; a detonation far more powerful than the devices I set could have caused. I didn't know that Giuli would be there." They sat, and the others gathered before them, uneasy to see the indomitable Portinari undone.

"So, Electra's tales about Sokaris are true? He exists?" Persephone asked hesitantly.

"Yes, he did." Nicolas looked at Electra. "Despite my centuries of stubborn denial, I have been wrong about that." A hint of pride and vindication flared in Electra's eyes. "I've come to believe recently that there are malevolent forces in the world that we can't see and don't understand. I believe they have the power to manipulate us to their will. Sokaris was one of them."

"Nicolas, superstition? From you?" Max questioned.

"I am a child of the dark ages, Max." Nicolas smiled weakly. "What do you expect?" Max returned a sad smile.

Nicolas looked around suddenly and asked what he had wondered since he stepped through the doors. "You all came to defend Venice. Why?"

Argus stepped forward, finally. "We came," he said helplessly, "as you asked. Remember, you said *gather what friends you can*. I told

Max what you said about Khaldun and going to destroy a god, and he put the rest together. We all thought that you were dead, but they came anyway. For you and Giuliana. Even some who said they would not." He gestured toward Persephone.

"We had to avenge her, Nicolas," said Electra. "She was no friend of mine, but she did not deserve this."

It seemed an honest statement, but Nicolas knew that Electra's motive was also selfish. Even now, she would use his grief, however she could, to achieve her goals. He knew that he could not and would not ever trust her. He had no strength to confront her now. But the time would come.

Eoghan said, "The loss of Giuliana... we could not let that go unanswered." Nicolas pondered Eoghan's words, which began to reveal a course of action before him.

Nicolas looked up and considered the vampires before him. Delphine was there, eyes aflame. Persephone, too, stood alongside her. It was strange but somehow comforting, to see the strength of his race gathered in this historical place of power. It was an uneasy alliance. There was distrust, but there was also respect that had come from their recent interactions.

He pulled Max aside, and the others' attention turned to attending to Argus and recounting their parts in the recent foray. As they moved away down the hall, he said to Max, "Was anyone else hurt?"

"Not that I know of, at least not seriously. Only a few made it to the villa, and they were dispensed with quickly. The others were sweeping the districts to clean up, but apparently, most of the revenants had all been commanded not to leave the Arsenale. It was a slaughter. Venice is clear. For now. It was a victory for you, Nicolas. What will you do with it?"

"What are you asking, Max?"

"Whether you've realized it yet or not, you are no longer an island. They followed you tonight when no one had been able to bring them together in a millennium. I never thought I would see such a sight again. It was a show of strength. Others will pay attention."

"Don't you start, too, Max," Nicolas sighed wearily. Max chuckled, but Nicolas held his gaze seriously. "I did learn something tonight about surviving alone. If I'd had the others around us before Sokaris gained strength, Giuliana might well still be with us. Have I been a fool, Max?"

"They've given you no choice, Nicolas. They were with you tonight, but there have been centuries when their behavior has been abhorrent. Our kind has rarely made good allies." He sighed. "You may not want to lead, but you took a stand tonight. That will make it difficult for you to continue to claim indifference."

Nicolas tried to identify what he felt. He was too raw to tell. Had he been indifferent? Reluctant to take a stand? Or loathe to put what he cherished at risk? He had always had his music and his life with Giuliana to protect. But now, what did he have to defend against the threat of his own kind? This time he recognized the edge of doubt creeping in. "Max, I must confess, I am unmoored. I have no idea how I will survive."

"Of course, my boy. I do not mean to press," he said sympathetically. "What will you do now? You know you are welcome in Salzburg."

"Thank you, Max. I may take you up on that soon. But tonight, I must return to Paris and see what's left of my life. It's time I claimed it."

———

THE NEXT NIGHT Nicolas stepped up behind the podium, which had been set up just outside the enclosed site of the Portinari Building ruins. There had been limited notice to the public, yet somehow a significant audience was present. The lights burned through the

Paris fog, leaving a hazy pool of illumination around Nicolas, expertly filtered to warm his ivory complexion to an almost human tone. He waited for the applause and cheers to subside, looking from one face to the next, searching for malice, but he found none.

Francois stood at the front of the crowd to his left with Paul, whose suspicious scowl was unsettling. Francois had no idea what Nicolas planned to say this evening. It had all happened too fast, but Nicolas had been determined that he should make this public appearance, afraid that, if he did not, it would be too easy to change his mind and slip away.

"Thank you for coming. It will be short. I just wanted to thank all of you who have shown Giuliana and me such warmth and support. We all miss her—I miss her—and there will always be a void..." The crowd was quiet while he searched for words.

"Truthfully," he said quietly. "I had thought to give up music after the season. There were too many critics." His eyes found Jules LeCourbe peering at him through his thick spectacles and wondered what he would say about this tonight. Then he realized he didn't care. "I had begun to believe what they said- that my music- that I... Well, you know what they said." He offered a self-deprecating smile before bending his head. "But that is not what Giuliana would have wanted."

His voice strengthened, and he looked up again and scanned the crowd. "And we will not fail her." He gestured to the rubble behind him. "We will rebuild. And there will be a new opera next season." He paused again for the cheers to subside. "This I promise: I will not let the detractors take that away from her, nor me, nor any of you."

The shouts of approval engulfed him in a wave. Nicolas straightened and pulled back his shoulders at the heartening sound. "No matter how it wears on us, no matter how badly the spotlight burns us, sometimes we have a responsibility to stand against the tide that has turned against us, lest that tide bring down all that we've built.

His eyes searched out Francois's, liquid with emotion, and locked on them. "All that we love."

He waved to the supporters and disappeared into the embrace of the dark night.

THE END

ACKNOWLEDGMENTS

Our thanks to John Adamus who helped make us much better writers. Thanks also to Heather Slawecki, for her remarkable work on the cover.

ABOUT THE AUTHORS

Joy Crozier is a Florida native and reformed accountant, who escaped to the great Northwest in 2013 to pursue farming and support the farm-to-table movement. Joy is a painter and an avid gardener. She is also a lifelong lover of books and is especially fascinated by the alternate worlds created in fantasy fiction. She has two smart, intuitive daughters, Ally and Cara, and an endlessly patient and supportive husband, Ken. She also lives with six high-energy English Springer Spaniels: Starbuck, Luna, Oliver, Leeloo, Mulder, and River.

Joseph Floyd is a Florida native born in Tampa. A retired research librarian from the University of South Florida, his areas of expertise included Women's & Gender Studies, Anthropology, and Art History. Joseph served on the editorial board of the *Tampa Bay Review* and is a past winner of the University of South Florida Annual Poetry & Fiction Contest. His work has been published in *Pleiades* and the *Tampa Bay Review*. Joseph still lives in Tampa with his husband and a very recalcitrant Maine Coon cat named Maxwell Edison.

Made in the USA
Columbia, SC
29 April 2023

15936191R00167